When Only HAPPILY EVER AFTER Will Do

A Novel

By the author of:

Turning Toward the Sun

Pushing Back the Storm

CEIL WARREN

All rights reserved. No part of this work may be reproduced or utilized in any form or by any means, electronically or by and information storage and retrieval system without prior written permission of the publisher. Editorial reviewers may excerpt 300 words.

Library of Congress Cataloging-in-Publication data is available.
ISBN Paperback: 978-1-7341279-7-3
ISBN Ebook: 978-1-7341279-8-0
BISAC categories:
Fiction/Small Town & Rural
Fiction/Romance/Later in Life
Fiction/Friendship

Westchester County, New York
Printed in USA

This is a work of fiction. All of the characters, names, places and incidents portrayed in this novel are products of either the author's imagination or are used fictitiously. Any resemblances to actual persons, living or dead, events or locales is entirely coincidental.

When Only Happily Ever After Will Do Copyright 2021 by Ceil Warren
Cover design by Asya Blue
Edited by Mark Mathes

Ceil Warren
Visit my website at: www.ceilwarren.com

Hello Fellow Reader:

Thanks so much for taking the time to read ***When Only Happily Ever After Will Do***.

If it's your first visit with the lively residents of Stones End, check out the first two books in the series, ***Turning Toward the Sun*** and ***Pushing Back the Storm*** sold on Amazon.

Following is an excerpt from books one and two in the delightful Stones End series.

And if you have a moment, please consider **posting a review or a rating** on Amazon or Goodreads.

Contact me anytime. I love hearing from fellow readers: contact@ceilwarren.com.

All the best and happy reading,
— Ceil Warren

Excerpt from *Turning Toward the Sun*

Arthur's life was a well-ordered and predictable one and he came to rely on the sameness of his daily routine. It gave him comfort like an old worn bathrobe you simply cannot part with.

But this day was different, and Arthur knew it. Trouble was lurking like a far-off twister charging right for you. He didn't see it at the start of the day. But before day's end his deep, dark secret would be a secret no more and life would change forever in the tiny village of Stones End.

Excerpt from *Pushing Back the Storm*

"I'm sorry, but I'm not seeing why this is an issue. Yes, I loved her, but I'm in love with you. You're overreacting, my dear. A cultural expansion of Stones End will be great for the village."

The thin dam holding back her broiling frustration shattered. "You didn't hear a word I said. I don't give a hoot about the cultural livelihood here. My concern is your former love interest. Who is an international opera star, drop-dead gorgeous and still has a body that doesn't quit. Now, will you please go home!"

It stunned Arthur into silence. He snatched his coat and ran for it.

Praise for *When Only Happily Ever After Will Do*

"Loved, Loved, Loved it! It was so engaging, I didn't want to put it down. Kept the suspense up to the very last word. I didn't see the end coming."

—L. Carpenter, Westchester, NY

Praise for *Pushing Back the Storm*

"In book two of Ceil Warren's Stones End Series, *Pushing Back the Storm*, Arthur's first love, Ana Felicia, takes up residence in Stones End. The move stresses Arthur's upcoming marriage and poses unforeseen problems for the villagers. Ceil carefully crafts a captivating story of powerful love and fierce friendships with surprising twists and turns that keep you guessing. As for Arthur, was it better to have loved and lost? You'll have to know the ending!"

— Anne Scavotto, Westchester, NY

"In her second novel of the Stones End series, Ceil Warren reacquaints us with the quirky, but loveable characters of the village. The arrival of a famous opera diva heralds a cloud of intrigue and foreboding that envelops not just Arthur, but the whole village. Unexpected revelations and events further add to the web of suspense that guides the reader through this most exciting adventure. With deep insight and humor into the intricacies of life and love, the author has created a book that is truly a joy to read!"

— Jacqueline Kutner, President
Bronx County Historical Society, Riverdale, NY

Praise for *Turning Toward the Sun*

"Feel-good book of the year! A rare pleasure when an author takes the reader into the soul of a character. I cherished this richly woven, witty, soul-searching journey as Arthur struggles to shake off his past and take a path toward an unknown future."

— M. Cardinale, Dutchess County, NY

"Loved it! I was completely captivated by this wonderful novel celebrating life and all its messy complexities. Profound, witty, engaging story that constantly moves forward with fast-paced, hysterical dialogue, heart-stopping, heart-aching, and stand-up-and-cheer moments. *Turning Toward the Sun* is filled with relatable characters: quirky, lovable, flawed. The story unfolds as 62-year-old Arthur receives an unexpected letter which causes him to wrestle past demons, fight to keep a 40-year-old secret hidden and attempt to find an answer to a decades-old question. Will he find the redemption and answers he seeks?"

— N. Dmytrijuk, Orlando, FL

Acknowledgments

Sending heartfelt thanks…

To my wonderful family and friends for always asking, “How’s the writing going?” Your enthusiasm and encouragement help more than you know.

To Mark Mathes (https://reedsy.com/mark-mathes), Editor Extraordinaire, for fixing my grammar and punctuation failings, and oh so patiently getting me to change passive voice to active. Your amazing insight brought this book to life. You are a joy to work with.

To Asya Blue (www.asyablue.com) for another stunning cover design and meticulous detail in formatting. You make what seems impossible look easy. I’m eternally grateful for your professionalism and awesome talent and your ability to make a painstaking process fun.

When Only Happily Ever After Will Do

CHAPTER 1
All's Right with the World

Arthur quick-stepped it into the kitchen and slapped Ari on the back. "Good morning, my dear brother."

"Well, someone's in a good mood. Finally."

"And why not? Constance has returned to Stones End. The wedding is back on. Ana Felicia troubles are behind us. And all's right with the world." He poured a cup of coffee and treated himself to some forbidden sugar.

Pulling jackets on over their pajamas, the brothers scuffed out to the front porch and sat on the bench named George. Arthur named his handcrafted bench after their father, who loved to build boats in Greece. The world fell away as Arthur looked beyond the trees to the Housatonic River. Crisp Connecticut air stung his cheeks with color. Autumn oak leaves and pine needles gave up an earthy musk and coffee fueled the promise of a brilliant day. A smile crossed his face. *Life is good.*

Ari eyed Arthur, hoping the subject wasn't a sore spot. "I know you and Constance wanted the wedding to be next weekend. How mad are you that I threw a monkey-wrench into the works?"

Arthur beamed. "To tell you the truth, I'm thrilled to wait for our sisters. It's a 16-hour flight from Athens to JFK, you know. To have Emily and Zoe at the wedding means the world to us."

"Glad to hear it, especially since they gave me strict orders to hold the wedding till they arrive. And you never want to go against the sisters."

Arthur briskly rubbed the hairs on the back of his neck. He needed a razor cut before the ceremony. And something for his nerves. He loved his sisters, but trouble was sure to follow.

"No, going against the sisters is never a good idea. Besides, this is my first time at this wedding stuff. I'm pleased that it will be a full affair. I know Constance had a grand wedding her first time around. I think she's happy to have another."

"Nobody seems to want my opinion," said George. "You and Constance should elope before you screw things up again."

Ari laughed, enjoying that their father's spirit lived on in Arthur's bench. He often wondered if he and Arthur kept George's spirit alive in their minds or if George was actually there with them. He knew his brother had been talking to their father for decades.

"Pop has a point. You're lucky Constance forgave you after your fling with Ana Felicia."

Arthur pulled his head back. "Fling? There was no fling! It was all a misunderstanding."

"There was that kiss," Ari chided.

"Well, yes. But Ana Felicia was doing the kissing."

"That's not what it looked like to me," said George.

Arthur's head shrunk into his shoulders. He gulped his coffee, pretending not to hear.

"And then Constance found Ana Felicia in your arms," said Ari.

"Twice," added George.

Arthur needed to change the subject—and fast. He waved a dismissive hand. "Well, it's all water under the bridge. Constance, good woman that she is, forgave me. And Ana Felicia is no longer a threat to her. Yes. All's right with the world. Our world."

"You didn't tell him?" said George.

Arthur stretched his neck tight. "Tell me? Tell me what?"

Ari shrugged not sure he should mention it. "I could be wrong, but it looks like Walter and Ana Felicia are starting up a..." He paused, trying to think of the right word.

Arthur's right eyebrow shot up. "Starting up what?"

"A relationship."

Arthur leapt from the bench. Ari pulled his legs out of the way of the coffee avalanche.

"Calm down. Maybe it's just a friendship."

"Either way, it means Ana Felicia will be hanging around. Constance won't like this. No, she won't like this at all."

Remembering their recent breakup sent a shudder through Arthur. Raised tempers, ugly words, the long separation. Months of agonizing over how to get his true love back. He couldn't lose her again.

"If Ana Felicia is with Walter, Constance will have nothing to worry about. Sit down. You're making me nervous," said Ari.

Arthur couldn't sit. "How can you say that? Ana Felicia moving here is what broke our engagement to begin with. Or are you forgetting?"

"No. I don't think anyone will *ever* forget that."

Arthur paced quick enough to cause sparks of friction on the wooden porch planks. Ari tucked his legs under the bench, keeping an eye on Arthur's erratic cup.

"I can't take any more upset. Why is there always upset? I got up this morning dreaming about our wedding and now I'm wondering if there will be one."

"Now, look what you've done, Ari. You broke your brother again," said George.

Father Gregory turned up the walk. "Good morning, gentlemen. Wonderful day, isn't it?"

Arthur shot him a stone-hard, wide-eyed look.

"Oh, God. What is it now?" Father Gregory covered his mouth, shocked that he'd taken the Lord's name in vain—and it wasn't even 8 o'clock.

Arthur's voice rose ten decibels. "Ana Felicia may still be in Stones End."

Father Gregory pulled on his collar that just got tighter. He glowered at Ari. "You weren't supposed to tell him. We don't even know if it's true yet."

Ari pointed at the bench. "It wasn't me. George brought it up."

The priest rolled his eyes. *Great. Now, Ari is talking to his dead father. Heaven help us.*

The crisp November air suddenly felt heavy enough to bury them in a blizzard of drama. Arthur paced. Ari sat with his hands on his head. Father Gregory felt around in his pocket for his rosary.

"Well, the only thing I can think of," said Ari, "is don't tell Constance. Under any circumstance."

Arthur spun around. "That's a terrible plan. You know I can't keep a secret from Constance to save my life. It's lying." He turned to Father Gregory. "Right, Gregory?"

Father Gregory ran a sweaty hand over his face. The high-speed boat race to stop Constance from lifting off at JFK jumped to mind. Boat pounding and pitching, white knuckles, nausea, terror. He pulled on his collar again. "Go for it, Arthur. God will forgive you."

CHAPTER 2
The Wedding Gift

Madge pushed a cup of coffee in front of Mrs. Kruchinski perched at the counter between Birdie and Rosie.

Mrs. Kruchinski clapped her hands together in full wedding-planning bliss. "I'm so pleased that Arthur and Constance are going with a traditional wedding."

"Me too," said Rosie. "I wonder if Constance has a wedding dress, yet? I should have something in my closet."

Mrs. Kruchinski worried about the appropriateness of one of Rosie's dresses. *A flamenco dancer's wardrobe is provocative, sexy even. That won't suit Constance at all.*

"And we have to plan the flowers," said Madge. "I was thinking of a fall-color arrangement. You know, plenty of orange, white and pale greens."

Birdie tried to jump in. Oscar yelled to cut her off. "It's not your wedding to plan, ladies. Arthur and Constance may have thoughts of their own, you know."

The women looked at him as though he were speaking Martian.

"It takes a lot to plan a formal wedding, dear," said Madge. "And everything has to be ready by the time Arthur's sisters get here."

"When do they arrive?" asked Rosie.

Deputy Caroline marched into The Café. "When does who arrive?"

"Arthur's sisters," Oscar called out.

"November 17th. Arriving at Kennedy Airport at 4:30 pm," said Caroline, in her official deputy voice. She shifted her leather harness with handcuffs, flashlight, and pistol out of discomfort and habit.

"How do you know that?" Mrs. Kruchinski demanded, her pride in knowing village news first dented.

Caroline smirked. "It's my job to know."

A low chuckle drifted from behind the grill. It was near to impossible to scoop Olga Kruchinski. The look of conquest on Caroline's face didn't escape Oscar.

Constance bristled through the door in her pink chenille bathrobe and matching slippers.

"Here's our bride-to-be," Oscar said. His head tilted as he recalled using that exact phrase two months ago. *Let's hope second-time's a charm, and we actually have a wedding this time.*

"I need your help." Constance's voice held a hint of urgency.

"What's the problem?" said Birdie.

"I don't know what to get Arthur for a wedding gift. It has to be something extraordinary."

Walter looked up from his morning paper. "That's easy. Get him a pocket watch with a sentimental inscription. He'll love that."

Constance shook her head. "No, needs to be grander."

"I know. How about a bench with an inscription?" said Rosie. "There's some song with beautiful lyrics about growing old together. Arthur loves benches. He'll be thrilled."

"They're already old," said Oscar.

Madge shot him a warning look. "That's enough from you. And mind your bacon. It's burning."

Constance laughed. "Leave him alone, Madge. After all, he's right. I don't feel old but 62 may qualify us as oldish." She turned to Rosie, "I love the idea, but still not grand enough."

Mrs. Kruchinski banged her cup. "Why do you keep saying that? Arthur doesn't need anything. I would think a sentimental token gift is appropriate."

"Trust me, it needs to be grand." Constance twirled the end of her thick, silver hair.

Madge looked at Mrs. Kruchinski and nodded in Constance's direction. Mrs. Kruchinski's eyes widened. They both knew the language of hair twirling.

"Constance, my dear, stop fidgeting. We'll help you figure this out," said Mrs. Kruchinski.

Birdie twisted around at the smack of Horace's mail sack hitting the cafe tile. Horace breezed over, swept Birdie into his arms in a grand gesture and kissed her good morning.

Walter lowered his newspaper and smiled. "Now, that's a pretty sight. Still not used to seeing you together, but a pretty sight all the same."

Horace released Birdie and threw his arms wide. "What's the topic of the day?"

The question was a safe one on any given day. The tiny village, with a population of 253 people, and two-block stretch of stores, did not lack vitality. There was always an issue to be discussed, argued, or manipulated in Stones End and the walls of The Café ran with its secrets.

"Constance's wedding gift to Arthur," said Walter.

"Don't worry," Horace squeezed Constance's shoulder. "Arthur will love anything you get him. Besides, you have a lot of wedding planning on your plate."

Mrs. Kruchinski's hand shot up. "You have no concerns there. We've got everything covered."

Constance stopped twirling her hair and stared blankly. *Uh oh* was written all over her face.

"The flowers will have a beautiful autumn theme," said Madge.

"And I have the perfect wedding cake picked out, which I will personally bake," added Mrs. Kruchinski.

"And there's a spectacular white dress in my closet if you need it," said Rosie.

Berris flitted in. Mrs. Kruchinski startled her by firing a question. Berris was naturally nervous and hated questions and certainly not in front of people and never before her morning jolt of caffeine.

"Just the person we need. Berris, how do you plan to do Constance's hair?" asked Mrs. Kruchinski.

Berris pushed her large red plastic glasses up her nose and examined Constance up close. "Now Constance, I know you like wearing your hair down, but I've been thinking about this, and a French twist will look stunning. Especially if we spray the twist pink."

Constance stood as still as a statue. She should have seen the hostile takeover coming.

Now, that's a Holy Crap look if I ever saw one, Oscar thought. He hoped he just thought it and didn't say it out loud. He glanced at Madge. *No, I'm good. If I said it out loud, Madge would have fired off a crucifying look.*

Walter noticed Constance's alarm as well and buried his head in the West Coast scores. A pained gaze on Constance's face brought Horace to her rescue.

"Hey, I have a terrific idea for a gift. Buy Arthur one of those wooden boat-building kits. They're miniature and he loves woodworking and boat building. You'll kill two birds with one stone."

"I love that idea," said Rosie.

Mrs. Kruchinski's cup stopped half-way to her mouth waiting for Constance's reaction. Constance looked pensive. The crowd leaned in hopefully. Then her brows drew together.

"Sorry, Horace. It's a wonderful idea but still not grand enough."

Mrs. Kruchinski's voice boomed. "There's that word again. Constance, you're overthinking this. Horace is right. Arthur will love whatever you give him. And we have bigger fish to fry planning the wedding."

Time to nip this group planning in the bud. Constance sucked in a deep breath and cleared her throat. *It's now or never*, she thought. *Be brave. Gently explain that Arthur and I want to plan our own wedding. Oh, but they live for this kind of event. No. Don't waiver. You can do this.*

"About those plans…" Walter cut her off. Constance blew a long exhale at the momentary reprieve.

"We need to reverse engineer this. If we know Arthur's gift to you, we can come up with a comparable one. So, what's he giving you?"

"A schooner." She didn't blink.

Birdie sputtered. "Are you talking about a real schooner? Not a model?"

"Yes. Three-masted, 50-foot, solid teak schooner that will soon be named: *The Constance.*"

Seven jaws dropped at the same time.

Walter broke the silence. "We're going to need a bigger present."

CHAPTER 3
Don't Tell Constance

Arthur was halfway down the stairs when he noticed his mismatched shoes and no socks. He marched back to his room. *It's going to be one of those days*.

It didn't sit right keeping the news about Ana Felicia from Constance. He and Constance weathered the recent storm, and their love was never stronger. They've only been back together three days and it already wiped out the memory of their two-month separation.

He couldn't wait till they were married, and all this worry was behind them. Extending their life past weekly Scrabble, dinner at The Café and movie night was something he daydreamed about. He longed to wake up next to Constance, go sailing with her, cook long leisurely dinners every night. His mind wandered to the thought of her company, how the scent of lavender swirled around her and holding her in his arms.

Arthur pulled on his socks and shoes and stomped his right foot. *They're wrong. I have faith in us. I'm going to tell Constance about Walter and Ana Felicia.*

He felt good about taking charge but knew not to tell Ari and Father Gregory. *It will just open a can of worms. And who wants worms*, he snickered as he scooted off the porch and down the path. "Have a good day," he called over his shoulder.

"Stop!" said Ari.

Arthur spun around. His brother pointed. "What's that?"

"What?" Arthur inspected himself. Was he wearing his bathrobe instead of his coat?

"That look on your face. I know that look. It says *I'm going to tell Constance*."

Arthur's eyes popped. "How the heck do you know that?"

"Never mind. Big brothers know. And I'm right, aren't I?"

Arthur charged back to the porch. "You two are wrong. I have faith in Constance and me. I'm about to start a life with this woman and lying, yes, it's lying," he waggled his finger, "is not the way to start. Besides, you know I'm not good at hiding things. I'll crack."

Ari pulled himself up to his full 5 feet 10 inches height. "You listen to me, Arthur. The wedding is less than a month away. Trust me, you can keep your trap shut for that long. And did you consider that Constance doesn't need the extra worry? You and she have a full-scale wedding to plan."

Father Gregory saw a ray of hope. "That's right. You won't have time to think about Ana Felicia's return or whether to tell Constance. The wedding plans will take up every moment."

They have a point. There will be plenty of diversions. And I don't want Constance worrying.

Arthur pointed at the pair. "Ok. But you'd better be right."

"Just keep saying: Don't tell Constance," said Ari.

Father Gregory repeated, "Don't tell Constance."

Arthur turned down the path to the village. *Don't tell Constance* echoed like an annoying tune that gets stuck in your head.

The pair watched Arthur hustle toward the village. Ari glanced at Father Gregory. "How long do you think he'll last?"

"A week."

"That long? I say he'll crack in three days."

George chimed in. "You're both wrong. Constance will know by sundown."

Father Gregory turned his eyes heavenward. *Great. Now I can hear George.*

CHAPTER 4

The Flashy and the Drab

Someone banged on the window of The Café. It was the flashy new assistant at Berris' beauty parlor, yelling, "Good morning." Madge and Mrs. Kruchinski nodded politely. Walter flapped his hand, and Oscar stretched over the counter with a smile plastered on his face.

Berris darted toward the door. "Gotta open the beauty parlor for Roxy."

Mrs. Kruchinski waited until Berris was out of sight. "Is it me or does Roxy stick out a bit…" she searched for a kinder word than she was thinking.

Rosie didn't hold back. "Too much."

The men wondered if the term *Stick Out* was a general one, or because Roxy wore extremely short skirts and low-cut blouses leaving nothing to the imagination. Either way, they were grateful for the big-haired, red-lipped, flesh-revealing sparkle of Roxy.

Madge's hands sat on her hips. "You want to pull your eyes back in their sockets, Oscar?"

Oscar spun back to the grill and flipped a crispy pile of hash browns.

Rosie crossed her arms and slanted an eyebrow. "In my country, Roxy is someone wives watch their husbands around."

The women's eyes shifted to the front window to better assess the threat.

Walter laughed. "Well, Roxy certainly is colorful. Did you know our Martin has taken a shine to her? His eyes glaze over every time he sees her. And they've been stepping out for a while now."

"That surprises me," said Constance. "I've talked to Roxy. She has a lot to say about makeup, hairstyles and celebrity gossip and Martin's interests are books, travel, and art. I wouldn't think Roxy is his type."

"Roxy's every young man's type," said Horace.

Birdie whacked his rock-solid arm.

"I know Berris' business surged when Ana Felicia opened her conservatory, but it's closed now. How can she afford to keep an assistant?" said Birdie.

"The surge kept going. Berris attracted a younger clientele who stayed. They love her hippie vibe, and they're nuts over her collection of spray-in color," said Madge.

"I'm happy for Berris," said Walter. He tucked his paper under his arm and strolled toward the door. "And I think young blood is good for Stones End." He winked. "Especially the colorful kind."

Walter turned back. "Constance, a taxi pulled up in front of your shop."

"A taxi! No one ever takes a taxi to Stones End," said Madge.

Mrs. Kruchinski almost toppled Madge and Birdie trying to get to the window first. A prim young woman in a tweed suit and sensible shoes emerged. Constance cried out, "Charlotte!"

Aunt and niece swayed back and forth in each other's arms while the driver unloaded two suitcases large enough to live in. Walter and Horace ran to help.

Constance held Charlotte's face. "Oh, let me look at you. Are you really here?"

"As soon as you called about getting back with Arthur, I hopped the first available flight. And I have strict orders from Great Aunt Prudence to keep you out of trouble."

Mrs. Kruchinski banged on the window and motioned for Constance to bring Charlotte into The Café.

"Run for it," said Horace, out of the side of his mouth.

"If you don't, poor Charlotte will suffer interrogation," said

Walter, straining to lift a case.

Constance grabbed Charlotte's shoulders and bustled her through the side door of the bookshop that led to her apartment.

Mrs. Kruchinski pouted. "I guess Constance didn't hear me banging."

Birdie rolled her eyes.

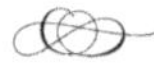

"I'm desperate for a proper cup of tea, Aunt Constance."

"Well, you've come to the right place. Come into the kitchen while I steep a pot. I don't want to miss a moment of catching up."

Charlotte dropped into a chair and launched an excited string of questions. "I'm dying to know what's been going on. How did Ana Felicia end up in the village? What broke you and Arthur up and how did you get back together?"

Constance marveled at her niece's energy. She certainly wasn't awake enough to rehash the full story. "You go first. I want to hear all the news from home."

Charlotte sighed. "Home is the same. Great Aunt Prudence still has bunions and a dry cough. There's a bake sale to raise money for the new church organ. And Agatha Potts won at bingo five weeks in a row."

Constance laughed. "How is it, The Cotswolds hasn't changed in 40 years? You poor thing. I'd forgotten what it's like to be 21 and ready to break loose and see the world."

"Oh, there's Arthur!" Constance ran to the front window and called down to the street. "Arthur, dearest. You'll never guess who just arrived from England."

Charlotte stuck her head in the window.

Arthur threw his arms wide. "That can't be little Charlotte. I'll be right up." He took a deep breath. It wouldn't do for Constance to see him in a nervous state. She might interpret it as wedding jitters. He climbed the stairs, repeating his assigned mantra. *Don't tell Constance.*

Constance gave Arthur a good-morning kiss and Charlotte beamed at seeing the happy couple together at last. She always thought they'd be perfect together.

"Now, let me look at you. Where are your pigtails?" Arthur teased.

Charlotte strung her arm through Arthur's. "Uncle Arthur, I haven't worn pigtails since I was six. Oh...I called you Uncle. I hope that's all right?"

Arthur's eyes warmed and a sense of family tugged at his heart. He patted Charlotte's hand. "Yes, my dear girl. It's more than all right."

"Darling, do you have time to join us?"

Arthur tensed. Breakfast was a danger zone. *Charlotte will want to know what's been going on. Ana Felicia will come up in the conversation. Get out now.*

"No, no. I'm afraid I'm late for work." He winced at the tightness in his voice.

Charlotte laughed. "You're the boss. You won't get in trouble."

"That's true. But if my printshop is not open when Martin arrives, he gets himself in a lather. We have a date for dinner, though. I promise. Have a wonderful day catching up."

Constance and Charlotte stood at the window, watching Arthur dash up the street.

"He's a keeper, Aunt Constance."

Constance's voice choked. "Yes. He is wonderful, isn't he? And to think, we almost lost one another."

"Are you going to tell me what happened or keep me in suspense?"

Constance didn't want to go into the sordid details and spit out an abridged version.

"Ana Felicia opened a conservatory for the arts here in Stones

End. I'm afraid I overreacted to the news of Arthur's first love being here every day. With all the loss in my life, I feared losing Arthur to her."

"That's understandable."

"All I wanted was to ask her intentions."

"Sounds reasonable. What did Ana Felicia say?"

"That's what Arthur and I fought about. He was dead against it. So, I never got to talk with her."

"Is that what broke you two up?"

"Yes. The argument got ugly, and in a childish fit of anger, I broke our engagement."

"How long were you engaged?"

"Less than 24 hours."

Charlotte's head snapped back. "That's got to be a record."

Constance laughed. "Trust me, it's not what I was going for."

"But you got your happy ending and now you and Arthur will be married in less than a month."

"Less than a month!" Constance spun around. "I have so much to do. That reminds me, I need your help with an issue. No, I need your help with two issues."

"That's why I'm here."

Constance did a high-speed download as though reporting a breaking news story. "My friends have taken over the wedding plans and I don't know how to tell them to back off without hurting their feelings. And I have no idea what to get Arthur for a wedding gift. And just as a reference point, Arthur is giving me a schooner."

Charlotte blinked several times before responding. "The first is not a problem. Trust me. I'll take care of it. The second is a little tricky. Wow. How do you top a schooner? But, not to worry. We'll figure it out."

Constance rolled her shoulders into a relaxed position. "You, dear, girl. You are exactly what I need. Steel yourself, though, when you take on the village ladies. They're a force of nature. Especially

Olga Kruchinski. I've shared stories about Olga."

Charlotte laughed. "Mrs. Kruchinski stories are my favorite. And don't you worry about me and the ladies. I've been battling Great Aunt Prudence for years, who, as you know, is formidable."

Constance wrapped Charlotte in a hug. "Did I tell you how thrilled I am to have you here?"

"Stop worrying, Aunt Constance. Your wedding will be..." Charlotte didn't finish her sentence. She moved closer to the window. "Who's that coming out of the bakery?"

Constance leaned out the window. "That's Martin, Arthur's assistant. I've told you about him."

Charlotte's head tilted dreamily. "You didn't tell me he's gorgeous."

Constance looked again. She never thought about it, but Martin was quite striking with his dark brown mop of hair, tall, lean frame, and perfectly squared shoulders.

"And, who's that?"

Constance jerked her head back to the window to see Roxy dash out of the beauty parlor and hang on Martin's arm. Martin lit up like a Christmas tree.

"That's Roxy. She's Berris' new assistant."

Charlotte looked like a balloon that just took a pin to its side. "Are they a couple?"

Constance hadn't considered the possibility of Charlotte and Martin. Her imagination galloped. *Charlotte is a much better match for him. She loves all the same things he does.*

One side of Constance said: *Stop it. Matchmaking is deplorable.* And she could hear Arthur's warning not to get involved. The other side sprinted toward the altar. *Who cares? If Charlotte marries Martin, she may stay in Stones End.*

Downplaying the Roxy connection seemed the path to take. "I don't think so. They have been seen out together, but I wouldn't say they are officially a couple."

"So, what's Martin like?"

Constance, swept up by the thought of family living in Stones End, clapped her hands together like an excited child. "Actually, my dear niece, Martin is perfect for you."

Charlotte glanced at the flashy Roxy, then looked to her very English, very tweedy appearance. "I'm a bit drab, aren't I?"

Constance followed Charlotte's stare. "Don't worry, dearest. Roxy is a momentary shiny distraction."

The color rose in Charlotte's cheeks at being read so easily and, at the same time, the thought of meeting Martin.

"Aunt Constance, I know you have to open the bookshop. I'll freshen up and take a walk around the village."

Constance smiled. She knew where Charlotte was headed.

CHAPTER 5
Is Ana Felicia Back?

Father Gregory shuffled through the village in a stupor. He heard hints of Ana Felicia and Walter starting a relationship but fluffed it off as gossip. He couldn't imagine Ana Felicia daring to show her face after the disaster she caused.

The distressing events of the past few months rattled his thoughts. It was hell living through Olga and Karl at each other's throats, Madge and Oscar barely speaking. And poor Martin was downright depressed with all the change in the village. Not to mention Arthur and Constance breaking their engagement.

Despite the hint of a brewing storm, he couldn't help but smile. Walter finding love with the opera singer he secretly adored for decades was good news, indeed.

Yes, he thought, *a match made in heaven. But please, Lord, not before Constance and Arthur walk down the aisle.*

The blustery day brought a chilled November wind. Father Gregory turned his coat collar against its bite. *Gonna be an early winter,* he thought.

He avoided The Café, not wanting to hear gossip about Walter and Ana Felicia. Or worse, have his congregants pump him for information which they were excessively fond of doing.

As he reached the fountain at the top of the village's two-block business district, he was grateful to see Horace sitting on a bench. Horace kept discussions as silent as the grave. And besides, he had insomnia and often walked in the middle of the night. If anyone saw Ana Felicia lurking, it would be him.

"Gregory, come sit a spell." Horace patted the bench.

Father Gregory lowered himself with a thump. "I'm glad to run into you. Do you mind if I share a concern?"

"Fire away."

"I've been hearing rumors about Ana Felicia and Walter starting up something. I don't know what. I haven't seen her in the village and chalked it up to gossip. Do you know…"

Horace cut him off. "It's true, all right. Two nights ago, I was out walking. It must have been near 2 am when I saw Walter and Ana Felicia. They walked to her car parked up the road out of view."

"Did they see you?"

"Walter did, on his way back to the barbershop. At first, he looked startled, then he was excited to talk about himself and Ana Felicia. It seems they formed a friendship toward the end of her time here that's grown into more. It sounds like they're falling in love."

Father Gregory pulled on his collar. Horace noticed the familiar motion and knew it signaled stress. He tried to remember if his friend ever took a vacation.

"Now, before you work yourself up, they know to keep a low profile. Well, at least, till after the wedding. Although Walter is disappointed that he can't bring Ana Felicia as his date."

"Just so you know, Arthur and Ari are aware," said Father Gregory.

"How did Arthur react?"

"He went ballistic, but Ari and I convinced him to keep the news from Constance."

Horace whistled. "That's a tall order. Arthur's an honest man. Good at keeping secrets but not so good at being devious."

"Agreed. It's a gamble he won't crack. But we gave him a good reason for keeping the news to himself. We told him that Constance doesn't need any more to deal with."

"That might work. He's crazy in love with Constance and won't want to upset her."

Father Gregory stood. Red and yellow leaves rained from the

trees in a sudden gust. He wrapped his arms around himself and stomped the coldness from his feet. “Do me a favor. Keep the Walter and Ana Felicia thing out of The Café.”

Horace doubled over in a wheezy fit of laughter. “Keep it out of The Cafe he says. This is Stones End we’re talking about. You might as well ask me to lasso a cloud.”

A smile crossed Father Gregory’s tired face. “We have to try, at least.”

Horace watched the retreating back of his battle-weary friend. *There goes an optimistic man if I ever saw one.* He laughed out loud. If five people already knew about Walter and Ana Felicia, keeping it out of The Café was pure delusion.

CHAPTER 6
The Bewitching Roxy

Charlotte pulled on dark-brown slacks and her fisherman-knit sweater heavy enough to hold off an Atlantic chill. She brushed her stick-straight, light brown hair. *Mousy*, she thought. *I have mousy-brown hair.*

Visions of Roxy's lustrous black tresses, dense enough to get lost in, did nothing for Charlotte's confidence, and Roxy's movie-star makeup diminished it further. Roxy resembled a dazzling gemstone that would burn through a London fog.

Charlotte bit her lips and pinched her cheeks, trying to raise color. She groaned at the lackluster result and again at her practical outfit. *Let's hope Martin likes me for my mind.* The thought had shades of Great Aunt Prudence's droning wisdom, making her skeptical that tactic ever worked.

It was nearly 10 am when Charlotte set off. The cheerful village perked her up. Colorful fits of autumn leaves swirled and tumbled down the street, skidded across shop awnings and painted every bench. Tantalizing scents from the shops raced through the chilled air. One moment homemade bread and cinnamon, the next bacon and coffee.

Her goal was to stroll uptown to the printshop and catch a closer look at Martin. Mrs. Kruchinski, who was leaving The Café as Charlotte passed, had other intentions. She commandeered Charlotte's arm and dragged her through the door.

"Charlotte, dear. Do you remember me? I'm Mrs. Kruchinski. You were a little girl the last time we met."

"How wonderful to see you, Mrs. Kruchinski." She hoped her

frustration at being sidetracked didn't show.

Charlotte made the best of her kidnapping. She delighted in matching faces to the people she'd heard about. Madge's fiery red mane and deep blue eyes did not disappoint. Oscar's backwards hat and plaid shirt were exactly how she pictured him. Birdie's silvery ponytail fit her rebel vibe. And Rosie moved with the precise movements of a dancer.

After polite conversation about her trip across the pond, the opportunity Charlotte waited for landed.

"I take it you're here for the wedding," said Oscar.

Charlotte rubbed her palms together and turned up the 21-year-old enthusiasm. "Yes. Isn't it marvelous that Aunt Constance and Arthur are finally getting married? I've designed their wedding in my mind a million times. Aunt Constance and I can't wait to start."

Charlotte delivered it like an air horn blast. A twinge of pity tugged at Oscar, seeing the defeated expression on Madge's face which spread like the flu to Olga, Rosie, and Birdie. But a counter-attack was inevitable and immediate.

"Now, Charlotte, dear," said Mrs. Kruchinski. "A formal wedding is a monumental occasion. You're going to need *plenty* of help."

Madge, Rosie, and Birdie didn't miss the cue lobbed at them like a stick of lit dynamite. They pelted Charlotte with their ideas for a half hour.

Charlotte waited for the ladies to run out of steam. "You're so kind. But please don't worry about the wedding details. Back in The Cotswolds…" She paused, allowing the moment to sink in. "I plan weddings for a living."

"Checkmate," drifted from behind the grill. Madge shot Oscar a murderous look.

Charlotte flashed a triumphant smile. *Poor kid.* Oscar knew Charlotte's polite slap down was deemed a minor setback to the ladies. They would rise like a phoenix from the ashes.

Charlotte breezed out of The Café, pleased she solved a problem for her aunt. She sprinted the two blocks to Arthur's printshop and paused. First impressions count. A panting dog wasn't a good one.

Glimpsing her wind-tossed hair in the window, Charlotte stuck her arm in her satchel up to her elbow, searching for the comb she knew she didn't bring. *I bet Roxy never left home without a comb.*

She took another peek. *Great. Rumpled, mousy hair.* There was no hope. She passed a hand over her head, twisted the knob, and came face to face with Martin sitting behind the counter.

He was on the phone with a customer and mouthed *I'll be right with you*. His strong eye contact and second glance made the back of her neck tingle. Charlotte flashed a dazzling smile and immediately feared she overplayed the moment. *I'm so out of practice.*

Feigning interest in a brochure, Charlotte studied Martin. His face had character, not a pretty-boy look, but intelligent, observant eyes and a natural smile. The tone of his voice rang sincere and his words precise. She imagined a finely organized mind under that mop of thick hair.

His herringbone grey sports jacket, white shirt and blue tie said he dressed for success. Although the bright turquoise tie looked like it belonged on a travel brochure for Miami. It screamed: Roxy!

The phone call ended. "Are you Charlotte?"

Her head drew back. "Yes."

Martin grinned and shrugged. "It's a small village. Word travels fast."

It captivated Charlotte how Martin was so much more than a handsome man. She got lost in his eyes that quietly took in all around him with a sense of awe. His confidence appeared firm, yet unpretentious. The type of person who could not easily be talked out of something he knew was right.

Her observations stirred a strong interest. Or was it desire?

Suddenly, she felt uncomfortable. Her emotions moved faster than where her mind wanted them to go.

Her eyes darted to his tie like a neon sign that demanded attention. Martin grabbed a bundle of papers and held them across his chest as though trying to hide a glaring stain.

A clumsy silence fell between them. Charlotte adjusted the satchel on her shoulder, then readjusted it. Martin shifted his weight from one foot to the other. The silence grew louder.

She clasped her hands tightly, as though clever words might leap from them. The ticking of the wall clock roared. *Say something before he thinks you're stupid.* She blurted out, "I like your tie."

Martin gripped the papers tighter. She wanted to snatch the words back. *Could this go any worse?*

"Thank you." He stammered. "It was a gift from a friend."

It had to be Roxy. Charlotte drew a small comfort that he called Roxy a friend and not a girlfriend.

Arthur wandered from the press room, holding a flyer. "Martin, I'm having trouble setting up this job and we need 400 copies ASAP." He squinted over his reading glasses perched on the middle of his nose. "Charlotte! What a pleasant surprise."

"I was walking by and couldn't resist popping in to say hello."

"Well, I'm glad you did. I see you've met my wingman." He leaned in conspiratorially. "Martin runs the place. I just show up and act busy."

Martin blushed. *He's humble.* Charlotte stifled a grin at the charming revelation.

Martin set the papers on the desk, removed his jacket, and stretched it across the back of the chair. Then he pulled on his printer's apron and methodically rolled up his sleeves. Charlotte marveled at his economy of motion. *I bet there's nothing out of place in his flat and he's never late for work.* Both qualities she admired.

"I'll jump right on this," Martin said. Then he turned to Charlotte. "It was lovely to meet you, Charlotte. I hope you enjoy your visit." Again, the strong eye contact, making her feel like she was the only person in the room.

Her eyes and mind still on Martin, Charlotte said, "I should let you get back to work."

Arthur peered at Charlotte, then at Martin, and back to Charlotte. His eyebrows raised. *Well, I'll be damned! She likes him. If Constance gets wind of this, she'll turn it into a matchmaking fest. Lord save us.* He grinned at the thought of young love all the same.

Charlotte tore her eyes from Martin as he dashed down the hall, then turned, and bumped into the front door. Martin stole a last glimpse before entering the print room. Arthur smiled. *And he likes her.*

"See you at dinner, Uncle Arthur. We can catch up then." Charlotte scooted out, rubbing her sore nose.

Arthur stiffened at the words: catch up. *Don't tell Constance,* echoed. He lumbered back to his office massaging a knot tightening in his stomach.

Charlotte planted herself on a bench by the fountain, threw her head back, and looked through the massive oak looming above. *I like your tie. Really, Charlotte. With all your fine breeding and education, that was the best you could do. Martin must think I'm a dolt.*

A reminiscent pang, like teenage disappointment, smothered her. *You're acting like a twit. Get your mind off Martin and onto planning the wedding.*

She momentarily soaked in the scene before her. It could have been The Cotswolds with the sprawling view of quaintness, but Charlotte saw a different picture. A modern vitality pervaded. Cyclists with neon-colored helmets raced, Fitbitted people jogged, the rush of feet in and out of shops invigorated. Even the dogs walked faster here. The energy was like a narcotic. Just what her jet-lagged brain needed.

She poked through her designer bag for paper and pen before the burst of mental clarity faded. Dress, veil, fittings, hairstyle, makeup, music for the church, music for the reception, transportation to the church, menu, flowers, decorating reception hall and church, table settings... The list rambled on and on.

Charlotte blew a deep sigh. She usually had over 6 months to organize an event of this magnitude. Pulling off a wedding in three weeks would be like climbing Mt. Everest in an hour.

She shoved the list into her satchel, like a disagreeable task to be dealt with later, then checked her watch. 11:23. She hoped to run into Martin on his lunch break. That is, if he took a lunch break and if his break was at noon.

Her practical nature kicked in. Was she acting like an adolescent nerd instead of an independent woman who controlled a lucrative event-planning business?

Her recent breakup loomed before her. It was a rough year hiding her broken heart from prying eyes. She wasn't sure she was ready to dive into the game of love again but didn't she, at least, deserve a spark of interest?

She checked her wristwatch. *Only 37 minutes,* she reasoned. *I have time and what's the harm in an innocent fling?* Great Aunt Prudence's logic barged in like an uninvited guest. *The harm is that he's someone who lives on another continent. And he's not British. Did you consider that, you foolish girl?*

Charlotte wrinkled her nose like a noxious smell passed and snatched her copy of *Sense and Sensibility* from her bag. If anyone could shut up Great Aunt Prudence, it was Jane Austen.

Just when Elinor Dashwood discovers Edward Ferrars is engaged, Martin padded across the green wearing a broad smile. Charlotte's pulse raced. Her waiting paid off. She ran a mental score: *Jane Austen, one. Great Aunt Prudence, zero.* She gave her hair a quick fluff and bounded off the bench.

"Marty, I bought our favorite soup for lunch." Charlotte jerked toward the interruption. Roxy, wearing a tight leather jacket, four-inch red heels, and a skirt that showed enough leg to make a nun faint strutted toward her. Charlotte looked back at Martin. His eyes gleamed with delight. Or was it lust? She couldn't tell.

Charlotte sank onto the bench. She stared at *Sense and Sensibility* lying on the ground. Suddenly, Martin's feet came into view, then his hand reached for the book.

"Sense and Sensibility." He couldn't contain a smile. "I'm excessively fond of Jane Austen."

Charlotte laughed at his clever attempt to sound like Willoughby's character. Martin smiled broadly, seeing his reference hit the mark and bowed like an Edwardian gentleman. "Your book, Madam."

Roxy's high-pitched whine shredded the enchanting moment. "Marty, it's cold out. Let's eat at the beauty parlor." She gave Charlotte a tight-eyed stare. "Who's your friend?"

"This is Charlotte, Constance's niece. She's come all the way from England for the wedding. Charlotte, this is Roxy."

Roxy tilted her head at Martin as though waiting for him to finish. Seeing that he was going to leave it there, she stuck her face toward Charlotte and pulled her words long: "His girlfriend."

Charlotte noticed Martin's jaw tighten. She rose and extended her hand. "It's nice to meet you, Roxy."

Roxy glanced at her hand like it was a diseased appendage. "Nice to meet you too," she said, without extending her own hand.

"Marty, I'm freezing. Let's go."

Martin winced. Charlotte couldn't tell which he hated more, being called Marty or Roxy's bad manners.

"Would you care to join us, Charlotte?" he said.

"I'm sure she has better things to do. Besides, I just bought enough for two." Roxy clutched Martin's arm so close she could have jumped into his pocket. Then, she reached up and slowly pushed the mop of hair from his eyes, letting her hand linger on his cheek. Charlotte recognized it as the classic marking-your-territory gesture all women knew.

Martin's eyes glowed like a pair of fireflies on a hot summer night. It reminded Charlotte of when she lost her first boyfriend to a Roxy-like cheerleader. He had that same bewitched look. *Give it up, Charlotte. You wouldn't know how to bewitch a man if you took lessons.*

Charlotte threw her satchel over her shoulder. "Thanks so much, but I'm afraid my 20-hour trip just caught up with me. Maybe another time."

Roxy steered Martin toward the beauty parlor, leaving Charlotte to stare at their backs.

Arthur, spying the scene from the printshop window, watched Charlotte scuff off alone. His heart broke for his soon-to-be niece.

Jet lag grabbed hold and Charlotte pushed one foot in front of the other. It didn't help that her spirit now matched her low energy.

She felt foolish about her reaction to meeting Martin and cringed at the thought of how she raced toward the printshop. What was she hoping for—Kismet? *That only happens in the movies. Great Aunt Prudence's wisdom wins again.*

Rejection spurred the painful memory of her fiancé dumping her. Ted had been cheating on her for six months. He had no intention of marrying her. By the time he plucked up the courage to tell her, it was two weeks before the wedding.

Charlotte's mother was crushed. She loved Ted and thought they were the perfect couple. But she stood by Charlotte and said she would handle all the cancellations. Charlotte insisted on doing it herself.

She cancelled the cake at the baker, the hall at the church, the organist, the flowers, the last fitting with the seamstress. Each call was another stab at her heart, her pride, her hopes, and dreams. Thinking about the pitying stares that were sure to come made her contemplate moving. She didn't know how she would bear it.

By the time she made the last call, she was numb. Wariness replaced heartbreak and she made a solemn vow to swear off love. She wasn't expecting Martin.

His eyes mesmerized her. They seemed to speak their own language, and it was one of kindness. The tone of his voice dripped sincerity. And it didn't hurt that he was smart, cultured, and funny. Charlotte ripped open the bookshop door. *And belongs to a woman who probably thinks Chaucer is a fancy name for a plate.*

Constance picked up the phone. "The Page Turner Bookshop. How may I help you?" Arthur filled her in on what he witnessed. Constance didn't know what to expect when Charlotte returned but seeing her niece scuff in with rounded shoulders and downcast eyes didn't surprise her.

"Sweetheart, you look done in."

"Just tired." Charlotte scanned a stack of best-sellers on the counter, avoiding eye contact.

"You need a nap, dearest. Go upstairs and I'll wake you for dinner."

"Good idea." Charlotte lingered, like something was on her mind. Constance chanced pushing. "How was your walk around town?"

Charlotte stretched across the counter and grabbed a homemade brownie. "You remember your comment this morning that Martin and Roxy are not officially a couple?"

"I do."

"Well, they're now official."

"Just because you saw them together doesn't mean it's in concrete."

Charlotte raised an eyebrow. Constance shrugged sheepishly. "It's a small village…"

Charlotte cut her off. "I know, and news travels fast. But it was more than seeing Martin and Roxy together. Roxy stated, definitively, I might add, that she is Martin's girlfriend."

Constance pulled on her chin. Charlotte couldn't read the posture. Was her aunt assessing the situation, or scheming?

"Did Martin agree?"

"No. He stiffened like a cardboard cutout."

"Sounds like the announcement caught him by surprise."

"He was gracious and invited me to lunch with them. But I could tell he wouldn't mind if I said no."

"You didn't say yes!"

Charlotte stared hard. "No one wants to be a third wheel, Aunt Constance. Besides, Roxy slithered up to Martin so close you couldn't tell where her body started, and his body ended."

"Oh, my. Martin is a reserved young man. I bet that made him uncomfortable."

Charlotte laughed. "Uncomfortable? His eyes turned dreamy, and he forgot to say goodbye before Roxy hauled him off."

Horace's words rang out. *Roxy is every young man's type.* Constance patted her niece's hand. "I'm sorry, dearest. Men can be jerks."

Charlotte pushed herself from the counter and gave Constance a peck on the cheek. "We're making too much of this."

"Are we? I can tell you like Martin. And I happen to know you two have a lot in common."

"Yes. But Martin has a girlfriend. Besides, I'm here to help with your wedding, not plan mine." She pulled out her To-Do list and handed it to Constance. "My pillow calls."

Her swollen ankles and feet felt like she pulled two anvils

across the room. Too tired to turn, Charlotte called over her shoulder. "The morning wasn't a complete disaster. The ladies are no longer involved in planning your wedding."

"That's wonderful."

Constance dragged her glasses from the top of her head and read the To-Do list. It felt as though the ground shook. *We're in big trouble.*

CHAPTER 7

Welcome, Charlotte

Ari turned his head at the sound of Arthur's screen door slapping shut. "Where are you off to?"

"Where are *we* off to is the question." He tossed Ari his coat.

Ari shoved his arms into the sleeves. "Are you going to tell me, or make me guess?"

"Constance's for dinner. I want you to meet her niece, Charlotte."

Ari laughed. "You mean you want me to keep you out of trouble."

Arthur smiled. "That too. Charlotte wants to catch up with village news. Ana Felicia is bound to come up. I need you to be the traffic cop. You know, steer the conversation away from the danger zone."

"The danger zone being Walter and Ana Felicia as a couple."

"And there's another. We can't talk about Martin."

"Martin? What trouble can he cause?"

"Charlotte stopped by the shop today. From what Constance told me, it was to meet Martin who she spied coming out of the bakery this morning."

Ari stabbed a finger into the air. "Should be an excellent match. Martin's always talking about living in England and Charlotte is from England. They're made for each other if you ask me."

Arthur grinned at his brother's oversimplified view of life. "If you tell Constance I said this I'll deny it, but they would make a wonderful couple."

"So, why is Martin off limits?"

"After Charlotte left the shop, she sat by the fountain. I suspect she hoped to run into him coming out at some point."

"And did he?"

"Yes. Only he was meeting Roxy for lunch."

"Aww. Don't tell me."

"Yep. Martin and Roxy scampered off arm-in-arm and Charlotte trudged home alone."

"Poor kid. So, the toxic zones are Ana Felicia, Walter and Ana Felicia and Martin." Ari ran a hand over his face. "We'll be tiptoeing through a field of landmines tonight."

They turned off the river path and headed toward the village. The moon rose over the church steeple in the distance as they crunched along the gravel road.

"Tonight will be tricky, but you can pull it off. You're good at this," said Arthur.

Ari slapped his chest. "I'm your man."

Arthur threw his arm around Ari's shoulders. "I don't say it often enough, but you're a terrific big brother."

"You never say it."

Arthur punched his brother's arm. "Well, I'm saying it now, damn it."

The brothers swatted and flicked at one another like when they were kids in Greece. Then Arthur yelled, "Race you to the village."

Ari, close on his heels, hollered, "No fair. You got a head start!"

Arthur reached the bookshop first and doubled over with his hands on his knees. In a ragged breath, he choked out, "I win!"

Ari limped toward him, holding his side. "I never could beat those bloody long legs of yours."

Both ignored the fact that their racing days were over.

Arthur pressed his finger to his lips. "Shhh."

"What?"

"Do you hear that?"

Ari cocked his head. "Sounds like St. Gregory's schoolyard at recess."

They climbed the stairs to Constance's apartment above the bookshop. The noise blared louder with each step. Squeezing past the group gathered at the door, Arthur scanned the jammed living room for Constance. Her hand shot up. "Darling, over here."

"What's going on?"

Constance threw her arms around his neck. "Isn't it wonderful? Madge and Olga pulled together an impromptu welcome party for Charlotte. Before I knew it, half the village showed up. Olga brought cookies, Madge brought sandwiches and salads and Birdie brought booze."

"Point me to Birdie," said Ari.

Arthur looked around. "And where's our guest of honor?"

Constance did a 360-degree turn. "There she is, talking with Rosie by the kitchen door."

"I'll say hello, then I'm off to find the food before it disappears."

Constance huddled in the living room corner with Madge, Mrs. Kruchinski and Birdie. She saw Martin stroll in alone. It didn't take him long to find Charlotte. The ladies glued their eyes on the young couple.

"Are you seeing what I'm seeing?" said Mrs. Kruchinski.

"They're adorable together. I've never seen Martin so animated," said Madge.

"Nice to see, for a change. When he's with Roxy, Martin does a lot of listening," said Birdie.

Arthur joined Oscar and Walter with a mile-high plate of sandwiches and potato salad.

Walter, a true romantic, was the first of the men to notice Martin and Charlotte. "Look how sweet they look together. Aren't they sweet, Arthur?"

Arthur looked over his shoulder. "I don't want this overheard by any of the female population, but yes, they make a wonderful couple."

Horace pushed in between Oscar and Walter. "What are we looking at?"

Oscar nodded toward Martin and Charlotte.

"Would you look at that? Our little Martin, chatting up a pretty woman," said Horace.

Arthur lowered his fork. "That pretty woman is my niece, Charlotte." He went for another mouthful, then lowered his fork again. "And we probably should stop referring to Martin as *our little Martin*. He's come into his own the past few years."

"That's true. Even in the past few months, he's dropped his quirkiness." said Horace.

"Yeah. He no longer dresses like he's from merry ole England. I suspect meeting Roxy had something to do with that," said Walter.

"It turns out, Martin has a fine mind for business. He single-handedly automated the printshop operation. It saved us so much time we doubled our clients. We're going to have to expand soon and hire additional staff."

Oscar slapped him on the back. "That's terrific."

"And if I get this five-year contract I'm working on, the sky's the limit. I'll promote Martin to Operations Manager."

"Great. Then maybe Martin can move from his shoebox-size apartment and buy a house," said Horace.

"Sounds like Martin is suddenly a prime catch," said Walter.

Arthur choked. "Please, Walter, don't let Constance hear you saying that."

Rosie elbowed her way across the room and sidled in between Constance and Madge. "I think love is in the air," she said, in a singsong voice.

Constance chewed the side of her lip. She could hear Arthur warning her not to engage in matchmaking. Her head tilted in her niece's direction. *But they're perfect together.*

"You're very quiet, Constance," said Birdie.

The second glass of wine loosened her resolve, and before Constance could stop herself, she shared Charlotte's interest in Martin and her encounter with him and Roxy that afternoon.

Mrs. Kruchinski bristled. "Not that I have anything against Roxy, but she's not right for Martin. Now, Charlotte, on the other hand…"

"Barracuda at 10 o'clock," said Birdie.

There was a collective turning of heads toward the door. Roxy strutted in like she owned the place and made a beeline for Martin, lashing herself to his arm. She didn't waste any time launching a dramatic tirade.

"You won't believe who came in at the last minute. Mildred Carson, for a pedicure, no less. I hate working on her feet. They're ugly."

Charlotte drained half a glass of wine in one long gulp. Making a sudden leap from a conversation about Charles Dickens to ugly feet was like being slapped by an unexpected wave. She scanned the room for someone to rescue her and locked eyes with Constance, who waved her over.

"Will you excuse me? My aunt needs something."

Martin strained his neck over the crowd watching Charlotte walk away. Roxy droned on about Mildred Carson's hammertoes.

Birdie poured more wine for Charlotte. She'd need it. Mrs. Kruchinski was poised to pounce. Charlotte barely got in a sip before she knew what hit her. “So, Charlotte dear, you and Martin seemed to have a lot to talk about.”

“Yes. We talked about our favorite artists and authors. And Martin was interested to hear about life in The Cotswolds and my new business venture. And he shared the exciting changes at the printshop and his desire to visit England.”

“Sounds like you two have a lot in common,” said Madge.

Charlotte glanced across the room at Martin. Roxy was playfully shoving a cookie in his mouth.

She turned back to the ladies. “Martin has other things on his mind.” She forced a nonchalant tone. “Let’s change the subject. Shall we? What’s new in Stones End?”

CHAPTER 8

There's No Such Thing as Ghosts

Charlotte wore a brave face that didn't fool Constance. Her niece could not hide the disappointment in her eyes. She stared pleadingly at Birdie to say something, anything.

Birdie blurted out. "Want to hear a strange story?"

"Always," said Rosie.

"The other morning when we had that drenching rain, I was walking Brownie in the village square. It was about half-past six. Brownie was sniffing around the fountain, when I saw something moving alongside the church up the hill."

Constance pressed her back to the wall, getting comfortable for one of Birdie's long stories. "What was it, an animal?"

"At first, I couldn't tell. The wind churned the fog into eerie shapes and played tricks with my eyes. So, I got as close as I dared."

"You're crazy, Birdie. I would have run for my life," said Rosie.

"No. I had to see what it was. I picked Brownie up and edged my way along the side path. It was then I saw a lone figure under a black umbrella. He walked with a lopsided limp, and it took him a long time to reach the rear of the church. When he got there, he stopped like he needed to rest, then turned into the cemetery."

Charlotte wrapped her arms around her middle. "You just gave me the chills."

"Please tell me you got out of there," said Madge.

"I should have but I was suddenly obsessed with what the man was up to. Who visits a cemetery at that hour?"

"Not to mention in the pouring rain," said Charlotte.

"I was afraid Brownie would bark if we got closer, so I ducked into the back door of the church and left him there. When I ran out, the cemetery looked like a place I'd never seen before."

Berris sauntered over and lurked at the edge of the group. "What was so different?"

"It always appeared peaceful to me, you know, graceful looking. But suddenly, I was terrified to go near it. The entrance appeared as a dark hole. I don't know why, but I had the feeling that if I entered, I'd never come out."

"At first, I couldn't see through the wall of fog. I held onto the hood of my jacket to keep the rain off my eyes. Then, his umbrella came into sight up ahead. He fought with the wind to keep it steady."

"A dark, foggy cemetery and you decided to follow a stranger in the rain." Mrs. Kruchinski shook her head.

"I knew to keep my distance." Birdie gulped a mouthful of scotch and water. Retelling the story clearly rubbed her nerves.

"So, what happened?" asked Constance.

"I inched down the path, pushing the heavy branches of the weeping willow from my face. It was hard walking on all the wet leaves. I kept slipping. To make matters worse, I was chilled to the bone. My instincts told me to run."

The women stood rapt in the eerie story. Berris shuddered. Madge pressed her right hand to her heart.

"The cemetery is creepy on a good day. All those old headstones covered in moss and weeds," said Madge.

"We're proud of our graveyard," admonished Mrs. Kruchinski. "It dates back to 1861. The first to be buried there were our Civil War heroes and generations of villagers since."

Berris twisted her hands so tightly, they pulsed red. "I'm with Madge. The place gives me the willies. Especially since it's haunted."

"Don't believe that story, Berris. It's made up," said Constance.

Charlotte dragged her eyes from Martin and Roxy. "Your cemetery has a ghost? Why does he haunt?"

"He's like the Sleepy Hollow ghost who looks for his severed head. Only our ghost is a young soldier looking for his missing leg," said Birdie.

Berris turned ten shades of pale.

"Uh. Let's stop talking about ghosts," said Constance.

Glancing at Berris, Mrs. Kruchinski obliged. "So, Birdie, who was the man in the cemetery?"

"No idea. I hoped some of you might have seen him around the village."

All heads wagged no.

"Can you recall anything else about his looks?" asked Madge.

"Hard to say. His face was hidden under the umbrella. It may sound silly, but he struck me as an old English gentleman. Maybe because he had on a tweed cap and those boots the Brits wear."

"Wellies," said Charlotte, stealing another glance across the room.

"Anything else you recall? Old, young, short, tall?" asked Constance.

"A shock of white hair stuck out of the back of his cap. And he used a walking stick to help move himself along. Overall, he gave the impression of a frail, old man."

They glanced at one another as if looking for answers.

"How mysterious," said Constance.

Birdie slanted forward. "There's more."

Berris' eyes froze in the open position. Mrs. Kruchinski grasped her wine glass with both hands.

"The wind let up, and I got a glimpse of him leaning against a tree at the end of the path. It looked like he needed another rest. But then he reached into the inside pocket of his coat and pulled something out."

Rosie gasped. "A gun?"

"Oh, Rosie. What made you think that?" said Madge.

"I thought the same thing," said Birdie. "And it could have been. Because he shoved the object into the outside pocket of his coat. Whatever it was, it weighed his coat down on that side. I don't know why, but the action struck me as sinister, and I turned back to see if any lights were on in the rectory."

"A gun? What would he need a gun for?" said Mrs. Kruchinski.

"You should have gotten out of there, Birdie. What were you thinking?" said Constance.

"I was thinking the rectory was stone cold dark, and there was no one to hear me scream if this creep tried to murder me. But just as I turned to run, he pushed himself from the tree. Suddenly, his steps quickened. He turned toward a row of headstones. And here's the strangest part. He went straight to Willie's grave, like he knew where it was."

"Willie's grave! My Willie?" said Constance.

"Yes. Your son's grave. I watched him for almost 10 minutes, but my teeth were chattering so badly I thought I'd crack a tooth. So, I hoofed it back to the church and bolted the door. My chest felt quivery. I couldn't tell if it was from fright or the cold. I stood by the window, waiting for him to leave the cemetery. But he never came down the path."

"What do you mean, he never came out? Where'd he go?" said Madge.

"Don't know. Vanished."

"A decrepit old man with a cane and a limp just vanished? That's impossible." said Mrs. Kruchinski.

"Agreed. I waited for the sun to come up. Then Brownie and I crawled over every inch of the grounds. Strange. He dragged his leg and poked his stick, yet the ground wasn't disturbed."

Mrs. Kruchinski stiffened, and Madge rubbed her arms like an icy wind blew through.

Rosie's eyes darted over each shoulder as though danger was near. Then spoke in a whisper. "You said he walked with a lopsided limp."

Charlotte tilted her head as she thought about what Rosie just described. "I see where you're going. You think he's the ghost with the missing leg. But he can't be. Birdie said this guy is ancient and the Stones End ghost is young."

"Well, if he lost his leg during the Civil War, he'd be ancient by now," said Madge.

Constance stared intently, then shook her head. "No. There's no such thing as ghosts."

Birdie drained her scotch and water.

"Did you report this to Caroline?" said Madge.

"Report what? The guy didn't do anything wrong."

Mrs. Kruchinski screeched. "He was standing over Willie's grave."

"That is odd. But not illegal," said Constance.

Caroline appeared, holding a bottle of water. She never drank alcohol while on duty. And she always considered herself on duty. "I heard my name. What's going on?"

Birdie related the story. When she got to the part about the cemetery, Caroline put her water down and reached for her notepad. She scribbled notes and asked questions, then scribbled some more.

"Well, there's nothing illegal here, but I'll keep my eyes peeled and ask around. I like to keep track of who's in the village. Maybe someone else saw this guy."

"Why do you suppose he stood over Willie's grave?" said Constance.

Caroline tapped her pen against the notepad. Folks rarely talked about when Constance lost her 12-year-old son, even though it was decades past.

"To tell you the truth, Constance, our historic graveyard attracts visitors. The tender age on your son's headstone catches the eye of many. I'm sure it's nothing."

Madge stared at Caroline. She wasn't buying it. But it pleased her that their painfully honest deputy sheriff offered a compassionate explanation. Mrs. Kruchinski wasn't convinced either but swallowed her words for Constance's sake.

Birdie squinted. Caroline glanced at her and wagged her head ever so slightly. Birdie knew what the wag meant: shut up.

The tall-cased clock chimed nine. Constance was glad to see the crowd thinning. It was a long day, and her feet screamed to be free of their tight-grabbing captors.

Charlotte excused herself to say goodbye to the last guests. Martin and Roxy had already left. It didn't surprise her. Roxy wasn't the house party type. A twinge of disappointment pinched that he didn't say goodnight.

Arthur snuck up behind Constance and wrapped his arms around her. She melted into his chest. "Looked like you ladies were scheming. I bet I can guess the topic."

Constance laughed. "You'll be happy to hear we weren't scheming."

"Did I hear a hanging *yet* at the end of that sentence?"

She elbowed him in the ribs. "For your information, smarty pants, Birdie was telling a ghost story."

Arthur released Constance and rubbed his bloodshot eyes. "Am I too tired to hear this?"

Constance spun around and kissed him. "Yes, sweetheart. Go home and get some sleep."

"Ari," Arthur yelled. "Where are you?"

Ari stepped from the kitchen, downed the last swallow of whiskey, and saluted. "Ready when you are."

Arthur shook his head. "How is it, no matter how much you drink, you're never drunk?"

Ari shrugged. "Thick Greek blood. It can absorb anything."

"Doesn't work for me," said Arthur.

"That's because you got Pop's British blood."

Charlotte applauded their brotherly banter. "You two should take this act on the road. You're hysterical!"

Arthur's arms opened wide. "Goodnight, Charlotte, my dear girl."

Constance pushed him toward the door.

Madge, Mrs. Kruchinski, and Rosie came out of the kitchen rolling down their sleeves.

"Everything's cleaned up and the dishwasher is stacked."

Constance gave them a group hug. "What would I do without you?"

Aunt and niece stood at the window watching the guests disappear into the night. Then Charlotte turned to Constance. "That story must have been rough on you. Are you alright?"

"Yes, dearest. I'm sure Caroline's right. It's nothing."

Charlotte covered a long, loud yawn. "We should get some sleep. Wedding planning starts tomorrow."

Charlotte scuffed off to bed. Constance poured herself a glass of wine and fell into a chair. *Why would a stranger stand in the drenching rain over Willie's grave?*

CHAPTER 9
When More Is a Bad Thing

The unsteady padding of feet heading for the bathroom drifted from the corridor. It was nice to have another heartbeat in the apartment. Constance thought of Willie and the decades of missed morning sounds from her son. She imagined them as banging and stomping. *Yes,* she thought, *Boys banged about, and girls padded around.*

The day headed toward a sharp uphill slant. Constance hunched over her coffee. *I should have passed on the last glass of wine.* She prayed to the caffeine gods to hit her with a jolt of energy.

A wet ring, from where she set her mug, stained the To-Do list. Constance blotted the coffee-brown circle with a napkin, then glared at the 47 lines of tasks blaring like a theater marquee. It was impossible for the two of them to tackle it in three weeks.

They needed help from the queens of planning, and Constance wondered how bruised her friends' feelings were. And it concerned her that Charlotte's confidence may be shaken by asking for help. What a discouraging thing to tell someone just launching a new career. And not just anyone, but her darling niece, who made a 20-hour trip to help her.

A hot swallow of coffee hit the back of her throat. The day was closing in and it wasn't even 8 am. Constance sighed and pulled out a flyer stuffed between the napkins. It was information on a boat-building kit. *Horace must have left it last night, dear man.* Constance looked heavenward and thanked the Lord for her amazing friends.

She still hadn't come up with a wedding gift for Arthur. *What will declare my love for him, our life, and our families?* She pressed her fists to her pounding temples. *I can't think about that now.* She shoved the flyer back among the napkins.

Leaning against the sink, Constance peered out the window. Shafts of sunlight broke through the grey ceiling of clouds and church bells tolled in the distance. Most mornings, the repetitive bong stirred a sense of tranquility. This morning, they rang out a disturbing image of a stranger hovering over Willie's grave. *Was Caroline right? Was he just another curious visitor?*

It made no sense. Her friends were alarmed. She read it in their faces. And why did Caroline take so many notes?

The questions twisted round and round, but she obsessed over only one. Who visits a graveyard at 6:30 on a stormy morning? Her mind kicked out the answer: no one.

Constance mentally changed the 47 tasks on the list to 48. *I have to make time to visit Caroline today.*

Charlotte drifted into the kitchen, stretching like a cat waking from sleep. "I shouldn't have had those last two glasses of wine. We have a killer day ahead of us." She sank into a chair and squinted one eye at the list, then swung it upside down and slapped it to the table.

Constance poured steeped tea into a cup with hand-painted pink roses. She set the cup and matching saucer under her niece's nose. "Drink this, dear. You'll feel better."

Constance waited for Charlotte to sip half a cup. Her grandmother's wisdom rang out. *Better to put unpleasant tasks behind you.* She slid in across from her and inhaled deeply.

"About this list, dearest... I was thinking... Now, please don't take this the wrong way... Because you know I have every confidence in you..."

Charlotte tilted her head as though struggling with a clue from the *New York Times* Sunday crossword. It made her brain hurt.

"Did I overlook something? Because we can amend the list and add anything you want."

Constance sputtered. "Add to the list? No, no. I was more thinking we might just have to cut it down some. Or maybe, just maybe, enlist the ladies to help with a few things."

Charlotte covered her face with her hands.

"Sweetheart, are you crying?"

"Thank God," said Charlotte.

Constance's back slammed against the chair. "You're not upset?"

"Upset? I almost lost my breakfast when I finished the list."

Constance released a hearty laugh. She threw the list into the air. "Let's go to The Café. We can celebrate our liberation from the list with a proper fry-up."

"Will the ladies be there?"

"Most likely. We can explain we need their support after all."

Charlotte's face scrunched. "What's the chance of them helping us now?"

Constance slipped her arm around her niece. "Not to worry. The women in this village never let one another down. Besides, they'll be thrilled to be back in the game."

Constance and Charlotte bustled into The Café arm-in-arm, chattering like two kids planning mischief.

"So, what are your plans for today?" said Mrs. Kruchinski. "I like to stay abreast, even though I'm not included." Her lips sucked into a sulk.

"For heaven's sake, Olga, you'll have them dripping in guilt. Charlotte is a wedding planner. She doesn't need our help," said Madge.

Charlotte flinched as though slapped. Constance pressed her hand and whispered, "It will be fine."

Birdie sensed what was developing and pulled up a chair to savor the spectacle. Constance was a straight shooter and would blurt out that they needed help after all. Charlotte, hopefully, wouldn't crumple under fire. But the true entertainment was how Olga would react.

"Charlotte and I realize we can't pull this wedding off alone. So, we're here to throw ourselves on your mercy and beg for help," said Constance.

Madge leaped off the stool. "Of course, we'll help."

"This is awesome," said Rosie. "I'll bring that dress around if you want to see it. I'm certain we can alter it."

Birdie gave Mrs. Kruchinski a wide-eyed nod that blared: *Don't be a misery.*

Oscar glimpsed the crossed arms and stiff lips on Mrs. Kruchinski and busied himself behind the counter. He had no stomach for carnage first thing in the morning. Walter ducked behind his newspaper, and Horace lowered his head over his bowl of cereal.

Mrs. Kruchinski's eyes narrowed. An uneasy silence descended. Charlotte suppressed a smile at a fleeting vision of her screeching, "Off with their heads!"

Birdie couldn't stand anymore. "Damn it, Olga. Say something!"

The impasse ended with the clap of Mrs. Kruchinski's hands, followed by her barking out orders like a drill sergeant. "Charlotte, you're in charge of Constance's ensemble."

"Madge, you take care of the flowers and help Oscar with the food."

Constance jumped in. "There must be lamb on the menu. Arthur's family loves lamb."

"I already worked out the menu," yelled Oscar. He poked his finger in the air. "And there will be lamb!"

Charlotte blinked at the extraordinary change of atmosphere. A moment ago, you'd need a machete to hack through the tension, and now the room soared with excitement.

"Walter, you coordinate the church music. And Rosie, you take the music for the reception."

"I'm on it," said Rosie. "A delightful mix to satisfy the old, young and sentimental."

"I'll manage the table settings and wedding cake. And we'll all pitch in decorating the village hall. That covers everything," said Mrs. Kruchinski.

"No!" Birdie bellowed.

Charlotte grabbed onto a chair as if an earthquake hit.

"No? What part is no?" said Rosie.

"We will hold the reception in the ballroom at the conservatory."

Constance stiffened her back like a sentry. "I'm not comfortable with that, Birdie. Will Ana Felicia give her permission? I haven't heard that the sale is final or even who bought the place."

"It's final, all right," said Birdie. "You're looking at the new owners."

"Owners? You and who else?" said Madge.

Walter peered from behind his Sports section. "Birdie, Rosie and I banded together and bought the conservatory. And we're stealing Ana Felicia's plan. I'll run a music and vocal program. Rosie will give dance instructions. And Birdie, of course, will head up the art department and gallery."

"And don't forget Horace. He's our legal consultant," said Birdie. Horace raised his spoon in acknowledgement.

"It's a dream come true for all of you. How positively wonderful," said Constance.

Oscar dashed from behind the grill and pumped Walter's and Horace's hands. "Congratulations. Couldn't be more pleased for you."

Madge folded her arms around Birdie. "You'll finally have your own gallery. Maybe now we'll see some of your work."

"Your wedding will be in a ballroom. Just like in the fairy tales," said Rosie.

"That's it," said Mrs. Kruchinski. "We'll meet in five days to report our progress to Constance and Arthur."

"Hey, what am I in charge of?" said Birdie.

Mrs. Kruchinski rolled her eyes. "The liquor. You're always in charge of the liquor. I thought that went without saying."

Birdie smiled and bowed. "Thank you."

"So, are we all set?" said Mrs. Kruchinski.

"Wait," said Charlotte. She fumbled through her satchel. "Arthur set up a wedding account at the bank to cover expenses. I'll ask him to include your names. That way you'll have money to cover upfront expenses."

Mrs. Kruchinski pulled back. She turned to Constance. "Looks like we need a wedding planner after all."

Charlotte beamed.

Walter stretched up on his toes. "There's another taxi out front."

"Another taxi? That's two in one week. What's going on?" said Mrs. Kruchinski.

A tall, delicate woman with short grey hair wearing a felt hat, beige coat buttoned to her neck and white gloves stepped from the taxi. She turned and extended her hand to the second passenger. A zaftig woman with wavy black hair flowing past her shoulders emerged.

Despite their youthful posture and energy, their faces reflected the wear of women in their mid-sixties. Constance strained to have a better look. "It can't be." Just as she reached the window, Ari appeared and shuffled the women inside.

"Constance," Ari called out. "Come meet my sisters Emily and Zoe."

Emily gave Constance a lengthy hug. "Constance, it's wonderful to meet you finally. I'm Emily."

Zoe wrapped Constance in a crushing embrace that almost lifted her off the floor. "You're as gorgeous as Arthur described you."

Constance brushed at tears. "I'm thrilled to meet you, at long last. Does Arthur know you're here?"

"No. It's a surprise. We realize you're both busy with full-time jobs, so we came early to take charge of the wedding arrangements," said Zoe forcefully.

Birdie blew an exasperated sigh. Mrs. Kruchinski's jaw hit her chest.

Constance sputtered. "How wonderful." Her hands reached for the top of her head to keep it from blowing off.

CHAPTER 10
What to Do with the Sisters?

Arthur sprinted straight for The Café when Ari called and wept at seeing his sisters. Mrs. Kruchinski held a handful of napkins at the ready, waiting for the emotional tidal wave to subside. The sight of the four siblings together after 13 years overwhelmed Ari. He grabbed the offered napkin and blew his nose loudly.

Oscar called out from behind the grill. "Breakfast is on the house!"

The door to The Café opened, blowing in a blast of chilly air, swirling leaves and Father Gregory. "Gregory, come meet my sisters," said Arthur.

Father Gregory extended his hand. "What a marvelous surprise. We weren't expecting you for weeks."

Ari laughed. "I don't trust these two. Coming early means they're up to something."

"We came early to help with the wedding plans," said Emily cheerfully.

"Not help," said Zoe. "Take charge."

Arthur felt the pressure when Constance put her foot on his. The signal was clear: do something. He loved Zoe. But he wouldn't wish her on anyone when she was hellfire bent on a plan.

"Now, you two are not to worry about the wedding. Constance and Charlotte have everything under control." Arthur squeezed Constance's hand. "Don't you, darling?"

Constance's eyes radiated thank you. "Yes, sweetheart. As a matter of fact, we just met with our friends and divided up who does what. So, you see, you can have a relaxing vacation."

"Absolutely not," said Zoe. "We came to help."

"Stop being a bossy-boots," said Emily. "I wouldn't mind a vacation."

Madge leaned into Oscar. "Looks like Zoe is a match for Olga."

"My money is on Olga," said Walter.

"I don't know about that," said Horace. "I wouldn't want to tangle with Zoe."

Birdie shook her head. "You're wrong. Olga can take Zoe to the mat."

Oscar reached into his shirt pocket. "Wanna put your money where your mouth is, Birdie?"

Father Gregory caught sight of the notepad. He remembered when Oscar took bets about Arthur. They wagered how long he could keep Ana Felicia and her secrets from Constance.

His finger wagged from across the room. Oscar lowered his hand and brushed his apron like he didn't know what the good priest meant. Madge lit up. Her face burned as red as her hair.

Horace choked down a howl. "You gotta give it to Gregory. He's determined to save us miscreants from perdition whether we like it or not."

Madge and Oscar served a smorgasbord of breakfast delights—mountains of pancakes, enough crispy bacon to satisfy a truck stop and, of course, Greek omelets oozing feta cheese and dotted with black olives.

Youthful reminiscing bounced around the table. Every story started with: *Remember when*. "Remember when Zoe was 18 and won the Miss Corso beauty contest. Emily was green with envy. Remember when Arthur and Pop restored the shipwrecked schooner."

Stories bounced from youthful hijinks to the pain of their

parents' deaths and landed on expanding the family business into a multi-million-dollar tourist enterprise on their Greek island.

Constance heard most of the raucous tales from Arthur through the years. But it was like watching a Broadway show hearing them told by the original cast. *This is my family now,* she thought. The warmth and contentment of a fulfilled life settled in her heart.

Mrs. Kruchinski joined Madge at the end of the counter. She nodded toward Zoe. "That one is going to be trouble."

Madge's tone was dismissive. "She'll be fine. Arthur and Constance let her know we're in charge."

Mrs. Kruchinski snorted one of her well-known *humphs*. "And you think it ends there? She's going to circle back to the wedding takeover. You'll see."

Without knowing it, Zoe didn't miss her cue. She banged on the table, causing the last crumbs on the empty plates to jump. "So, back to why we've come. I'll need to see the wedding hall and meet with your caterer. Emily, you're good with floral arrangements." She turned to Constance. "Do you have a florist in Stones End?"

Mrs. Kruchinski elbowed Madge. "What did I tell you?"

Arthur dragged a hand over his face. "Now, Zoe. I've already told you. Constance and Charlotte have everything covered."

"My dear brother. We didn't sit like Mediterranean sardines in a flying tin can for 16 hours to do nothing when we arrived in Stones End."

Her sister jumped in. "And we didn't come to cause trouble. If Constance has everything in hand, then leave it be." Emily feigned a stern look. "Besides, I've been dying to get a peek at Arthur's operation." Emily turned toward her brother, wearing an innocent smile. "We can help you instead."

Constance glanced at Arthur. His eyes bulged so far off his face, she feared they'd pop out and roll onto the table.

Ari scowled at his sisters. "Give it up. This Good Cop/Bad Cop act of yours won't work. Arthur's printshop is off limits, as is the wedding.

Now, you two just simmer down. Relax and stop causing trouble."

The room braced for the tornado that was sure to hit.

Emily put on her best aggrieved look. "Well, Zoe. I guess we'll just settle into Arthur's house and putter around." Zoe jumped on her cue like a consummate actor. "You're right, Emily. I'm sure we can find *plenty* to do there."

The sisters glared at their brothers, waiting for them to break.

"I'll never find anything in my house again," mumbled Arthur.

"Hell, you'll be lucky if they don't pick it up and move it to another location," said Ari.

Mrs. Kruchinski glanced at Madge and Birdie. "Damn, they're good."

"Best I've ever seen. We should take notes," said Birdie.

The sibling showdown threw a tortured silence over The Café. Father Gregory tugged his collar for the second time that morning. Walter held his paper like a shield in front of his body. Horace, who normally loved the drama, rubbed his moist palms against his shirt.

Constance knew she had to do something. But what? If she let the sisters plan the wedding, she'd hurt her friends' feelings. Who did she owe her loyalty to? Family or friends? But her friends were her family for the past 40 years. *This is impossible.*

A small, but confident voice cut through the tension. "I know how Emily and Zoe can help," said Charlotte. "They can run the bookshop while Aunt Constance and I shop for her wedding ensemble."

Constance brightened. Her shop was open six days a week, leaving her to cram household chores, grocery shopping and cooking in on her day off. Leisurely shopping was a dream.

Constance leapt from her chair. "That's brilliant!" She turned to the sisters. "Will you do it? I could teach you the operation in a couple of hours." She clasped her hands together as if praying. "It would be a tremendous help."

"Wonderful idea," said Emily. "We'll give you the gift of time."

Zoe stood. "It's a great plan. Come and show us your layout."

Madge, Mrs. Kruchinski, and Birdie slapped a high five.

"Terrific idea," called out Mrs. Kruchinski.

"Way to go, Charlotte," added Birdie.

Horace whispered to Walter. "Look at them. Salivating at the thought of getting rid of Zoe."

"Can't say I blame them. Can you?"

Horace grinned. "Phew. That was a close one."

"It's settled then," said Constance. "And thank you."

Ari glared at Arthur, who refused to meet his stare. Both knew the plan had disaster written all over it.

There was no time to thwart the plan. The ladies were moving toward the door. Ari scooted in next to Arthur. Father Gregory leaned in.

"This will not end well," said Ari.

"There's no stopping it now."

Constance turned and blew Arthur a kiss. He forced a weak smile.

"My poor Constance. She won't know what hit her," said Arthur.

"What are you talking about?" said Father Gregory. "Your sisters are astute businesswomen. What could go wrong?"

"I can't say it, Ari. You tell him."

Ari spoke in a monotone drenched in dread. "Zoe has a penchant for reorganizing."

For the third time that day, Father Gregory tugged at his collar. He knew how meticulous Constance was with the layout of her shop. "I take it that's a bad thing."

"She won't recognize the place."

Father Gregory stared blankly. Ari caught his hand on the way to his collar and patted his shoulder. "Stop tugging, Father. I'll plant myself in the bookshop today and do battle with Zoe. Anyone have a sword and shield handy?"

"You'll need it," said Arthur. He tried for a laugh but could only manage a nervous chuckle.

Horace smiled as he slid the strap of his mailbag onto his shoulder. "No pressure, Ari. Just your brother's wedding and the future of your family on the line."

"Let's look on the bright side," said Walter. "Maybe your sisters will have great ideas for Constance to consider."

Birdie chased after Horace. "Or maybe, Ari will die on the battlefield."

CHAPTER 11

Scheming and Matchmaking

Ari scrutinized his sisters while Constance explained the layout of the bookshop. Their sideways glances, every now and then, made the three cups of coffee he had that morning churn into acid. He smelled their scheming from across the shop. And whatever it was, they were doing their best to keep it hidden.

"Well, that's it," said Constance. "It's not a sophisticated operation. My primary source of income is the procurement of rare books and manuscripts which I sell mostly to European collectors. I manage those sales over the internet. So, don't worry about them."

"Now, Constance," said Zoe. "If we think of any changes that might boost sales, do you want us to run them by you or just go with it?" She took care to keep her tone casual, like it didn't matter either way. Ari knew better.

The question stopped Constance in her tracks. Her hands shuffled invoices and credit card receipts on the counter to stall. She'd always been protective over the shop, never considering expanding because she'd have to hire staff. And staff meant relinquishing control over the thing she held dearest since her son's death.

But these were Arthur's sisters who were already put off helping with the wedding or getting their hands on the printshop. Surely, she could trust these seasoned businesswomen who took their father's ragtag boatyard that barely put food on the table and turned it into a wildly successful tourist business. And, besides, they traveled a great distance, leaving their families to help.

She looked up, surprised to see Ari motioning a clear *Don't Do It* signal. But if she didn't, there was the threat of them turning

Arthur's house upside down. Arthur loved order. He couldn't handle the chaos. And a groom ready to commit homicide won't do.

Protecting Arthur was the turning factor. She decided to take one for the team. *What harm could these sweet ladies do in a couple of weeks,* she reasoned.

Constance waved nonchalantly. "Just go with it. If I can't trust my sisters-in-law, then who can I trust?"

Ari shut his eyes tight. He had his work cut out for him.

"You're saving me. I didn't know how I was going to manage the bookshop and wedding. A million thanks." She turned and looked around the shop. "Now, where is my wonderful niece?"

Charlotte popped up from behind the counter. "Are we ready to head out?"

Constance pulled her aside. "Charlotte, would you mind if we started fresh tomorrow? There's something I need to tend to this afternoon. And I don't know about you, but my head feels like a marching band has taken over."

"That's fine, Aunt Constance. I'll get started on the place cards for the tables. It's a personal touch I offer my clients. I hand paint each one. I was thinking of a diner scene for Madge and Oscar and bakery goods for Mrs. Kruchinski's card."

"What an enchanting momento. Everyone will cherish them."

"I'll pick up the blank cards at the stationery store and spread them out on your kitchen table."

"Arthur has every variety of paper stock known to man. Just stop by the printshop, there's a drafting table in the back room you can use." Constance nudged Charlotte. "And if Arthur's not there, I'm sure Martin will be happy to help."

A moan escaped Charlotte. "Please don't start that again. Martin is with Roxy. I'm here to help with your wedding. And when it's over, it's back to The Cotswolds."

"And Great Aunt Prudence's dry cough and bunions?"

"There are worse things in life," Charlotte snapped. Her words came out snippier than she intended, but she needed the matchmaking to stop. Her aunt's needling rankled, but she shuddered to think of the ladies joining the cause.

She yanked sunglasses from her satchel, shoved them on crookedly and waved goodbye. "See you at dinner."

Charlotte stomped up the stairs to her aunt's apartment to get her watercolor kit and brushes. *Poor Aunt Constance. She doesn't deserve to get the brunt of my hangover. I should apologize.* She turned back toward the bookshop. Then, stopped again. Her head throbbed. *I'll make it up to her tonight.*

Constance hoped the myriad of distractions would drive away her worry about the stranger in the cemetery. But no such luck. Of all the graves, why Willie's? It wasn't like his headstone was in the front row. It was almost at the back wall of the cemetery.

She strolled uptown, hoping to find Caroline alone in the station office. Stones End may be a quaint, tiny village, but their deputy sheriff's skills were high caliber. She was certain Caroline jumped on the report of a suspicious stranger in their midst.

Suddenly, Constance yelled. Her purse flew into the air. Martin grabbed her right arm to save her from hitting the pavement.

"Constance, I'm so sorry. Are you alright?"

She brushed her hands over her jacket. Martin retrieved her purse.

"I'm fine, Martin. No damage done." She nodded toward the beauty parlor. "Have you switched from Walter's barbershop for your haircuts?"

Martin stammered. "Uh, no. I was visiting with Roxy… and Berris."

"I see." She couldn't miss an opportunity to mention her niece. "Charlotte will use the printshop to design hand-painted place cards. Do you have time to set her up this afternoon?"

"Of course. I'll make the time. Charley is very talented, isn't she? Runs her own business and an artist too. My goodness."

"Charley?"

The color rose on Martin's cheeks. "Yes. When we talked at her party, I called her Charley. For some reason, it seemed natural. Then I realized it might not be appropriate and asked if it was ok."

"What did she say?"

Martin's eyes drifted as if recalling a pleasant memory. "She said it was more than ok."

More than ok floated on the air like a beautiful melody. Constance smiled broadly. *Charlotte should be getting to printshop right about now.* She turned to Martin.

"Are you heading back to the shop?"

"Yes. But can I walk you to where you're going first? I don't want to leave till I know you're alright."

"I'm perfectly fine, Martin. You run along."

Martin glanced at his ringing phone. Constance saw Roxy's name pop onto the screen. *For heaven's sake, he just left her.* He said a quick goodbye and took the call.

Constance peered in the window of the beauty parlor. Roxy stood in a miniskirt, leather, knee-high boots, and a tight sweater. *No wonder Martin is enamored. She looks like Jessica Rabbit.*

It didn't sound like Charlotte had gone off Martin. *Maybe she's just being practical.* Great Aunt Prudence's rigid outlook on life most likely rubbed off on her. Or perhaps the heartbreak of her former fiancé getting cold feet two weeks before the wedding was still raw.

She reached the fountain and saw Martin sprinting across the square toward the printshop. The scene reminded her of George Bailey running through Bedford Falls with his jacket and scarf flapping behind him. All that was missing was snow.

Charlotte was just entering the shop, and he called out to her.

She turned and waited for him. Then, stole a glance in the window and ran a hand through her hair the way women do when guys are watching.

Constance smiled. *Yep. She still cares.* She watched them enter the printshop chatting like two lovebirds. *They're perfect for each other,* she sighed. *There's got to be a way to bring them together. Charlotte will kill me, but maybe it's time to consult the ladies.*

CHAPTER 12
Business or Pleasure?

"Let me take your coat, Charley."

Martin lingered over the delicate scent of peonies clinging to Charlotte's coat. He imagined a secluded English garden where he and Charley explored. It brushed the moment with a sense of calm.

Charlotte was lost in her own moment. *He called me Charley again.* Just the sound of it seemed to establish a private connection between them. She felt her resolve against romance thawing.

"So, Constance tells me you're designing hand-painted place cards for the wedding."

She couldn't hold back a chuckle. *Dear Aunt Constance can't help herself.*

Martin looked confused. He didn't see the humor.

Charlotte flicked her hand as though shooing a fly. "Don't mind me. I just thought of a funny thing my aunt said."

She pulled out a small portfolio from her satchel and showed Martin proofs of her designs. They were watercolor scenes of the seaside, woodlands, and village streets.

He studied each card carefully, pointing out images that delighted him. She loved the attention.

"Charley, these are magical. Very Beatrix Potter-like."

"You think so?"

"Indeed. I like to sketch but my drawings aren't works of art like these," he said. His eyes focused on each sketch, and not on her. She was ok with that. Her work did not have attention like this since art school.

"You sketch? I'd love to see your work."

"Oh no. It's amateur stuff. Nothing compared to your artistry."

"Artists are their own worst critics. Please. I'd love to see them."

He reached behind the counter and produced a large manilla folder. "Promise you won't laugh?"

"Promise." Charlotte opened the folder. Her eyes widened. "Martin, these are exquisite. And look, they're all scenes of Stones End."

Martin peered over her shoulder as Charlotte studied the drawings. "I used to sketch buildings when I lived in the city. But they always struck me as cold."

"I can't picture you in a city. Which one?"

"Manhattan. I was born there."

"Now, that surprises me. When did you move to the village?"

"When I was 13."

"That must have been traumatic. A teenager leaving his friends."

"Actually, it was wonderful. I didn't have friends in the city. My nose was always stuck in a book."

"Why did your family move?"

"Divorce. My mom wanted a complete change afterwards, so she moved us here. Her sister lives in Darien. Dad escaped to California."

"Do you miss Manhattan?"

"I love the culture, but I found living there sad. So many talented people with larger-than-life dreams and no promise of ever being noticed. Here in the village, it's easier for dreams to come true. People care about each other."

Charlotte laughed. "Sometimes a little too much, I'd imagine. The Cotswolds has the same challenge."

Martin smiled broadly. "Yes. It can get a little tricky keeping your personal life private. But worth it in the end. Don't you think?"

He fixed a warm gaze like she was the only person on the planet. It was flattering and unnerving at the same time. She pulled herself back to the moment.

"Yes. Worth it in the end."

It was building again. That fluttery sensation in the pit of her stomach that comes when you fall in love. *Are you crazy? Martin is with Roxy. Give it up.* She thought of Ted and how loving a man who doesn't love you in return is torture.

Martin reached for Charlotte's portfolio and brushed against her arm. It was like an electric shock hit her. Time stopped for a single blink of the eye and there was just the sensation of Martin's touch on her skin.

Martin stepped back briskly. *He felt it too,* she thought. He cleared his throat and opened her portfolio.

"Now, I know these are all one of a kind, but have you ever considered mass producing them? Arthur has old print presses and state-of-the-art laser printers that could turn these out like they were originals."

"I'll have to give that some thought."

"I hope you do. These would sell like crazy."

Charlotte picked up a card of palm trees where colorful parrots perched. "Do you really think so?"

"I'm sure of it." Martin spun around and faced Charlotte. She saw his enthusiasm brimming. "Think of it. You could market them as single cards or box sets or both. And if you expand to pictures that appeal to different countries, cultures…" He threw his arms wide. "My goodness. The possibilities are endless."

Charlotte raised her hand like a stop sign. "Wait a minute. We're talking about breaking into an established, highly competitive greeting and note card industry. What is the chance of my cards standing out in a field of what…millions?"

"These will. Trust me. I've seen the junk on the market. Nostalgic scenes that stir the buyer to dust off a treasured memory. But don't you see? Your cards will evoke new memories. They're not cards to save in a shoebox and look at every ten years. They're enchanting, magical works of art that people will want to send, frame and savor."

She clapped her hands. "You make this sound exciting. I'm already imagining Black Forest scenes, The Alps, the Taj Mahal. And all done in watercolors with a charming, Old-World feel. Then, there are hobbies. People are passionate about their hobbies."

"Yes. Yes. There's golf, tennis, cricket…"

"And we haven't even tapped into life events, Martin."

"Of course. Births, graduations, weddings…" Martin suddenly stopped and gave Charlotte one of his fixed stares. "Did you just say *we*?"

Charlotte stuttered, "Sorry. Just a figure of speech."

"Oh…" Martin stared at the floor. "I'm sorry to hear that, because…" He examined his shoes. Scruffy Topsiders. So much for first impressions.

"What?"

"I hope this is not presumptuous of me, but I've never believed in a venture as much. And I'd be willing to invest in the start-up—with you."

Charlotte's head jerked back. "Partners?"

"Yes, partners. Or just as an investor if you prefer."

Silence replaced enthusiasm. The idea thrilled Charlotte. But was it possible to separate business from pleasure?

Her reaction made Martin feel like a poacher. "There's no pressure to invite me in on this, Charley. But, please, think about expanding your business to include your amazing cards. And if you want to explore the production and distribution possibilities, talk with Arthur."

A phone rang. Martin dug in his pocket. His face brightened seeing Roxy's name on the screen. "I'm in a meeting. Can I call you back? Yes, we're still on for tonight. I'll pick you up at seven."

Was it her imagination, or did their meeting just end on a note of Martin scouting business for the printshop? It took that single thought for Charlotte to realize that part of her excitement about starting up a venture with Martin was the promise of romance. His idea was brilliant. But could she keep business separated from her desire for pleasure?

CHAPTER 13
The Ghost Is Alive

Constance pulled open the door to the sheriff's office. "I'll be right with you," yelled Caroline from the back room. Constance jumped when Mortimer repeated, "I'll be right with you."

"You scared me, Mortimer!" Constance patted her thumping chest.

"Hello, Constance. I don't see you here often."

"Yes, it's been a long time. I know you're busy, but I'm curious to know if you found who the stranger in the cemetery is?"

Caroline was tempted to say no because she had nothing confirmed. But what she discovered might help her friend's peace of mind. "Please, sit."

Constance glanced around as she took a seat. She wasn't surprised to see an obsessively neat office. It did surprise her, though, to see family pictures and animal knickknacks tucked among the police manuals, handcuffs, pepper spray, and bound reports on the shelves. Their deputy was not known to have a soft side.

Caroline thumbed through a tidy stack of municipal notices and incident reports and pulled out a single page. "I did ask around in Kent. Our mystery man has been seen a number of times. I say mystery man because he seemed to pull the same disappearing act as he did at our cemetery."

"How so?"

"Hikers saw him up at the waterfalls, struggling along the path. They turned back after a short time to see if he was alright, and he was nowhere to be seen. Then a woman saw him limping toward a bench in town. She was concerned he might topple over, so she waited till he sat."

"Did she speak with him?"

"No. She ducked into the shop for a minute and when she came out, he was gone."

"How is it possible for an elderly man with a pronounced limp to disappear like that?"

"That part's not a mystery. He obviously turned off the path into the wooded area at the waterfalls. And he must have left the bench and disappeared into a shop. But he seems to have a pattern of disappearing when anyone notices him. Which is suspicious behavior in my book."

"That wasn't the case in the cemetery. Birdie kept out of sight."

"He might have sensed someone following him. I know it isn't possible for someone to sneak up on me."

"Is it likely to have such a heightened sense of your surroundings in a rainstorm?"

"Normally, I'd say no. But Father Gregory reported the back gate to the cemetery broken. So, he didn't want to be seen leaving by the front path."

"This is giving me a bad feeling." Constance fidgeted with the heart pendant around her neck.

"It's got everyone in Kent talking."

"Anything else? Were you able to find out who he is?"

"The owner of the bistro saw him going into the post office with a package. I spoke to the postal clerk and had her pull the mail record. The return address listed a woman in the town."

"He's probably staying with her. Were you able to check her out?"

"Well, here's where the mystery gets darker. I was on my way to do just that when the clerk called after me. She hadn't noticed the name on the return address, at the time she just checked that there was one."

"So, what was strange?"

"The name of someone who died last year."

"Oh, my God."

"I went around to the place, and it was deserted. There were boards over the doors and windows. As far as I could see, no one was staying there."

Constance didn't know what to make of the story and asked the deputy to continue to investigate.

"There's really nothing left to look into until this guy shows himself again. No one has seen him in the past week in Kent or Stones End. So, let's hope he was someone passing through and is now gone."

Constance knew she said that for her benefit and that she didn't believe a word of it. She walked to the door, then turned back. "Please keep me informed. The thought of this strange man standing over Willie's grave gives me the shivers."

"Will do."

"By the way, what was the name on the package?"

"Kathleen MacGregor was the dead woman, and the package was addressed to Ian MacGregor in Scotland."

The color drained from Constance's face. She grasped the doorframe.

"Are you alright?"

"Yes. Yes. I'm fine." She grabbed her handkerchief from her purse.

Caroline guided her back to the chair in front of her desk. "Let me get you some water."

Constance used both hands to hold the cup. *Her hands are shaking,* thought Caroline. *She knows something.*

She sat upright and leaned across the desk. "Is there something you want to tell me, Constance?"

Her back stiffened. "Good heavens, no! Why would you ask that?"

"Because you look like you've just seen a ghost."

CHAPTER 14
Lightning Strikes

The moment Constance walked out the door of the bookshop earlier that morning, ideas shot around the room like lightning strikes in the middle of July. Stock had to be rearranged. The coffee and treat counter moved. Wi-Fi must be added.

Ari tried to beat back the ideas but was met by a high-speed locomotive threatening to squish him like a bug.

"Ari, who's the handyman in this village?" asked Emily.

"Olga's husband Karl. He's a landscaper who runs a fix-it business on the side."

"We need to call him. And do you know who's the internet provider?" said Zoe.

"I wonder if Karl is also an electrician. We'll need more outlets when we expand the coffee bar," said Emily.

"And we're going to create a children's storytime area. So, you must move some of these bookcases for us," said Emily.

Ari pressed the sides of his forehead. "You should talk to Constance first."

"Constance gave us permission to run with changes," said Zoe.

His voice climbed from brotherly concern toward hysterical. "I'm sure she meant minor adjustments, not a major renovation. And just how do you plan to do all of this under her nose? She lives upstairs, you know."

Emily latched onto Zoe's arm. "You have the honor of telling him. It was your brilliant idea."

"This is the best part. We'll book Constance and Charlotte

into The Plaza Hotel in Manhattan for four days. It will be our wedding gift."

Emily jumped in. "They'll have three full days of shopping topped off with a spa day. Full treatment—facials, massages, refreshing drinks. That way Constance will be relaxed when she sees our fabulous changes."

Ari pulled his hand over his face. "You might want to tell the spa to slip a fistful of Valium in those refreshing drinks."

Zoe wagged her finger at Ari. "Not a word to Constance."

"Or Arthur," added Emily. "Now, run along and find Karl for us."

Ari dug in. "Have you considered that your changes might flop? This village reeks with quaint and you're proposing a cutting-edge layout. It might work in LA, San Francisco, or the East Village. Constance will hate it, and the villagers might show up with pitchforks."

Zoe threw her hands up and stormed off. Emily countered his concern in a sister's patronizing voice. "You're talking to the women who turned Pop's tired boatyard into what it is today."

Ari bristled. "I'd like to think I had something to do with the success. My efforts generated hundreds of clients. I steered deep-sea fishermen to our fishing excursions. Honeymooners to our romantic voyages. Loads of tourists to the dinner cruises."

"Yes, brother dearest. But if Emily and I didn't reorganize and expand, there'd be no capacity for the crowds we take in," said Zoe.

Ari opened his mouth, then shut it. He hated when they were right. And damn it they were always right.

"Why are you acting like we're sabotaging Constance?" asked Zoe.

"Because I have the feeling that you're sabotaging Constance."

"For heaven's sake, Ari," said Emily. "Look around this place. Yes, it's charming, but charm is something people work into their lives when they have a spare moment. We're talking about jamming this place with customers."

Zoe explained the vision. "Think of it. An internet station with a counter and stools across both front windows where young and old will be plugged into their electronic devices drinking, eating, and reading. Wait. Bar stools? What about wine and beer?"

"People attract people, Ari," said Zoe. "Monthly emails will list upcoming discounts. If you love espionage, you'll mark your calendar for when your favorite author is on sale. Parents will bring their tots every Thursday for story time and buy the book we read because it's now their child's favorite. And a licensed plush animal."

"Don't you see? Creating a reason to stop by is better than waiting for customers to make the time to soak up *quaint*," said Emily. "Constance is sitting on a gold mine here and right now, she's making a pittance from it."

Ari raised a suspicious eyebrow. "How do you know how much Constance makes?"

"Well…" Emily couldn't bring herself to finish.

"I hacked her financials," said Zoe.

"You what?" Ari dragged his hand across his glistening forehead.

"Oh, stop fussing. We won't tell anyone," said Emily. "Constance is family."

"Besides, poor Constance is living frugally when she could live comfortably. We're going to do this for her. We've all tasted frugal living, and it's no fun. Bargain hunting for clothes, buying cheap cuts of meat and lots of casseroles."

"Lord. Remember those bloody casseroles? Most of them were fish." said Emily.

"Now, off you go. And remember, not a word to anyone," said Zoe.

Ari staggered toward the door. *Constance will divorce Arthur before they're even married.*

"By the way," yelled Zoe. "The renovation is your wedding gift."

Ari clutched at his heart. *And my wife is going to throw me out of our bedroom.*

CHAPTER 15
No Trust to Be Found

Charlotte struggled to concentrate on her place cards for the wedding. She hunched over Martin's sketches at the drafting table in the art room of the printshop. An idea was creeping to the front of her mind. Suddenly she screamed, "Martin!"

Martin appeared instantly, like he was beamed in on a transporter.

"I have a spectacular idea. But it would depend on you agreeing."

"Absolutely. What exactly am I agreeing to?"

"Using your drawings to create a village scene for the wedding hall. That is, if we can blow them up to say, six or seven feet."

"Sure. We can enlarge them to any size you want. What are you thinking?"

"You have a sketch of every shop in the village. We can display the enlarged sketches down the opposite walls of the hall. It will look like the wedding is being held on Main Street."

"I'm loving this," said Martin. "We can bring in planters and artificial trees."

"Yes. And run sky-blue fabric over the area decorated with lights."

"Charley, this is outstanding. Shopkeeper guests can sit at tables in front of the sketch of their storefronts."

"And we can connect the two vertical rows with a long table at the top for the wedding party and one at the bottom for non-shopkeepers, like Father Gregory and Caroline. Now, how will we stand them up?" said Charlotte.

"Not a problem. We'll mount them on cardboard and attach a cutout stand. Wait. The village is colorful. Will my black and white sketches have the right effect?"

"I've thought of that. We don't have time to colorize them. How about splashes of color to make them pop?"

"I can help. Just tell me how you want it."

Charlotte wondered how his decision would sit with Roxy. She could use his help but didn't want to cause trouble between them.

"This will take a lot of time, Martin. I'll understand if you can't commit."

He didn't hesitate. "No. I'm in. Let's run over to the conservatory ballroom and take measurements. That way we can calculate what size we need for the enlargements."

He shoved a tape measure into his jacket pocket while Charlotte threw her bag over her shoulder. They turned for the door at the same time. Their bodies crashed.

Martin grabbed onto her as she reeled back a step. Their faces were inches apart. Martin's eyes softened, like he was seeing Charlotte in a sensual gauzy light. Charlotte stared into their warmth. The sublime moment of passion kept him from releasing her. It was both tender and raw and impossible to deny.

You're making it hard not to fall in love with you, Charlotte thought. She stepped back. Her eyes were downcast. "We should go." Her voice was husky, and she blushed at the tone telegraphing her aroused feelings.

They left the shop in silence and were no sooner out the door when they heard Roxy's irritating whine.

"Where are you two going?" Charlotte could hear the attempt at a casual tone, but detected a cutting edge that only other women sense, like how only dogs can hear a dog whistle.

"Glad you're here, Roxy," he said. "Afraid I'll have to cancel our dinner tonight. Charley and I need to work on an art project for the wedding."

Roxy jabbed her thumb like she was hitchhiking. "Can I speak to you, Marty?"

"Excuse us, Charley."

Martin followed her like he was being pulled to the principal's office. Charlotte couldn't hear their conversation, but it was clear from the slash of her mouth that the queen bee wasn't happy.

"You're cancelling a date to be with this British babe? And when did you start calling her Charley?"

"Please understand, sweetheart. Charley, uh, I mean Charlotte came up with a terrific idea on decorating the wedding hall and she needs my help. Remember, she's Constance's niece, and you know I'd do anything for Constance and Arthur."

"How long is this project gonna take, anyway?"

Charlotte saw Martin trying to get a word in and failing. Roxy was raking him over the coals.

"The scope of the project is massive. So, the better part of three weeks."

"Three weeks! And you expect me to just sit home while you're teaming up with her?"

"What are you talking about? Charlotte will return to England after the wedding. You make it sound like I'm having an affair with her. I'm just helping to make her aunt's wedding special. That's all."

"You're so naïve. I see the way she acts around you. All that hair fluffing and how she jumped off the bench when she thought you were coming to see her."

"I assume that's a joke. She is a sophisticated businesswoman. Trust me. She has no interest in a country bumpkin like me."

"Well, I insist that we still have lunch together—every day. And I'll stop by each night to keep y'all company."

"Lunch it is. But coming by each night is not a good plan."

"I beg your pardon! Not a good plan?"

Martin took her hands in his. "You'll distract me. I won't get anything done."

Something told Roxy not to push this. She didn't want to look unreasonable in the eyes of the villagers. *These people have a weird bond. And Berris will be mad if I drive away customers.*

Roxy fell into his arms and gave him a kiss. "Ok, sweetie. But remember, you're my country bumpkin."

Martin joined Charlotte.

"Everything alright? If this is going to be a problem…"

"All good." He forced a smile. It had *Roxy is not going to drop it that easily* written all over it.

Charlotte didn't like that Martin resembled a whipped dog. She was tempted to string her arm through his as they walked off. Maybe if the bitchy Roxy thought there was competition, she'd be nicer to Martin.

Great Aunt Prudence's wisdom barged in again. *Two wrongs never make a right.* And her all-time favorite also rang out. *Remember, you're a lady.*

Charlotte yielded to the sage advice with a sigh. She called over her shoulder. "Thanks, Roxy, for loaning me Martin."

"Just remember to give him back."

Her tone was sharp enough to cut through steel.

Roxy stood cross-armed, watching them saunter off toward the conservatory. *It may be time to see where I stand with Marty. I don't trust that one.*

Ari called Karl and asked him to stop by the bookshop, then trudged back to Arthur's house. He needed advice from George.

"We've got a problem, Pop."

"Let me guess. Your sisters?"

"How do you know they're here?"

"It's a small village. Word gets around."

Ari didn't know how George knew it. *He's a bloody bench on*

Arthur's porch. But, somehow, he always knows what's going on.

"They're yanking the bookshop into a 21st century media experience. Books are an afterthought with these two."

"You're forgetting your sisters know what they're doing. I'm not saying they should barge ahead without consulting Constance. But you'll see, everything will turn out alright."

"I don't have the same confidence. And here's another thing. Zoe and Emily forbid me to tell Arthur. Now, how am I going to hide this from him? I hate being put in the middle."

"Well, get used to it. Your sisters are famous for doing just that."

"Thanks, Pop." Ari slumped. "Everyone will hate me. Constance for not stopping them. Arthur for not warning him. And get this, my wonderful sisters are sticking me with the bill for the damn renovation. And I'm dead against it."

"Now, that *is* a problem. Those girls sure can spend."

"Glad you find this amusing."

"Lighten up, son. I told you. Your sisters know what they're doing. You can trust them."

"Aren't you the optimist? Personally, I wouldn't trust those two as far as I can throw your old boat."

When Constance returned from her meeting with Caroline, she snuck in the side door to her apartment. A twinge of guilt pinched at her sense of obligation that Arthur's sisters were downstairs working in her shop. But she desperately needed time to absorb what Caroline shared.

The tall-cased clock chimed one. *It's five o'clock somewhere.* She popped a cork from a leftover bottle of wine.

Kicking off her shoes, Constance fell into her favorite armchair. The thought of sleep seduced her, but anxiety from her meeting fought off its advances.

Caroline could explain the stranger's disappearances but showed concern that they were on purpose. Whatever the mystery man is hiding, he's set on keeping it a secret. And a dead woman's name on the return label spooked her.

He must be staying in that abandoned house. Although it isn't like Caroline to miss a clue. Constance sat up abruptly. *Caroline never misses clues. She found out his identity and didn't want to tell me.*

The thought alarmed her. She poured more wine. *This makes no sense. Why would she keep it from me?* Constance shoved her feet in her shoes. *I must talk to her again.* Suddenly feeling ridiculous, she kicked her shoes off.

You're paranoid. Caroline will think you're crazy.

Constance finished her wine. Her head felt heavy, and she rested in the chair. *MacGregor. The name of the only person I know in Scotland. And he's been dead for decades. What could this possibly do with me—and Willie?*

Is Caroline right? She said no one has seen him in almost a week. Maybe it's nothing. Stop overthinking it, Constance. There must be a million MacGregors in Scotland.

She closed her eyes. The stranger towered over Willie's grave. *Caroline isn't telling me everything.*

CHAPTER 16
Dripping in Secrets

Berris peered over the top of her glasses as Roxy stormed into the beauty parlor. Berris was easily thrown by the mood of other people. And Roxy's aura seared with anger.

"That was a quick visit with Martin."

"He's too busy for me. With Charlotte." Roxy spat out Charlotte's name as though it were a filthy word. She flung her jacket over a chair, and it tumbled onto the floor amid swirls of hair snippets in every color.

"What are they working on?"

"Who cares? But it will take them three weeks and Marty and I are on hold till then." Roxy paced with her hands jammed on her hips.

Berris pushed the glasses up the bridge of her nose. She glanced at her appointment book, trying not to be pulled into the negative energy whipping around Roxy. "Three weeks? I bet it's something for the wedding."

"I suppose. But three weeks is too long for my Marty to rub elbows, and God knows what else, with another woman. Don't you think?"

"Why are you worried? Martin's a gentleman."

"Marty doesn't worry me. It's that British bimbo."

"British bimbo?" Berris let loose a whimsical chuckle. "Charlotte's sweet. She won't steal Martin."

Roxy squeezed her eyes shut. *Berris always misses the obvious.* She leaned across the counter and made a declaration. "I intend to approach Marty about where we stand."

"What does that mean?"

"I need to know how serious our relationship is."

Berris slapped shut the hair-style magazine in front of her. "Are you talking about marriage?"

Roxy exhaled an exaggerated sigh. "Of course, I'm talking about marriage. We've been dating for over a month. And now that this bimbo is threatening us, I'm going to push the idea."

"Be careful what you wish for," Berris said in a sing-song voice, then meandered off like she forgot Roxy was there.

Roxy scooted after her. "Berris, please don't mention our chat with anyone. It will be our secret. Ok?"

Berris stooped for Roxy's jacket on the floor, shook it off and hung it on the wall peg, then drifted off, humming a nameless tune.

Roxy examined herself in the mirror. She freshened up her fire-engine red lipstick. Then fluffed her billowing hair that added two inches to her height and smoothed her slender hips as if preparing for a beauty pageant showdown. *Marty's a catch. I'm not losing him to that flat-haired, skinny bitch.* Her eyes tightened to slits. *It's time to take control.*

The ringing phone woke Constance. She answered in a husky voice. "Hello, dearest. Where are you?"

"At the shop with Martin. We're working on a surprise for you and Arthur. So, I won't be home for dinner," said Charlotte.

Constance jolted upright. "That's lovely. But you need to eat."

"We'll grab something from The Café. Don't wait up."

The thought of Charlotte and Martin working and dining together brought Constance fully awake. She rubbed her palms together and whooped, "Hope lives."

The clock chimed five. *Lord, I slept the afternoon away. Poor Emily and Zoe.* Constance pulled on her shoes and dashed downstairs. *I must work on my sister-in-law skills.*

"I'm so sorry I left you alone today. Is everything alright?"

"Smooth as glass," said Zoe.

The bell on the door jingled. Constance whirled around to catch Arthur and Ari strolling in.

"Darling, you're home early," said Constance.

"Can you believe Charlotte and Martin threw me out?" Arthur planted a kiss on her cheek.

Emily smiled. "What are those kids scheming?"

Arthur dropped his voice. "Very hush-hush. Locked in the back room like they're plotting to steal the crown jewels."

Constance laughed. "It's a wedding surprise for us." Her eyebrows lifted.

"Don't you raise those beautiful brows at me, young lady. They're just working on a project. Not planning marriage and a family of twelve."

"Spoil sport. I choose to be hopeful." She swung around to Emily and Zoe.

"I owe you an apology. Today got away from me. I promise to check in from now on."

Zoe nodded to Emily, whose blue eyes glinted like sun kissing the Mediterranean.

"We have a surprise for you, too. We booked you and Charlotte into The Plaza Hotel for the next four days."

Zoe grinned, seeing Constance light up like a kid on Christmas morning. "A bride deserves to be pampered."

Constance drew them into a group hug. "It's the best gift ever. I can't wait to tell Charlotte."

Arthur flicked at a tear, watching the women he loved share an affectionate moment. Ari wasn't crying. He wrestled with the echoes in his head. *Don't tip off Constance. Don't warn Arthur. And definitely don't tell the wife.*

"Charley, grab your jacket. We have to go," said Martin.

"Go where? We just started."

"It's 6:15, and The Café closes at 6:30. If we don't hustle, we'll miss dinner."

Charlotte and Martin tore across the village square. She stopped to catch her breath as they approached the two-block business district.

"You go. I'll catch up."

He extended his arm. "Give me your hand."

A warm feeling spread when his firm, strong hand touched hers. The sensation was strangely familiar. She wondered how something new could trigger familiarity. She tried to think of what it reminded her of. It was like an image caught in the flash of a lightbulb, then gone.

"Ready?"

Charlotte nodded. His grasp tightened. They raced the full length of Main Street, skidding to a halt in front of The Café. Madge, who just flipped the Open sign to Closed, yanked open the door at the sight of the out-of-breath pair.

"You two look like you've run a marathon."

"We did," Charlotte gasped.

"Is it too late to grab supper to go, Madge?" he said.

"It's never too late for you two," said Oscar. "Have a seat. Burgers, omelets or sandwiches?"

Charlotte and Martin answered in unison. "Omelet." Then laughed at their shared taste.

Madge swung around at someone banging on the door. "Olga, what's wrong?"

"I'm here to beg for my supper. It's inventory night. Karl's working late too and can't bring me something to eat."

"Come in. Oscar will whip something up for you."

Mrs. Kruchinski spied Charlotte and Martin. Her eyes flared like she just won the lottery.

"Hello, Mrs. Kruchinski," said Charlotte.

"And what brings you two here?"

"We're working on a project for the wedding," said Martin.

Mrs. Kruchinski rushed them like a bull seeing red. "I'm the head of the planning committee. So, you young people need to say what you're up to."

"Sorry, but it's a secret," said Charlotte.

Mrs. Kruchinski dropped her purse with a bang. "No. No. I can't have any secrets lurking. Tell me what you're planning."

Charlotte patted Mrs. Kruchinski on the hand. "It's a surprise for everyone, including you."

Her voice softened. "A surprise for me? Only Karl tries to surprise me." She smiled. "And I always guess what he's up to."

"Well, you won't guess this one," said Martin. He winked at Charlotte.

Madge pulled Mrs. Kruchinski to the counter. "Come on, Olga. One secret floating around Stones End won't kill us."

"Speak for yourself."

Caroline rubbed her eyes. They felt gritty. She killed the day researching MacGregors in Dumfries, Scotland, hoping to uncover someone with family ties in the United States. Those who popped up didn't match the age of the mystery man whom eyewitnesses pegged around 80ish.

She cracked the cap on a bottle of water. "What am I doing wrong, Mortimer?"

"What am I doing wrong, Mortimer?" echoed. She stroked the breast of her African grey parrot perched on the edge of her desk. "You don't know either, do you?"

"Wait." Caroline's fingers hovered over the keyboard. She punched in the name: Constance Whitestead, Dumfries, Scotland. Nothing. *No, that's her married name.* She spun her chair to the filing cabinet and plucked out a folder: Whitestead, Constance, nee: Fernsby.

She swung back to the keyboard and entered Constance Fernsby. Something popped onto the screen. Caroline leaned in. "Whoa!" She banged against the back of the chair hard enough to topple it. "What the hell?"

Mortimer screeched. "What the hell?"

Caroline snatched the phone and called Scotland Yard, across the pond, and a time zone six hours later. "Hello, Dad. I need your help with another case."

"I'm fine, luv. And how are you?"

"Sorry, Dad. No time for chitchat. This is serious."

The kitchen clock read 7:32 am. Constance called out to Charlotte. "There's no time to make breakfast, dearest. I'll dash to The Café and pick up food for the train."

"Ok. I'm almost packed."

Charlotte grabbed her phone and dialed Martin. "Good morning. It's Charley. Did I wake you?"

"Not at all. What's going on?" Martin lied. He overslept after a torturous night on the phone with Roxy whining about Charlotte.

"I found out last night that my aunt and I will be visiting Manhattan for four days. We leave shortly. This will screw up our schedule, won't it?"

Martin swung his legs over the side of the bed and scratched his head. "Let me think. No, we're good. I can use the time to print the enlargements."

The tension in her neck melted. "You're a lifesaver. I owe you one."

Martin laughed. It had a playful, boyish quality that made her smile.

"You don't owe me. Just have a good time. I'll keep the presses rolling."

"Anything you want from the city?"

He didn't hesitate. "Pretzels from the street vendor."

"You got it."

Oscar did a double take when Constance whizzed through The Café door.

"Who died?"

Constance stopped. "That's the strangest greeting I ever heard."

"Constance Whitestead, in all the years I've known you, you hardly ever set foot in here before 10 am."

She smiled. "Good point, but I have an early train to Manhattan." Constance turned to Madge and Mrs. Kruchinski. "You'll never guess where Charlotte and I are heading?"

"Grant's Tomb?" said Oscar.

Horace scrambled in and interrupted before she could answer. "Has Caroline been in yet?"

"What's wrong, Horace?" said Madge.

Horace opened his mouth, then shut it when he noticed Constance. "Nothing's wrong. I just need to talk to Caroline."

Constance thought it odd that Horace clammed up when he saw her.

"Don't tell us nothing's wrong. You not dropping that bloody mail sack at the front door tells us something's wrong," said Mrs. Kruchinski.

Oscar worried Horace was suffering from one of his seizures. His forehead was a mass of wrinkles, and his eyes were clouding with that far-off look.

"Here you go, Constance. Breakfast for you and Charlotte." Oscar handed her a bag but didn't take his eyes off Horace.

The door blasted open. "Shake a leg, sweetheart. You'll miss the train," said Arthur.

"I want to hear what Horace has to say first," said Constance.

"You go. I'll fill you in later," said Madge. "Wait a minute. Where are you off to?"

Constance beamed. "Four days at The Plaza. I can't wait. I've never been there."

"If I didn't love you so much, I'd be jealous," said Madge. "Now, go and enjoy yourself."

"Take lots of pictures," said Mrs. Kruchinski.

"Forget the pictures. Steal some of those fancy soaps for me," said Madge.

The door no sooner slammed shut when Mrs. Kruchinski turned on Horace. "Ok. Spill it."

Horace dropped his leather bag and crossed his arms. "I'm waiting for Caroline."

"Here I am, Horace," said Caroline.

Madge jumped back a step. "You scared the heck out of me, Caroline. I didn't hear you come in."

"What's up? You folks look spooked."

Horace jerked his thumb toward the back table. "Can we talk in private?"

"Oh, no you don't," said Mrs. Kruchinski. "If something peculiar is happening in the village, we have a right to know."

Birdie bolted through the door just as Mrs. Kruchinski bellowed. She glared at Horace.

"Constance is in danger. No time for secrets."

CHAPTER 17
A Lurking Danger

Caroline flipped open her incident notebook. A fleeting thought of sharing what she knew entered her mind. Her father's advice countered it. Investigating friends or family in the village takes diplomacy, patience and never sharing your evidence—with anyone.

"Tell me what happened."

Birdie nodded an encouraging look.

"It was a little before two and I couldn't sleep. So, I took Brownie for a walk."

Madge elbowed Mrs. Kruchinski and whispered. "Now, why would he take Birdie's dog for a walk in the middle of the night? Sounds like they're shacking up."

Mrs. Kruchinski returned a stern look.

"Brownie and I rounded the corner on Main Street. At first, I thought I was imagining it. You don't expect to run into anyone at that hour. But there was a man standing in front of Constance's shop."

Mrs. Kruchinski choked on a gasp.

Madge leaped from the stool. "Wait, there's Arthur. He needs to hear this." She ran to the street. "Arthur, we need you."

Arthur shuffled in behind Walter and Rosie, who beat him through the door. "Good morning, my good friends."

"I thought you were taking Constance and Charlotte to the train?" said Oscar.

"Ari drove them. What's so urgent?"

Horace repeated what he told the others. Arthur clenched his jaw. His eyes darted back and forth like danger was near enough to touch.

Walter and Rosie sensed an ominous vibe and planted themselves at the counter without saying a word.

"Go on, Horace," said Caroline. She kept a sideways glance on Arthur, whose jaw threatened to shatter under the pressure of his clenched teeth.

"What struck me as odd was that the man wasn't peering into the shop. He stared up at her apartment window. That didn't sit right."

"What man?" whispered Rosie.

"The mysterious guy from the cemetery," said Madge.

Rosie made the sign of the cross.

"I started walking toward him when a cat ran in front of me. Brownie bolted after the darn thing. It was a good five minutes before I lassoed him. I hustled back to Main Street. By that time, the guy disappeared."

"Do you think it was the stranger in the cemetery?" said Walter.

"Birdie described him hunched over and leaning. It's him. And he had the same coat and tweed cap she saw. And Wellies."

Oscar stepped from behind the grill and stood by Madge. She turned. "That's him, alright."

"Did he see you?" said Caroline.

"He did. He turned when the cat screeched."

"Can you recall his facial features?"

"His cap was pulled low, so I couldn't make out his face. The light from the streetlamp lit his scarf. It was swaddled around his neck loose-like and trailed down the front of his coat."

"What color was the scarf?"

"Don't know. I'm color blind. But I'd recognize the pattern anywhere. It was that Scottish plaid. What do they call it?"

"Tartan," said Walter.

Horace pointed. "That's it. Tartan."

"You should have called me, Horace," said Caroline.

"I was going to call, but I forgot my phone. By the time I got back to Birdie's, one of my episodes hit. I fell asleep in the living room chair and didn't wake till morning."

Caroline glanced at Arthur. His lowered head and eyes made her wonder what he was thinking. Did he imagine Constance being kidnapped, or worse, murdered? She laid her hand on his shoulder. "It's going to be alright, Arthur. I won't stop until this is sorted out."

Arthur raised his eyes to meet hers. "Find this guy, Caroline. If something happens to my Constance…"

"This creep won't hurt Constance," said Oscar. "Not on our watch."

"Right," chimed Walter. "We'll mobilize around Constance day and night until she's out of danger."

"Caroline, can we distribute a poster warning the village to look out for this man? You know, one of those Boleros alerts," said Madge.

"BOLO," said the deputy. "Be On the Lookout."

"Yes. The more eyes searching for this guy, the better," said Mrs. Kruchinski.

Caroline pulled her hand down her face. She knew this crowd well. They already pushed the panic button and had no intention of letting up until she made an arrest.

"I know this is hard, but the man has done nothing wrong. Standing in a cemetery and in front of a bookshop is not illegal. And we don't have a crime, so he can't be a suspect."

She held her hand up against the rising push-back.

"I know what you're going to say. Both circumstances are suspicious. And I agree. But I repeat, not against the law. We can't have people calling the sheriff if they see an old man with a limp. In case you haven't noticed, we have more than one old man in this village who wobbles."

"So, what you're saying is that we have to catch him breaking the law?" said Rosie.

Arthur slammed his fist on the counter. "And suppose that's too late for Constance?"

Caroline tucked her notebook and pen in her uniform pocket. "I want you to listen carefully. Here's how we're going to proceed."

Madge nudged Oscar. "Take notes, sweetie." Oscar whipped out his notepad.

"It is highly unlikely this guy…"

Arthur burst out, "I don't want Constance to hear any of this. She'll worry herself sick."

Caroline took a step toward Arthur. "I have news for you. This guy already worries Constance."

"What? How do you know?" said Arthur.

"Because she visited me yesterday."

"And what did she say?" asked Mrs. Kruchinski.

Caroline hesitated. She wondered again if she should she share what she told Constance about the mystery man. The group was teetering on hysteria. The information might catapult them over the edge. She played it close to the vest.

"She's worried why this stranger stood over Willie's grave."

"So, what's the plan?" asked Walter.

"Constance is surrounded by people during the day. And this guy only surfaces in Stones End under the cover of darkness. So, I'll stay with Constance and Charlotte at night."

"That's unnecessary. Constance and Charlotte will stay with me. They can have a bedroom for themselves. My sisters, Ari and I can take the other two rooms."

"Good plan. Now, Arthur. I know how you feel about telling Constance. But she needs to be on her guard. So, where is she now?"

Arthur's eyes widened. "Oh, my God. She and Charlotte are on the train to Manhattan."

"Constance and Charlotte are out there alone," gasped Mrs. Kruchinski. The murmuring reached an out-of-control level.

Caroline's voice boomed. "Calm down, folks."

All eyes locked on the deputy.

"At this point, we're talking precautionary measures. I need to remind you, this man has done nothing wrong. It could just be a coincidence that he stood over Willie's grave. He's not the first stranger to do so. And maybe he knew someone who once lived above the bookshop."

"Ack," spewed Mrs. Kruchinski. "Pure twaddle."

"Maybe. But the fact remains: He has not threatened Constance or anyone in this village. Hell, he's not even spoken to anyone."

No one noticed Father Gregory slip in. Madge jumped when he spoke. She rubbed her chest to slow her pounding heart. *People have got to stop sneaking up on me. They're going to give me a heart attack.*

"We need to listen to Caroline," said Father Gregory. "What she just said is fact, and besides, she knows what she's doing. Think of it, this man may mean no harm to anyone. Yet here we are, ready to tie him to the stake if anyone spots him. Let's not act like an angry mob."

"Well-said, Father." Caroline turned to Arthur. "Now, what time are Constance and Charlotte due back tonight?"

Arthur wrung his hands as though each were trying to comfort the other. "They're not coming back tonight. They're staying at The Plaza for the next four days." He whipped out his phone. "I'll call Constance and tell her to return immediately."

"Hold on. Let's think this through logically. There are millions of people in Manhattan. They're safe during the day," said Caroline.

"I agree with Caroline. I was in the city last week. Packed stores, jammed restaurants, and over-crowded sidewalks. I had to wait on a line to cross the street," said Walter.

"Tell them to eat dinner at the hotel. The Plaza's security staff is excellent. I'll notify them about this man and ask them to keep a close eye on Constance and Charlotte," said Caroline.

"Suppose they want to go out at night?" said Arthur.

"They shouldn't. Get them to stay in their room after dinner," said Caroline. "Make something up if you have to."

"That won't be a problem, Arthur. Constance and Charlotte plan to shop till they drop. They won't have energy for nighttime adventures," said Birdie.

Caroline studied Arthur. His posture was rigid. "So, we're good with not ruining their trip?"

Arthur nodded tentatively.

"Just one more thing. Who knows Constance and Charlotte are in Manhattan?" asked Caroline.

"My sisters, Ari and me," said Arthur.

"And us here," added Birdie.

"Good. Let's keep it that way. If anyone asks where Constance is, tell them she's shopping for the wedding. Remember. Tell no one she's in the city."

Heads nodded in agreement.

"I'm heading back to the station. You have my cell phone number. Call if you hear or see anything. Day or night."

Caroline hustled toward the door, then swung back and pointed a finger at Mrs. Kruchinski. "No emergency council meetings."

"No emergency council meetings," Mrs. Kruchinski repeated.

"By the way, Caroline. What did you tell Constance when she visited you?" asked Rosie.

"That I was looking into it."

"And are you? Do you know who this creep is?" asked Arthur.

Caroline looked him in the eye. "No. I don't know his identity yet." Which was the truth, she reasoned. But after what she discovered, she sure as hell had her suspicions.

CHAPTER 18
A Tense Village

An emotional volcano erupted when Caroline left. A stranger roamed in their midst. A stranger who might harm one of their own. The anxious group huddled, speaking over one another.

Mrs. Kruchinski roared, "Wait!" She peeked over her shoulder to make sure Caroline hadn't doubled back, then dropped her voice. "My house. Tonight. 7:30."

"You can't be serious. Didn't you just promise Caroline no emergency council meetings?" said Father Gregory.

"It's not an emergency council meeting." She glanced again at the door. "It's a secret one."

Father Gregory yanked his collar hard enough to snap it off.

"I'll be there," said Walter.

"We need to tell Martin. If anyone's lurking around, he'll notice," said Birdie.

"No," said Mrs. Kruchinski. "Just us."

Birdie opened her mouth to push back, but Mrs. Kruchinski waggled her finger.

"What about Berris?" said Madge.

"Certainly not," said Mrs. Kruchinski. "We'll spend the entire meeting reviving her."

"Well, I'm bringing my sisters and Ari," said Arthur. His expression said he wouldn't be challenged.

Mrs. Kruchinski nodded.

"I don't like this," said Father Gregory. "We're not detectives. Let Caroline do her job."

"Please, Gregory," said Arthur. "I'll go mad waiting on Caroline. Having a plan among ourselves will make me feel better."

Ari breezed in. "Well, the gals are off. And boy, were they excited."

Blazing eyes met him. "What? What the hell is it now?"

Karl popped his head into the bookshop. "All clear?" he whispered.

Zoe yanked him in and flung the door shut, then scanned the street to see if anyone caught him entering.

"Sorry, Karl. But this project is top secret," said Zoe.

"Good luck with that," Karl chuckled, opening his toolbox. "It's hard to keep a secret around here. Easier to solve world peace."

Emily clapped her hands. "Oh, it's good to pick up another accent. Where are you from, Karl?"

"Vienna, and I was just thinking the same. Now, how is it you ladies and Ari speak with a Greek accent and Arthur doesn't?"

"Because our father was British, and he and Arthur spent most of their time together."

Zoe wiped her palms on her work apron. "Time for work."

"Right you are. I'll just grab the shelves out of my truck. I varnished them last night, so they might be a touch tacky."

Emily sprinted to the window. "A delivery truck, Zoe."

"What did you order?" asked Karl.

The sisters fell into each other, laughing. "Everything!"

A delivery man wheeled a dolly through the front double doors. "Where do you want this?"

"Against the rear wall," said Emily.

Karl slid his cap back and scratched his head. "That's a lot of boxes."

"There's a ton more," said the guy with the dolly.

Karl gave a low whistle. *I don't want to be within 50 miles when Constance returns.*

Arthur turned toward the bookshop. "We should tell Zoe and Emily what's going on," he said to his brother.

Ari grabbed his arm and steered him in the opposite direction. The last thing Arthur needed was to witness the shop being transformed into a cyber showroom that looks like something out of a sci-fi movie.

"This morning doesn't need more drama. Let's tell them before the meeting tonight."

Deep in thought, Arthur didn't notice the large delivery truck parked across the full length of the double-windowed shop. The brothers scuffed up Main Street in worried silence. When they entered the printshop, Ari glanced at his brother.

"You're letting your mind run wild, aren't you?"

Arthur stared at Ari like he forgot he was there.

"I'm trying not to, but I can't find the off switch."

Ari wrestled with thinking the worst himself.

"Does Caroline have what it takes to protect Constance? Or uncover what's up with this creep? I mean standing over the grave of her son and then staring up at her apartment in the middle of the night is weird. Right?"

"Caroline's top notch. She learned from her father who's a Scotland Yard detective. Plus, she has a cop's instinct."

"I can hear the *but* banging around in your head."

"Yeah. But she can't be everywhere. I'll feel in control when we develop our own plan. And it would be better if Martin was in on it. The kid notices everything and we need all eyes on deck."

"Why do you think Olga didn't want him to know?"

"Good question. Let's ask it again tonight."

Martin checked the time, then quickened his pace. It was his turn to pick up lunch, and he was one minute late. Roxy wasn't one to be kept waiting.

Even in his haste, he noticed a change in the village's pulse. Caroline sat in her cruiser at the head of the two-block business district. She drove the cruiser in the village only when something was wrong. And why was she just sitting there?

As Martin sprinted toward The Café, he spied Mrs. Kruchinski standing at the bakery window. Her head swiveled back and forth like she was at a tennis match. He couldn't recall a time when she wasn't behind the counter. He passed the barbershop and was unnerved to catch Walter doing the same. And when he reached The Café, Madge opened the door for him. What were they on the lookout for?

Martin crept in, like someone was following him, then glanced back toward the door before sitting at the counter.

"What's going on?" he asked Oscar.

"Nothing. Why do you ask?" Oscar didn't meet Martin's gaze. Something the ever-observant Martin didn't miss.

"Something's not right. I can feel it." Martin glanced toward the front window. "There she is again. That's the third time this morning."

"Who?" Madge jerked her head in that direction.

"Caroline. She's been circling the village all morning," said Martin.

Madge exchanged a worried look with Oscar. Keeping Martin out of the loop was like steering a bloodhound away from a bloody rag.

She tried to put Martin off the scent. "Birdie's dog got out. She must be looking for him."

Oscar spoke in an unusually chipper and loud tone. "What can I get you, my friend? Or are you waiting for Roxy?" Madge rolled her eyes at his clumsy attempt at diversion.

Martin studied Madge, then Oscar. The pair stood stiffly, like praying not to be caught in a lie.

"Fine. Don't tell me. But you know I'll find out."

Martin grabbed soup and a salad for Roxy and a turkey wrap for himself to go, then dragged his feet toward the beauty parlor. He was in no hurry to return to last night's phone conversation with Roxy, which practically made his ears bleed.

Birdie and Brownie scampered toward him. Martin bent and petted the white, fluffy head. "Glad you found Brownie."

"Don't know what you're talking about. He wasn't lost." Brownie spotted a squirrel scampering up a tree and pulled Birdie past him.

Martin glanced toward The Café. Madge ducked out of the window. *She lied to me. Whatever's going on is big.*

The sheriff's cruiser rolled up the weedy, overgrown driveway of Kathleen MacGregor's deserted house for the second time that week. The long curls of peeling paint reminded Caroline of a snake shedding its skin. Shutters hung twisted in sad neglect and the grime-caked windows seemed like the owner died decades earlier instead of months ago.

Caroline wondered who Kathleen left the house to and why they hadn't claimed it. And if no one claimed it, then who bothered to board it up? Records indicated Kathleen was a childless widow.

She checked every door and boarded window to see if she missed anything. Still no way in that she could see, but Caroline was reluctant to leave. Her gut told her the mystery man had something to do with this house.

The November sun was setting fast. There was no point rummaging around in the dark. As she steered carefully out of the overgrown driveway, Caroline saw a pinprick of light through one of the front window boards. She shoved the gearshift into Park and inched back toward the house, undoing the safety strap on her holster as she neared.

"Is anyone in there?" Silence.

She banged on the front door before edging closer to the front window and squinting through the slits between the boards. She pointed a flashlight. Her father's voice echoed in her head: *Never put yourself in a vulnerable position*. Yet, there she was alone, at dusk, shining a light into a deserted house.

A twig snapped off the right side of the porch. Caroline pulled her pistol and swung the flashlight onto the area. Dry leaves rustled. The flashlight caught eyes glowing back at her. She let out a ragged laugh as a possum waddled off.

Returning to the cruiser, Caroline sat with her eyes locked on the front window. The setting sun cast the house in a backdrop of purple and orange, but no flickering light. Did she imagine it? Or did something glint in the low-lying sun?

She shook her head and backed down the driveway. "I know what I saw. Someone is in that house."

The old man blew out the candle in the study and inched toward the window. He spied a sheriff's squad car through the boards and the same deputy who nosed around a few days before.

Despite being able to see his breath in the air, a trickle of sweat rolled off his scalp. Another candle flickered in the front room, but he dared not move. Minutes stretched to imagined hours as the deputy walked around the property. His muscles tightened, listening to doorknobs shake and boards rattle.

Finally, a car door slammed shut. He scrambled to the parlor and pinched the candle's flame between his fingers.

His head tilted toward a sound out front. Boots hit the squeaky wooden porch again. A ragged breath snagged in his throat as the deputy called out. He slithered into the corner and curled his body against the wall. His eyes followed the shadow at the window.

A sliver of light traveled around the room and fixed on the candle he just extinguished. The old man folded his body further into the darkness, trying to shrink himself as small as possible.

His head jerked toward the clop of boots retreating off the porch, then crunching on gravel. The old man let out a long sigh as the squad car drove off.

CHAPTER 19
The Disappearing Ghost

Martin watched a dazed Arthur wandering from room to room, shuffling and reshuffling invoices and flyers on his desk and calling Constance two times in three hours. *He's worried about her,* he thought. And Martin worried about Arthur.

"Mr. Covington, is everything alright? You're not yourself this afternoon."

Before Arthur could answer, the bell on the shop door jingled, and Ari made a beeline for the office. He had just come from the bookshop where Zoe and Emily were like twin tornadoes leveling everything in their path. Installing electronic charging stations, moving bookcases and reading chairs and the storytime area setup was underway.

The sisters covered the front windows with brown paper and assigned Ari to keep prying eyes away. He sat on the bench in front of the shop all afternoon and assured half the population of Stones End that Constance knew about the renovation and that all would be revealed tomorrow.

Getting Mrs. Kruchinski to move on was like trying to push a mountain back a few feet. It took Ari 20 minutes to finally convince her that Constance approved the renovation. Maybe not convince, but he did wear her down enough to go away. Now, all he had to do was keep Arthur from walking by.

Ari swept into the printshop. Arthur sat with shoulders rising to his ears and Martin furrowed his brow. "What's going on?"

"Martin wants to know what's bothering me," said Arthur.

Ari plopped into the chair in front of his desk. He knew Arthur wanted to tell Martin the news of the stranger standing in front of the bookshop in the middle of the night. He agreed Martin should know but heard Mrs. Kruchinski's resounding *No* in his head. Should they find out her reason before bringing Martin on board?

Before he thought it through properly, Arthur gestured toward the other chair. "Have a seat." Martin listened to the new development, then stared at his lap.

Arthur asked him to be on the lookout for the stranger, then noticed Martin's hung head. "What is it, Martin? Do you know something?"

Martin stared out the window. This situation appeared more threatening. Should he tell Arthur what he saw? Maybe he should spare him more worry and just tell Caroline. His thoughts jumped to Constance in the city. *Was she safe? Oh God, Charley is with her.*

"Martin?" said Ari.

He rose abruptly. "I'll keep a close eye on things. Not to worry." He suddenly had an urge to call Charley. Martin made it halfway to the door and heard, "Hold on there, Martin."

He swung around to see Ari pointing at the chair. "Sit down, my friend, and tell us what you know."

Martin cursed under his breath for giving himself away. He looked at Ari, then Arthur. "The guy wasn't only stalking Constance's place; I saw him in front of your house as well."

Arthur jumped up. "When? How?"

"I woke at 4:30 and couldn't get back to sleep. There's a lot on my mind lately. So, I took a walk along the river to relax. That's when I saw the guy standing on the riverbank looking toward your house."

"Did he see you?" said Ari.

"Yes, but only because I called out to him."

"You shouldn't have done that. This guy could be dangerous," said Arthur.

Martin smiled. "I think I can handle an old man with a limp.

Anyway, I started walking toward him but had to go around that small bend in the river right before your house. When I cleared the bend, he vanished."

Ari shifted forward in his chair. "How long did it take you to walk around the bend?"

"Maybe a minute. But you lose sight of Arthur's house for a few moments."

Arthur banged his fist so hard he caused a paper avalanche. "How the hell is this guy getting away so fast?"

Martin leaned his head back and stared at the ceiling. "How indeed? After the bend, the river runs straight for quite a way upstream. I would have seen him."

"Unless he turned onto the path into the village," said Arthur.

"He couldn't have made it to the path in a minute. Not with his limp. Besides, I ran up ahead and didn't see him heading into town," said Martin.

Ari ran his hand over the top of his head. "Maybe Birdie is right. Maybe the guy is a damn ghost."

"Martin, do you have time to run and tell Caroline your update? Arthur and I will walk along the river to see if this guy left any clues."

He dashed across the village green. It was shortly after 5 pm and Caroline just returned from Kathleen MacGregor's house when Martin walked in. He briefed her, and she had the same reaction as Arthur, making Mortimer's wings flutter when her fist struck the desk.

"Sorry, Martin." She stroked her African parrot's chest. "And you, too, Mortimer."

Martin flicked his hand. "I know. This disappearing act doesn't make sense." He strode toward the door. Then paused and snapped his fingers.

"What?"

Martin returned to her desk in one stride. “I know how he’s been disappearing. It’s really quite obvious.”

Caroline’s eyes widened. “Of course.” She grabbed the phone. “Dad, it’s me. We’re no longer looking for a dead man.”

CHAPTER 20
Everyone Is Lying

Ari whizzed into the printshop and saw Arthur at his heavy oak desk with only a Tiffany lamp lighting the office.

"It's 6:30. Just enough time to choke down some food before the meeting at Olga's."

"I have to call Constance first."

"Have you talked with her today?"

"Three times."

"Three times? She'll guess something's up."

"Well, it's going to be four. I have to be certain she and Charlotte are not leaving the hotel tonight."

"Fine. Just remember, you agreed not to spoil her trip. We'll explain what's occurred when she returns. Right?"

Arthur nodded as he punched her number.

Constance and Charlotte lay on the king-sized beds in the Edwardian Suite at The Plaza like two wounded warriors from a shopping competition.

"Is it sacrilegious to have swollen feet in such an exquisite place?" said Constance.

Charlotte giggled. "And this was only our first day."

The chirp of a cell phone made them jump, triggering a landslide of packages from bed to floor. Constance flipped through her oversized purse and grabbed at the phone.

"How was shopping, darling?" said Arthur.

Constance laughed. "I think someone is missing me. How many calls is this today, three, four?"

A weak chuckle escaped his throat. "Any luck with finding a wedding dress?"

"Yes. I've narrowed it down to three. Now I just have to try each one on a million more times before we have a winner."

"I imagine roaming all over Manhattan exhausted you. Why don't you have dinner sent up to the room?"

"Actually, we're dining at the most adorable Irish pub we saw today."

Arthur placed his hand over the phone. "They're going out for dinner."

"Stop them. Caroline said they shouldn't leave the hotel at night."

"Arthur, are you still there?"

"Yes, yes. You two should conserve your energy. Remember, you have three days to go."

Ari shot him a thumbs-up.

"Yes, dear. But it's Charlotte's first visit to Manhattan and I want it to be chock-full."

"Constance, it's not safe for two women to traipse around at night."

"Oh, Arthur. It's the city that never sleeps. Besides, we'll be back by nine."

"I don't think that's a good plan."

"Plan? Why would we need a plan?"

Arthur covered the phone again. "I can't get her to agree. What should I do?"

Ari pulled on his chin. "I'm thinking."

"Are you talking to someone, dear?"

"Uh, Martin. Sorry, he needed something."

Ari shoved his hand over the phone. "Tell her you'll take her to dinner tomorrow."

"How about I take you and Charlotte to dinner tomorrow? That way, you can rest up tonight."

Another pause.

"Are you still there, sweetheart?" she said.

"Yes, yes. It was Martin again."

"You're acting funny. Is everything alright?"

Ari saw Arthur's eyes tighten with panic. "Did she go for it?" he asked.

Arthur shook his head, then tapped his pen rapid-fire on the desk.

"Arthur?"

"I'm still here. Horace told me the story of the stranger standing over Willie's grave. It's got me nervous. That's all."

Ari made a slashing motion across his throat. "You're giving it away," he whispered.

Constance stood abruptly. "Has there been an update?"

"No, no." Arthur winced at the lie. "I don't know why you didn't tell me about it." It occurred to him that Constance hadn't shared her visit with Caroline, either. The revelation made him uneasy, like there was more to the threat. He chanced drawing it out of her. "Did you hear anything new?"

She twirled the end of her hair and sputtered: "How would I hear? I've been in Manhattan all day." She cringed at the lie. But the truth was a story she didn't want to tell Arthur—or anyone.

A longer pause fell as both wrestled with what to say. Constance looked over at Charlotte, who was emitting low whiffling sounds in her sleep.

"Well, sweetheart, Charlotte settled the matter of dinner. She's sleeping like a baby. Poor dear. I forgot she's dealing with jet lag from London."

Arthur's sigh of relief reached through the phone.

"It's settled then. Have dinner in your suite. Then kick back for a relaxing night—in the hotel."

"Something is up, Arthur. I can hear it in your voice."

"Good night, darling. I'll talk to you tomorrow." Arthur hung up.

Constance tiptoed out to the sitting area, picked up the hotel phone, and ordered two salmon dinners and a bottle of wine. She gazed down upon the nameless crowd below and wondered how many lives carried dark secrets. *It must be easier to hide from your past in a city this size,* she thought.

She worried that someone saw her leaving Caroline's and would tell Arthur. She could imagine the speculation. Arthur knew more than he was telling. *So do I,* she thought. *Both of us keeping secrets. It's not proper for two lovers heading to the altar.*

She realized Madge never called about Horace's report to Caroline. Constance dialed her number.

Madge stared at the name on the screen. "It's Constance," she said to Oscar. "She's calling to find out what Horace said this morning."

Oscar spun around. "Don't pick up."

Madge couldn't ignore her friend. "Hi, Constance. Did you find a dress yet?" Oscar leaned in.

"Not yet but getting closer. Actually, I was calling about what Horace saw this morning. He was acting mysterious. Did he say anything about the stranger in the cemetery?"

Oscar pulled back. "Don't tell her," he whispered. Then leaned in again.

"Uh, no. Just some graffiti on the back wall of the post office."

"That's odd. Why wouldn't he share that with everyone?"

"Hang up," Oscar mouthed.

Madge whispered. "Start calling me like something's wrong."

"Are you still there, Madge?"

"Yes. I'm... Constance, have to run. Something just crashed in the kitchen and Oscar is shouting. Will catch up when you get back." Madge hung up.

"That was close," said Oscar.

Madge covered her mouth.

"What?" asked Oscar.

"I've lied twice today. First to Martin and now Constance. I'll have to go to confession tomorrow."

Martin overheard Arthur and Ari speak about the meeting at Mrs. Kruchinski's before they left the shop. His exclusion confused him, and the reason piqued his curiosity. Did they suspect his involvement in what was going on? The notion was preposterous and left him resentful and annoyed. He had a good mind to show up and confront them.

He absentmindedly walked to the cramped kitchen in the back of the shop and pulled a steaming bowl of tomato soup from the microwave. Crumbling saltine crackers over it, he mulled over the unsettling events of the day.

The strange man standing on the riverbank staring at Arthur's house, Madge lying to him, Caroline stuffing a fat folder on her desk into a drawer when he entered her substation. It was evident that she was investigating the mystery man and amassed a generous amount of data. And Arthur knew about the meeting and didn't tell him. Wasn't that a form of lying?

As he blew on a hot spoonful of soup, he remembered that he and Caroline knew something no one else was aware of. She cautioned to keep it to himself. It felt like more lying.

CHAPTER 21

The Secret Council Meeting

"Who are we missing?" said Mrs. Kruchinski.

Madge glanced around Olga and Karl's living room, crammed with friends. There was Birdie and Horace perched on the love seat. Arthur, Zoe and Emily, shoulder to shoulder on the couch. Ari and Rosie sat on the cushioned ledge in front of the fireplace. She, Oscar, Karl, and Olga sat on folding chairs.

"Looks like we're all here," she said. "Wait. Walter and Father Gregory are missing."

"And Martin," said Birdie. "We're missing Martin." She disagreed with excluding him and wanted the issue addressed. If they called him now, Martin would come running.

Arthur, who was of the same opinion, jumped in.

"Care to tell us why he's not invited, Olga?"

All eyes focused on Mrs. Kruchinski, who folded her arms across her chest.

"I trust Martin. But the only new person in the village since this maniac showed up is Roxy. And her, I don't trust."

"Roxy!" said Oscar. "You're kidding. Her thoughts don't wander past Martin and pop-culture."

"Don't be so sure," said Mrs. Kruchinski. "She's as calculating as they come."

Karl sprang up at the sound of the doorbell. "There's Walter and Father Gregory."

Conversation screeched to a halt at the sight of Caroline

marching into the room. Mrs. Kruchinski leapt from her chair and sputtered, "Who tipped you off?"

"No one. It was never a matter of *if*, just a matter of *where*."

Karl threw out his arms as if surrendering. "Well, you caught us." He motioned toward his chair. "Have a seat, deputy."

Caroline refused to sit. She stood over the group, glowering like they were disobedient children. Mrs. Kruchinski tapping her foot was the only sound. Even Horace, who normally enjoyed the village drama, sat staring at the beige carpet. Zoe and Emily were the only ones who dared look at Caroline.

"So, out with it. What are you planning—round-the-clock stakeouts, breaking out the sniper rifles, standing ready with barrels of tar and sacks of feathers?" said Caroline.

"Give us some credit as civilized people," said Birdie. "And if you must know, we were discussing why Martin didn't get invited."

"Olga suspects Roxy is in cahoots with the mystery man," said Madge.

"Roxy! Are you insane? Roxy is the last…" She stopped at the chime of the doorbell. Karl scampered off and returned with Father Gregory and Walter. The somber tone in the room stopped them. It felt more like a wake than a council meeting.

Karl disappeared mumbling, "I'll fetch more chairs."

"So, what were you discussing so solemnly?"

"Olga is concerned about Roxy," said Oscar.

Walter let loose a howl. "Roxy! Roxy involved…" His uncontrolled laughter kept him from finishing.

"Thank you, Walter," said Caroline. She turned toward Mrs. Kruchinski. "Roxy's involvement is a stretch for me too."

The village ladies eyed one another. They agreed on one thing: no one trusted Roxy.

"Laughing matter, you say. Then explain why Roxy saw this maniac leaving the graveyard and didn't tell anyone?" said Mrs. Kruchinski.

Caroline whipped out her notepad. “How do you know that?”

“Because I stopped in the beauty parlor yesterday to see Berris and overheard Roxy telling a friend on the phone.”

“What was Roxy doing out at 6:30 in a rainstorm?” asked Horace.

“And the guy left through the rear gate. The only thing beyond is a warehouse,” said Oscar.

“My warehouse,” said Karl.

“Not so laughable now, is it?” said Mrs. Kruchinski.

“Did you stop at your warehouse that morning, Karl?” said Caroline.

“Yes, at 6 o’clock. I left by 6:15.”

Caroline flipped through her notes. “You first saw the stranger at 6:30. Is that correct, Birdie?”

“Thereabouts.”

Caroline spun around to Karl.

“Did you lock up when you left?”

“No. Roger, my warehouse manager, was due in at seven. I left the door unlocked.”

“Roger’s a recent hire, isn’t he?”

“Yes. I don’t how long he’ll last. He’s already lost his warehouse key, which is why I opened up for him.”

“Still think we should include Martin?” said Mrs. Kruchinski, looking very satisfied. “His girlfriend is very questionable.”

The room was hushed. Madge stood. “Yes, I do. Martin wouldn’t share information with Roxy. I’d stake my life on it.”

“Really? Do you share what you’ve heard with Oscar?” said Mrs. Kruchinski.

Madge opened her mouth, then closed it. She shared everything with Oscar because she trusted him implicitly. Does Martin trust Roxy in the same way?

“The situation is getting muddier,” said Arthur.

“We started with word of a mysterious man standing over Willie's grave. Horace also saw the same man looking up at Constance's apartment in the middle of the night. Then, Martin tells me he saw him on the riverbank staring at my house. And now, Roxy caught sight of him leaving the back gate in the cemetery and she didn't tell anyone." Arthur shook his head. "Where's this leading to?"

"Wait. Did you just say this creep was in front of your house?" said Oscar.

"Yes. Martin told us this afternoon," said Ari.

Mrs. Kruchinski turned on Caroline. "Were you aware of this?"

"Yes."

"And were you planning to share this update with us?" said Birdie.

"It wasn't my plan," said Caroline, through clenched teeth. She shot Arthur a pinched-lipped look.

"What else are you not telling us?" asked Rosie.

The air burned with suspicion. One more accusation would ignite an emotional bonfire. Caroline was a cop who knew everybody's business and she was someone who kept secrets. Need to know, her detective dad drilled into her, even if the people who needed to know were friends.

Father Gregory didn't like the angry vibe. He sprang from his seat. "Stop this! Caroline is dedicated to serve and protect us. She doesn't deserve to be treated like the enemy. Listen to us. Suspecting Roxy. Not trusting Martin. And what do we have to base this on? Nothing. No crime has been committed."

"Are you saying none of this stuff worries you, Father?" said Rosie.

"Of course, the suspicious behavior of this stranger needs to be dealt with. But this meeting is about how to protect Constance. Not about pointing fingers."

"Gregory's right," said Arthur. "There's no call to turn on each other." Arthur stood in front of Caroline. "Crime or no crime, there is a threat, and we came together to address it. So, what are we doing about it?"

Horace stretched to his imposing height of six foot one, tucked his thumbs into his vest pockets, and stood in the middle of the room. Birdie hadn't seen him take his barrister stance in decades. Her eyes smiled at the impressive sight.

"I'd like to speak on behalf of my friend, Martin. Now, Olga has spread seeds of doubt about Martin's loyalty. She seems to think he would put Constance in jeopardy to share gossip with his girlfriend. I beg to differ."

"Here, here," Birdie yelled.

"Martin, as you know, has keen observation skills that go far beyond picking out a stranger in a crowd. Skills we need right now. He tunes into changes in posture, eye movement, tone of voice, thereby making it impossible to get a lie past him."

The color rose on Madge's face, remembering how she lied to Martin.

Horace moved around the room, looking each person in the eye as if they were jurors in a murder trial.

"It's laughable thinking we can keep what's going on from Martin. Martin will find out whether we tell him or not. And he'll keep his observations from Roxy if asked. He's devoted to every one of us, especially Constance and Arthur. So, I put it to the floor. Do we include Martin or not? I vote, yes."

Birdie, Madge, and Rosie jumped up, applauding. Oscar put his two fingers in his mouth and let loose a shrill whistle.

Arthur pushed off the couch and shook hands with Horace. "Thank you." He turned to the group. "I vote yes, as well."

Caroline blew her traffic whistle. The group came to attention. "Is it unanimous?"

Mrs. Kruchinski didn't flinch under the glaring eyes. Finally, she batted her arm. "You win. It won't hurt for Martin to be on his guard with Roxy." Karl hugged his irascible wife.

"Listen up, folks," said Caroline. "Here's how we're going to proceed. I'll bring Martin up to speed. Arthur will do the same with Constance and Charlotte when they return."

"Constance and Charlotte will stay at my house until the wedding," said Arthur.

"Let me know if Constance balks at the idea. I'll park the cruiser in front of her place every night."

"And we'll all take turns keeping an eye on Constance during the day," said Walter.

"Don't worry about that," said Zoe. "Constance will be with Emily and me in the bookshop when she returns." She punched her right fist into her left palm. "Trust me. No one will harm her on our watch."

"No one," repeated Emily and Ari.

Arthur's chest swelled. His family circled him and stood ready to guard and protect the woman he loved.

The group dispersed as a mobilized force. Arthur, Ari, and their sisters were the first to say goodnight. Birdie and Horace continued along the river path to Birdie's house. The rest trudged toward town, jumping at every snapped twig and shimmering shadow.

The last two heading home were Caroline and Father Gregory. "You were unusually quiet tonight, Father. What's on your mind?"

Father Gregory stopped and faced Caroline. He wanted to see her eyes when she answered. "Be honest with me, Caroline. Are you seeing an actual threat here?"

"Yes." Her eyes didn't lie.

CHAPTER 22
Locked Doors

Zoe and Emily collapsed onto the mushy, rolled-armed couch in Arthur's living room. The antique mahogany mantle clock chimed nine. Arthur knelt at the stone fireplace and lit sticks of cedar kindling, then coaxed flames around the pine logs with a bellow. Soon, the cozy room smelled like a campfire.

"Olga is a tough customer," said Emily. She flicked her feet, sending her shoes flying across the braided rug.

"I like her," said Zoe. "She makes things happen."

"You would. You're just like her," said Ari.

Arthur plunked down on his worn leather recliner and basked in the company of his siblings. *They haven't changed since we were kids.* He wondered if they noticed a difference in him.

He and Emily were similar, both tall and lean and even-tempered. They were the worriers. The methodical thinkers. Zoe and Ari refused to entertain worry. They made decisions quickly and faced life head on.

For all the bickering between the sisters, Arthur knew they were thick as thieves. God help anyone who tried to come between them. Emily would hit them with her scorching brilliance, and Zoe would just hit them.

Through the decades, he followed the prosperity of the family business from America. The raw business sense came from Zoe. She was the idea generator. Emily possessed the financial genius to spin ideas into reality. And they were so efficient, they made the impossible appear easy.

Arthur had flown solo for so long in life, he'd forgotten what it was like to have co-pilots. He was the youngest, and the presence of his siblings made him feel secure. He never wanted them to leave.

"So, what do you make of the situation? Are we overreacting?" asked Arthur.

"No," said Zoe. "Don't know what this stranger is up to, but my gut tells me he's trouble. We just don't know what kind. Could be serious, could be nothing. Always plan for serious."

"I agree," said Emily. "I don't sense his intentions are life threatening. If that were the case, he would have struck by now instead of popping up here and there. If he were planning something dastardly, why give people so many chances to identify him?"

"Excellent point. And this fellow is ancient. Not much chance of him attacking anyone," said Ari.

"Agreed. But Roxy's 21," said Zoe. She twisted around to Arthur. "You know her best. Is it conceivable she's in cahoots with this guy?"

"She showed up over a month ago. So, no one knows her that well. She's rough around the edges."

"Rough enough to be a bodily threat to Constance?" asked Emily.

Arthur raked his hands through his salt and pepper hair. "I don't want to think about that."

A strained silence weighed in.

Zoe nudged Emily and nodded in Arthur's direction. Arthur's neck sank into his shoulders, and he drummed his fingers on the arm of his chair.

Emily spoke tenderly. "Don't worry, little brother. We're here with you. Among the four of us, nothing will happen to our darling Constance."

Ari smacked his hands together. "That's right. Remember the Covington Runoff?"

Arthur's eyes blazed bright at the memory. "I'll never forget you all charging over the hill into the boatyard."

"I wasn't there. What's the Covington Runoff?" said Emily.

"We've told you the story a million times," said Ari. "It's when the rival boatyard came to trash our schooner."

Emily scooted to the edge of the couch. "It's my favorite. Tell it again."

"They caught me alone. There were seven thugs swinging clubs and sticks. I needed help and bolted for town," said Arthur.

Zoe sprang off the couch. "And we stampeded in like the cavalry..."

Arthur leapt to his feet. "Mom, Pop, Ari and Zoe thundered down the dirt hill to the boatyard wielding clubs. Mom swung her mop handle. I snatched a hammer..."

"That's right," said Ari. "Arthur charged the thugs before we reached him. You should have heard him, Emily. He let loose a battle cry like a Greek warrior."

"We heard Arthur's call to arms and howled like a swarm of banshees. Those sons-of-bitches took off like the devil himself was chasing them," said Zoe.

Ari puffed out his rib cage. "Yep. No one messes with the Covingtons."

"I was never prouder to be a Covington. Until today. All of you standing up to defend my Constance," said Arthur.

"Our Constance," said Emily.

Zoe lumbered from the couch. "It's getting thick in here. I'm off to bed before someone cries for a group hug."

She kissed Arthur's cheek. "Quit worrying. We've got this covered."

"You have the face of Madonna and the heart of Medusa," laughed Ari.

Zoe turned toward the stairs. "Not the first time I've heard that."

Emily bolted off the couch. "I'll never pass up a group hug." Arthur laughed and extended his arms. The three gathered in an embrace. Arthur whispered. "Thank you."

"For what?" said Ari.

"For always being there."

Emily flicked her hand. "That's what family are for." She gathered her tossed shoes and scuffed off.

The brothers dragged themselves out to the porch. Ari gave a satisfying stretch, releasing some of the day's stress.

"Wonderful to have my kids under one roof," said George.

"Wonderful," said Ari.

"Let's not let so much time pass before we see each other again," said Arthur.

"We'll plan the next reunion before I return to Greece," said Ari.

"Would be nice if Arthur shows Constance our homeland," said George.

The brothers sat with contented grins, gazing upon the moonlit river through the pines.

It wasn't long before they scanned the waterfront for the stranger and strained their ears toward every nocturnal sound.

"So, what do you think, Pop? Are we in trouble here or not?" asked Ari.

"Hard to say," said George. "Whatever this guy's planning, he's taking his damn time. We just have to wait and outfox the bastard in the meantime."

"Is our strategy to safeguard Constance strong enough?" asked Arthur.

"Yes. She'll have protective eyes on her at all times."

"What about this Roxy angle? Any chance she's involved?" asked Ari.

"I have no idea. She's calculating. Good at getting men to do her bidding," said George.

"Martin is proof of that. She's cast a spell over him. He can't see she's shallow," said Arthur.

Ari and George roared. "Those are hormones."

Arthur grinned. "Maybe so. But is she the devil in disguise?"

"I'd say it's the other way around. If she is involved, how did this creep recruit her?" said George.

Arthur's head jerked toward his brother. Ari returned a grim look, then glanced past Arthur.

"Don't move."

"What is it?"

"He's across the river by the birch trees."

Arthur barreled off the porch and sprinted sure-footed to the edge of the bank. The Housatonic flowed fast, creating a night mist. Ari, unfamiliar with the terrain, lagged as he maneuvered the gnarled tree roots, rutted ground, and craggy grass.

"Do you see anything?" said Ari, reaching his brother, out of breath.

Arthur squinted into the darkness. Ari followed his stare.

"Nothing. Sure it was him?"

"Too far to be sure. But someone was standing there."

Arthur tore back to the house and dialed Caroline.

"On my way. Do not pursue this guy!"

"I can't figure out what this guy's up to," said George. "Lurking around Constance and her shop and now here. Who's the target of his attention?"

Arthur's eyes widened. He hadn't considered that he might be the target. He turned toward Ari who was sweating—on a 40-degree night.

It was a half hour before the phone rang. "He got away," said Caroline. "I cruised the area. No sign of him."

"Damn it! What's this guy playing at?" said Arthur.

"He's gone now. Try to grab some sleep. I'll keep a close watch tonight."

Ari patted Arthur's shoulder. "I'll pour a nightcap."

"No. I'm heading to bed." He turned toward Ari. "You should do the same."

The brothers turned toward the stairs. Arthur stopped, stepped to the front door, and turned the lock.

Karl shut the light in the bathroom and crept toward the bed. Olga sounded like a submarine sending sonic pings into the atmosphere. Lights across the river blinded him. He clutched his binoculars. A buzzing from the nightstand sounded. Horace's name appeared on his cell phone.

"Are you watching this?" asked Horace.

Karl raised the binoculars. "It's Caroline in her cruiser. She's spotlighting the river."

"You think Arthur's seeing this?" said Horace.

"Hopefully, he's sleeping by now. Let's not upset him. Caroline's on it."

"Mystery man strikes again," said Karl.

"You're probably right. I'd better run before Birdie wakes."

"Yeah. Thank God Olga's out."

"Horace?"

"Yeah."

"Lock your door."

"Damn straight!"

The light in the printshop was on when Caroline returned. The clock in the village square showed 10:27. She stalked in and hollered Martin's name.

His head popped out from the art room. "Is everything alright?"

"Can you spare a minute? I need to share something with you."

Martin bounded toward the front counter. "I know about the

council meeting tonight," he said. His lips pressed tight.

Caroline nodded. "That's why I'm here."

Martin exploded. "Why was I left out? It doesn't make sense."

"No one wanted to exclude you. The worry, and it wasn't unanimous, was that you'd share sensitive information with Roxy."

Martin's jaw hit his chest. "What's the risk of talking to Roxy? Everyone in the village will find out, eventually."

"She saw the stranger leaving the cemetery through the rear gate that morning. So, speculation shifted to why she was there and didn't mention it to anyone? She had to hear him breaking the lock on the gate."

Martin tilted his head to the side as he analyzed the revelation. "Is this hearsay or confirmed information?"

"Confirmed. Olga overheard Roxy telling a friend."

Martin folded his arms and leaned his fist on his chin. His eyes bore a remote stare. Caroline couldn't interpret his reaction.

"What are you thinking?"

"I don't know what to make of this. The notion that Roxy's involved seems absurd. You have my word, though. I won't discuss events with her."

Caroline turned on her boot heel to leave, then hesitated. "One more thing. You'll be included in council meetings going forward. And that was unanimous."

The news pleased Martin. Then his smile disappeared. "Is Constance going to be alright?"

Caroline paused. "I can only guarantee safety."

He trained his eyes on the deputy while she crossed the village green. After she entered the substation, he peered up and down the street several times, then did something for the first time while working. He locked the shop door.

Charlotte roused long enough to devour her salmon dinner, then plodded back to bed. Constance stood at the window, knee deep in memories. The old feeling that she was cursed pricked at her like a thorn bush that refused to die. Believing in the curse kept her from encouraging an amorous relationship with Arthur through the years. And now she wondered if she was bringing tragedy to his doorstep?

She crossed to the couch and pulled a photograph of Arthur from her wallet. *I'll never survive if anything happens to you, my love. Our friends worry for me when it's you who's in danger.*

CHAPTER 23
The Grand Opening

The sisters bustled into the kitchen with a sinful amount of energy for 5:33 am. "Good morning, Ari," they chanted in unison. Emily pressed the button on the coffeemaker while Zoe jammed slices of bread into the toaster.

The kitchen screamed of a bachelor with minimalist taste. The silver flecked quartz counters sat atop oak cabinets and held only the essentials—coffeemaker, toaster, a neat stack of napkins and white ceramic sugar bowl.

Ari leaned his elbows on the sturdy pine table in the middle of the room and shifted one eye toward the clock. "May I ask why you're up so early? It's still dark out, for heaven's sake."

Emily answered from behind the refrigerator door as she hauled out milk, orange juice, berries, butter, and jam. "We could ask you the same question, brother dear."

"I just got off a Skype call with Ruthann. What's your excuse?"

"We spoke with her yesterday. Your wife is at the end of her rope caring for her mother," said Zoe.

Ari rubbed the stubble on his face. "I know."

Emily set the chilled cornucopia on the table and patted Ari's shoulder. "Big day today."

Ari stiffened. "Oh God. Is it the grand opening, already?"

Zoe slapped the back of his head. "Quit being negative. The bookshop looks spectacular. We've blitzed social media notices and hung flyers everywhere."

"We expect a huge turnout. College kids are already filtering home for their American Thanksgiving break," said Emily.

"And the Christmas shopping season has begun," said Zoe.

"Are you telling me you've finished the renovation in one day?"

"Of course not. What's left is minor. All things you can handle," said Zoe.

Ari hunched over his oversized coffee mug. "I'll give Arthur a heads-up before he leaves for the office. It won't do for our kid brother to collapse in the gutter clutching his chest."

Emily laughed. "You're so dramatic. Where do you get that from?"

"Maybe because you two pull heart-stopping antics."

Zoe shoved the last bit of toast in her mouth and washed it down with a gulp of orange juice. She pointed to the ceiling as she swallowed. "Arthur's moving around upstairs."

Emily seized her half-eaten toast. The pair raced through the door like bank robbers who just set off an alarm.

Arthur scraped into the kitchen in slippered feet. He roared out a yawn. "Did I hear the sisters?"

"Yep."

"It's 6:15. Why so early?"

Ari gestured to a chair. "Sit down, Arthur."

Arthur mumbled, "I hate when you say that. Always means trouble." He raised his hand like a traffic cop. "Don't talk till I get caffeine in me."

Ari grinned. "Meet me on the porch."

A maxed-out feeling crept in. Arthur lingered at the kitchen window, wondering what Constance was doing. His visions of her were so clear, it felt like she stood beside him.

Smiling at the fact that his soon-to-be bride was not a morning person, he imagined tiptoeing around the house, trying not to wake her. Stooping over the bed to kiss her goodbye. Rushing home with joy instead of facing cooking dinner for one.

Only two more weeks. Armed with his coffee mug, he headed for the porch.

Arthur eased himself onto George, taking care not to spill his favorite drink of the day. Ari glanced at Arthur's half-full mug. He settled his eyes on the river and waited for him to finish his coffee.

Grateful for a few moments of tranquility, Arthur savored the sweetness of the pre-dawn air, the soothing rush of the river, and sitting next to his big brother with Pop.

It was rare for Ari to sit still and rarer for him to look sad. An unwelcome reality dawned on Arthur. He hunched forward and leaned on his knees. "You're going home soon, aren't you?"

Ari kept his eyes on the river. "Ruthann needs me. I'm leaving the day after your wedding."

Inevitably, Ari must return to Greece. But hearing the actual date plucked a sad heartstring.

"What are we going to do without Ari, Pop?"

"Your brother's merely a phone call away. And now that Ari's on this Skype thing, you two can gab face-to-face."

Arthur chuckled. "How do you know about Skype?"

"I keep up with technology." George hesitated, then added, "Get it over with, Ari."

Arthur bolstered himself with a swig of coffee.

"It's about the shop. Zoe and Emily went overboard and did a complete facelift. I haven't seen the result, but I'm certain it's unrecognizable. The unveiling is today."

"Now, before you lose it, son, remember your sisters are businesswomen who know what they're doing," said George.

Arthur glared at Ari. He raised his cup, lowered it, then sucked in a deep breath.

Ari waved a hand in front of Arthur's face. His brother didn't blink.

"He's broken again, Pop."

"Arthur!" George yelled. "Say something."

"It's fine. It's all going to be fine," said Arthur.

Ari pushed his face close to Arthur, as if examining an alien substance.

"Why are you so calm? I thought you'd hit the roof."

Arthur answered like a talking robot. "Constance gave her permission. Pop trusts our sisters. Good enough for me."

"So, you're not even a little anxious about her reaction?"

"Constance gave her permission. Pop trusts our sisters. Good enough for me."

"Yep. He's broken."

"He'll snap out of it. The changes will be a triumph. You'll see," said George.

"Love your confidence, Pop. But I still say Constance won't like it and the shop won't be jammed like a rock concert."

Ari waved his hand again in front of Arthur. Still no response.

"Arthur! Turn everything off. Caroline will find out what this nut is up to. The bookshop is in expert hands. And, in case you've forgotten, you're getting married in two weeks. Switch gears and start thinking about that."

Ari whacked Arthur in the arm. "Excellent advice."

"Have either of you taken care of changing the name on the schooner? Or its christening as *The Constance*?"

The brothers studied each other for an answer. Arthur brightened. "Let's christen her before the wedding."

"Makes sense. It's her wedding present. I'll take care of the name change for you. I know a guy."

Arthur grinned. His brother seemed to know more people than Arthur met in the four decades he lived in Stones End.

"I'll create the template. You'll have it by the end of the day," said Arthur.

The brothers sprang off the bench and hustled through the front door. Arthur poked his head back out. "Thanks, Pop."

The screen door thwacked shut before George could respond. He answered anyway. "That's what fathers are for."

George granting permission to stop thinking about the many distractions energized Arthur and Ari. The picture-perfect day further boosted their spirits as the brothers ambled toward the village. The early morning bounty overflowed with autumn trees stretching toward a sharp blue horizon. Birdsong welcoming another rise of the sun and brisk air, tinting their cheeks with color.

They rambled along, debating about painting *The Constance* on the stern of the schooner. Each had strong opinions regarding font, italics, border style. Soon voices roared and arms flailed in amicable competition.

The argument ground to a halt at the sight of a dozen people gathered in front of the bookshop. Arthur checked his watch.

"It's 7:40. What's going on?"

Ari threw back his head and howled at the sight of multicolored balloons floating like a dancing rainbow, and Zoe calling out to the crowd like a carnival barker.

"Grand opening at 10 am. Bring your friends. Free books, treats, and toys for the kids."

Arthur edged closer to the shop. Emily stood behind a table serving free coffee and pastry. Zoe shoved a flyer into the hands of the early morning joggers and dog walkers.

Oscar darted out of The Café door balancing a coffee urn. Mrs. Kruchinski streaked across the street bearing a pink box. "I've brought more."

They found Arthur and Ari on the sidewalk. "You two are helping?" said Arthur.

"And why not?" said Mrs. Kruchinski. "The new bookshop must be a success."

"Or we're all in trouble with Constance," said Oscar.

The closed white shades across the shop windows hinted of a bounty of hidden treasures beyond. "Has anyone seen it?" said Arthur.

"Karl has. But I couldn't wrestle anything out of him. And believe me, I tried," said Mrs. Kruchinski.

"Brave man," murmured Horace, wandering over.

"Your sisters approached Olga and me to supply daily sandwiches, pastry and donuts. We worked out a price. Constance needs to approve it, of course," said Oscar.

"Well, I want a glimpse," said Arthur. He moved toward the shop door and heard Zoe holler, "Stop!"

"No sneak peeks. Come back at ten," said Emily. Zoe ran to block the door.

Ari steered Arthur aside. "Let them have their moment. Besides, I'm not sure we can take them."

Karl drove up in his flat-bed truck loaded with hardy mums, sedum, pumpkins, and bumpy-fleshed gourds. "Do you need my help today, ladies?"

Emily yelled, "No, Karl, but thanks for asking."

Arthur stuck his head in the side window. "What's it look like inside? They won't let me see."

Karl flashed a broad grin. "Sheer magic!" He honked and rode up Main Street.

The grand opening produced stress for Caroline. It was a perfect opportunity for the mystery man to slither into the village. Trying to figure out his next moved frustrated her because there was no way to know who he targeted.

She staked out in the squad car with eyes trained on the bookshop. Martin tapped on the window and made her jump.

"I heard about last night. Discover anything?"

"Yes. I confirmed your theory of how he vanishes."

Martin shook his head. He knew he was right.

"You have any spare time today? I could use another set of eyes." Caroline motioned toward the bookshop.

"I have a lot of rush jobs to finish but I can give you my lunch hour."

"I'll take it."

Martin sprinted toward The Café for coffee and hoped to find Roxy at the beauty parlor for a good morning kiss and snuggle. It was a paltry attempt to appease Roxy who was beyond the ranting stage over his late hours. He dreaded the next two weeks.

Ari burst in looking for Arthur. "Grab your jacket. We can't miss the grand opening."

Arthur peered at the clock. "Where did the morning go?" he mumbled. "I need ten minutes. What's it looking like?"

"You won't believe it. The line is a block long waiting for the doors to open."

"One of us should be there. Go, I'll come as soon as I can," said Arthur.

Ari yelled as he passed the front desk. "Can you spare Martin?"

"Yes. Twenty minutes."

Martin and Ari rushed out in a blur.

Twenty minutes later, Arthur pulled on his jacket as Martin ran back in. "Well?"

"I don't want to give it away," said Martin, but Arthur could see him bursting with excitement.

"Tell me. I don't want to be blindsided."

He raised his fists to the sides of his head and shot his fingers open. "It will blow your mind!"

Arthur didn't know what that meant.

Newspaper deadlines, rush jobs and designing the template for *The Constance* cluttered Arthur's mind as he hurried toward the bookshop. And all had to be finished before he headed for Manhattan to take Constance and Charlotte to dinner.

Arthur's pace slowed as he saw Caroline sitting in her cruiser. He called out good morning, but she didn't turn. Her presence reminded him of the man across the river last night. Maybe it was good that the women were out of town.

Not knowing what to expect, Arthur approached the shop warily. Would the place look too modern, too crowded with garish displays, lighting that blinded?

He reached the shop and stared in amazement. Old and young crowded the oak counters across both front windows. Bobby Carlton, a third-year college student, appeared to be teaching old Mr. Ferguson something on his laptop.

Wires snaked out of every charging station. Earbudded people read, necks stretched over laptops. iPad cases propped open. Water bottles and snack plates littered the countertop.

Arthur entered the shop. Zoe was ringing up sales and didn't notice him. The crowds made it difficult to take in everything. No sign of Emily or Ari.

The oak bookcases that always rested against the right wall now formed a horseshoe. A low teak bench with metal legs sat in the middle of the horseshoe and groups of people perused books standing at the cases and sitting on the bench.

Beyond the books was a gauze tent strung with white fairy lights for the storytime area. Arthur estimated the area to be 15 feet wide and 10 feet deep.

Emily performed somewhere inside the magical tent. Arthur peeked in. It was like looking upon a fairy tale. Glittering stars, moon and sun cutouts hung from the ceiling. Low sky-blue and grass-green plastic benches stenciled with familiar story characters outlined the perimeter and animal-shaped bean bags covered the floor.

Every inch of bench and bean bag held a child. Emily sat on an oversized red velvet winged chair, reading a story about a friendly monster under the bed. The children's faces were lit with wonder.

Arthur pulled his head out of the tent and gazed to the left, where four overstuffed armchairs faced each other. The newly covered chairs held grey and white plaid slipcovers, and two antique white pole lamps illuminated the reading area.

"They did it again. It's magnificent," said Ari.

Arthur spun around to face his brother. "There you are. Look at this place. Enchanting! Did you see the storytime area?"

"See it? I put it together." Ari thrust out his chest.

"And the bookcases nestled together? You feel you're in a private library on someone's estate."

"Will Constance love it?"

Arthur did a slow 360-degree turn. "She'd be crazy not to. The only concern is she'll need an assistant. Not big in her book. Maybe she'll see it's time to grow."

"Zoe's been at the cash register since the door opened."

"The dust will settle. I wonder what future sales will be?" asked Arthur.

"Hard to say. But our sisters carved out daily, weekly and monthly activities to keep this place hopping."

Arthur laughed. "We terrified ourselves for nothing."

"Pop was right. Trust the sisters."

Arthur stroked his chin.

"What are you thinking?"

"Tomorrow's headline. *The New Page Turner Bookshop. Where literature and technology weave an enchanting spell.*"

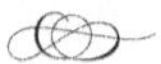

Caroline glanced at her watch and broke into a trot. She had one minute to relieve Martin. She reached the cruiser and ripped open the door.

Martin sprang from the driver's seat, wiping lipstick off his mouth with the back of his hand. Roxy stumbled out the passenger door.

"You were supposed to be watching the bookshop, not making out with your girlfriend." The veins on Caroline's neck bulged.

Martin's face turned the color of Roxy's ruby-red lipstick. "I was not making out. Roxy leaned over to kiss me goodbye. I did not take my eyes off the shop for the past hour."

"He didn't, Caroline. I swear," said Roxy.

Caroline shot a blistering stare. "That's deputy to you." Martin was certain if Roxy didn't move, she'd burst into flames. Caroline spun back to Martin.

"What were you thinking, letting your girlfriend sit in the cruiser?"

Martin's voice cracked. "I would never do such a thing. Roxy jumped in, uninvited. I demanded that she leave. She leaned over to kiss me goodbye. She wasn't in the car for one minute."

Caroline turned on Roxy. "Don't you have somewhere to be?"

Roxy turned tail and ran like a scared rabbit. Caroline rolled her eyes at the sight of her running in four-inch heels.

"Sorry, Martin. My nerves are on edge. Anything to report?"

"Nothing. Although, there are a lot of people I don't recognize."

"I'm seeing the same. Arthur's sisters did a media blitz to the surrounding areas. Mention free giveaways, and people come running."

Martin gave a lopsided smile. "If you still trust me. I'll give you a break at five."

Caroline returned the smile. "Thanks."

He loped toward The Café for a takeout tuna sandwich. "And don't worry," he called out, "I'll lock the cruiser doors this time."

Charlotte and Constance walked sideways through the door of the Edwardian Suite at The Plaza, forcing their packages through the opening. They limped to the blue silk couch in the living room. Constance pried the shoes off her bulging feet and scrunched her toes through the thick-piled carpet.

"You shopped like someone possessed, Aunt Constance. I can't believe we have your entire wedding ensemble, and it's only 4 o'clock on our second day," said Charlotte.

Constance's manic shopping was on purpose. She felt a pressing need to return to Stones End. Arthur was acting strangely. Madge hung up quickly last night, and she couldn't reach Olga or Birdie all day. Was their questionable behavior linked to the stranger in the cemetery? She had to know what was going on.

Feeling guilty about cutting their trip short, Constance justified it with good intentions. She would make it up to her niece before Charlotte returned to England.

"Dearest, would you be terribly disappointed if we went home early? Arthur's acting funny and I'm worried it's about the changes his sisters are making in my shop. We can catch an early morning train."

Charlotte perked up at the suggestion. She was eager to see how the wedding project was coming along. The more honest reason that she missed Martin nagged her. She daydreamed about his floppy hair, the sexy tone of his voice, how his eyes danced when a brilliant idea struck, the warmth of his hand in hers...

The last image sent tingles down her arms. She dug in her satchel and whipped out a train schedule. "We can easily make the last train tonight and grab a taxi at the station."

"Tonight? Wonderful. I'll call Arthur and cancel dinner. Are you sure you don't mind?"

"Not at all. This will give me a few days of wedding prep time back."

Constance smiled as she packed. *Charlotte's not fooling me. She's returning because of Martin.*

Constance fell into Arthur's arms at the train station. "You are such a dear for picking us up. We were happy to grab a taxi."

"Nonsense. I wouldn't hear of it. Besides, you're in my arms a half-hour sooner."

Charlotte's eyes pooled, gazing at the happy couple carrying on like teenagers in love. She longed for that kind of happiness. *At this point, I'd settle for half of what Aunt Constance and Arthur have.*

When they pulled into Stones End, Arthur stopped the car in the village square by the fountain. "There's something I need to tell you."

Constance drew back.

"Your shop…uh, looks different."

Constance sputtered. "Have your sisters made changes already?"

"They sure have." Arthur pulled out his handkerchief and wiped his brow.

"The grand opening was today."

"Grand opening!" Her eyes bulged like a bullfrog.

"Now, sweetheart, before you say anything, it was a fantastic success."

Constance leaned forward and stared out the windshield.

"Constance?"

"Why is Caroline sitting in her cruiser?"

Arthur re-wiped his brow. "That's a story for later." He started the car. "Let's get you home. Ari and my sisters are waiting to show you the changes. I think you'll love them."

As they pulled away, Charlotte glanced out the back window of the car toward the printshop. Her pulse quickened. The lights were still on.

Her friends yelled, "Surprise!" as Constance walked through the door. Struck dumb with how different the shop looked, she took in the changes—counters and stools across the windows, her bookcases rearranged, a glass-doored refrigerator stacked with water bottles, juice and energy drinks, cappuccino and espresso machines.

Arthur and his family stood silent as she explored the storytime tent and reading area.

Horace whispered to Birdie. "If that doesn't make her fall in love with the changes, I don't know what will."

Emily chewed on a cuticle and made her finger bleed. Zoe folded and unfolded her arms repeatedly, like they were in the way. Ari glanced at Arthur, who shrugged. "Give her a minute."

Constance turned and absorbed the feel of the unfamiliar look, then shook her head. "How did you accomplish all this in two days?"

Emily sounded on the verge of tears. "You don't like it?"

Constance sobbed. "I've never seen anything so beautiful." She ran toward Zoe and Emily. Zoe was so relieved she didn't resist a group hug.

The sisters did a high-speed data dump. Constance could barely conceal her shock looking at the cash receipts. "This is what I usually make in a week!"

"Count on opening-day volume dropping by 70% going forward," said Emily. Constance looked up, trying to calculate the effect on earnings.

Zoe smiled. "Even with the drop, you'll almost double your cash flow."

Before she could react, Emily and Zoe pointed to a scrolling slideshow of pictures on two iPads at the counter. Candid shots, posed shots, brief video clips rolled by. The dancing balloons, mesmerized children, animated ladies in the reading corner sharing magazines, men studying maps, young and old shoulder-to-shoulder at the window counters.

She brushed more tears as Mrs. Kruchinski hollered. “Come get cake.” She plunked down a two-layer sheet cake decorated with the image of The Page Turner before Constance. Father Gregory, who had a sweet tooth, was the first in line.

“It’s a shame Martin is missing this. He loves cake,” said Arthur.

Charlotte tried her best to sound casual. “I’ll take him a piece. I’m not at all tired.”

The ladies all gave a knowing nod as Charlotte dashed out the door.

Madge and Oscar took their cake to go, congratulating Constance and the sisters, saying it was past their bedtime.

Birdie, Horace, Rosie, and Walter ate their cake in the reading area, then offered their congratulations as well. “You’ve got a smash hit on your hands,” said Walter.

Karl wrapped his arms around Olga. “How about heading home, *meine liebe*? It’s been a long day.”

Birdie hugged Constance. “It’s stunning!”

Horace gave Constance a peck on the cheek and handed her a paper bag folded at the top.

“What’s this?” asked Constance.

“Don’t know. Someone left it behind one of the reading chairs.”

Constance opened the bag. Arthur caught her before she hit the floor.

CHAPTER 24
A Cracking Tension

Walter ran into the street. His arms waved over his head, hollering for Caroline, parked by the village square. The squad car peeled out, leaving skid marks. Seconds later, it screeched to a halt in front of the bookshop. Madge and Oscar dashed out, seeing Caroline.

"He was here. In the bookshop," said Walter.

Caroline barreled in and saw Constance sitting on a bench with Arthur handing her a cup of water.

"Constance, are you alright?" She looked at Arthur. "Do we need an ambulance?"

"Ambulance! No, no. I'm perfectly fine. Just too much rushing around, that's all," said Constance. Her pale face and shaky hands said otherwise, making Arthur hover like a nervous hen.

Ari pulled Caroline aside and handed her a tartan scarf. The worn blue, grey and green scarf was large enough to wrap around the neck and flow to the waist. It felt smooth, like cashmere, but thicker and had two gold tassels sewn into one end. Her darting eyes found Horace.

"Is this the pattern the man in front of the bookshop wore that night?"

"Yes."

"Are you certain?"

Horace didn't hesitate. "Positive."

"Where did it come from?"

"Somebody left it in a paper bag behind a chair," said Walter. He pointed to the four armchairs in the back of the shop.

Caroline turned to Ari, Emily, and Zoe. "I don't suppose you saw who left it?"

Heads nodded, no.

"Wait, maybe the camera did," said Zoe. She gestured toward the scrolling screens on the counter. "We shot dozens of photos and videos today. I'll email them to you now."

Caroline punched her email address into Zoe's phone and returned to check on Constance. Arthur was updating her on the stranger's appearances—he was seen in front of her shop and Arthur's house and across the riverbank last night.

Caroline listened to Arthur share the recent events. Something hit her ear wrong. Walter said Constance almost passed out when she saw the scarf. Why? Arthur hadn't related the story of the stranger yet. And when he did, he didn't mention the scarf. He just related that the mystery man stood outside her shop. Could it be a coincidence and Constance was indeed overtired? The deputy sat quietly and observed her friend.

It didn't make sense that Constance was woozy from too much rushing around. The woman she knew had boundless energy and stamina. And the lightheadedness came upon her when she saw the scarf. Caroline knew the scarf was the key. Her gut told her. She called Walter over.

"Did Constance look tired when she came back?"

"Not at all. And once she saw the changes to her shop, she was flying high. She and the sisters were whooping it up."

Caroline turned slowly back to Constance.

She didn't faint because of too much rushing around. She recognized that scarf and knows the man who left it.

"Why didn't anyone tell me?" said Constance.

"We wanted you to have a worry-free trip," said Father Gregory.

Arthur patted Constance on her clammy right hand. "I want you and Charlotte to stay with me tonight. You two can share a room, Emily can share with Zoe and Ari and I will bunk together," said Arthur.

Constance pleaded. "I need to be in my own bed tonight, sweetheart."

"Please, darling."

Caroline tugged Arthur's sleeve. "I'll stay in the shop. I need to study the photos. If that's ok with Constance."

Constance stood, holding onto Arthur's arm. "Perfect." She kissed Arthur's cheek. "I'll be under the watchful eye of our deputy."

The thought of Constance staying in her apartment alarmed Arthur. He didn't want her under Caroline's watchful eye. He wanted her under his eagle eye, where he and Ari could take turns sitting outside her room all night, guarding her over breakfast, chaperoning her into the village. There was no chance he'd recognize his thoughts as paranoid while he was feeding off them.

Charlotte ran up Main Street, then slowed down, imagining Great Aunt Prudence's reprimand that it wasn't ladylike to run. Her practical nature pushed love interests away, but her heart pulled them back. She took off running again.

It surprised her to find the printshop door locked. She worried that Martin was out with Roxy. She knocked and peered through the window, praying he would appear.

"You're back!" said Martin, his eyes bright with welcome.

"Brought you some cake and New York bagels." She intended to offer a casual, professional smile. One that said, *just stopped by to see if you needed help.* Instead, she felt her lips peel back to reveal every tooth in her mouth. She handed him the goodies and hoped that it was enough of a distraction from the heated color rising up her neck.

Martin eyed the treat like he hadn't eaten in a week. He was excited to show Charlotte his progress on the wedding project, but the thought of sugar and salt hitting his taste buds pulled him toward the kitchen.

"You'll have to share this with me."

She laughed. "I was hoping you'd say that."

They sat at the tiny metal table only big enough for two, laughing every time their hands bumped, diving for more cake.

"Tell me what you thought of Manhattan, Charley."

She regaled him with her impressions of the city—energy pelting from every direction, the uptight faces of businesspeople, the casual stroll of dog walkers, bicyclers managing death-defying maneuvers through traffic, the sea of taxis that looked like a swarm of yellow-jacket bees.

Martin hung on her every word, gesture, smile. Why hadn't he noticed until now her eyes of light sapphire? Or that her hair resembled sun-kissed honey?

He found himself comparing Charley to Roxy. His girlfriend's dark, sensual looks commanded attention, while Charley's invited attention. He didn't know which was more desirable.

When he was with Roxy, he couldn't take his eyes off her. Or believe his good luck that this raven-haired beauty chose him. She was the type who only muscle-bound jocks got to date.

People noticed him when he was with Roxy. He didn't know why, but it made him feel important. His parents never noticed him nor did his schoolmates. It was as if he spent his life peering into a party from an outside window. A party he was never invited to.

So why was his heart pulling toward Charley? She was out of his league. He looked around the cramped kitchen in a tiny nowhere village and thought: *What hope do I have of dating a smart, fun, successful European woman? She'll probably marry some hot-shot lawyer from London or a Greek billionaire.*

Charlotte noticed Martin was drifting and admonished herself for rambling on about the city where he grew up. She was boring this cosmopolitan man who knew New York City well enough to be a tour guide.

Suddenly, she felt foolish getting caught up in the imagined intimacy of sitting inches from one another, eating late-night cake, Martin calling her Charley again and that flattering attentive stare of his. *He probably stares at everyone like that.*

Her fork dropped to the plate and her hope with it. Once again, she reminded herself that Martin was with Roxy. *Why can't I keep that simple fact straight?* She tried, in vain, to stop the answer from tumbling forward. *Because you're falling in love with this floppy-haired, humble, smart, immensely endearing man whose laugh sounds like a little boy.*

"Are you too tired to see how our project is shaping up?" he said.

She stood and stretched, thankful for the chance to think about the wedding and not Martin. "Absolutely."

As they turned past the front counter toward the art room, Martin did a double take out the window.

"We've got to go—now!"

"Why? What happened?"

"Caroline left in her cruiser. Something's happened."

He grabbed her hand and pulled her through the door and across the town square. They saw the patrol car in front of the bookshop and raced toward it.

Charlotte burst through the door and screamed, "Aunt Constance!"

Constance threw her arm into the air. "Here, dearest, here."

"Are you alright? What happened?"

"The stranger from the cemetery was in the shop today," said Constance.

"Why do you look pale?"

"It's nothing. A bit of a dizzy spell, that's all."

"Well, no wonder. We ran around like lunatics for two days."

She brought Charlotte up to date on the mystery man's movements while they were in the city. Charlotte turned ashen.

Arthur approached Caroline. "Where are you going to study the photos? Not at the middle counter, I hope."

"No. I'll move the iPads to the window counter in full view of the door to Constance's apartment. And the back door is alarmed, so that's not a problem. The whole village will know if he comes in that way."

Martin cocked an ear in their direction. "I'll help you, Caroline."

"I won't say no to that."

Father Gregory hollered for everyone's attention. "It's been a long day, folks. Why don't we all head home and let these good people get some rest? I know the tension is building about our mysterious visitor, but let's not forget, we have a joyous event in a couple of weeks that needs planning."

Relieved for a segue to a happier topic, Birdie yelled, "Here, here, Padre."

"You're right, Father. We'll leave the sleuthing to Caroline. Starting tomorrow, wedding plans take center stage," said Mrs. Kruchinski.

A round of *goodnights* ensued. Constance watched her friends huddled together as they left and wondered what they were saying.

"How is it possible that no one noticed a limping old man in the shop today?" said Madge.

"It doesn't make any sense," said Rosie.

"I'll bet he wasn't in the shop at all. I think his accomplice planted the scarf," said Birdie.

The three women gave one another an icy stare. "Roxy!" said Mrs. Kruchinski.

Constance pulled down a strongbox from the highest shelf in her closet and sat on the edge of her bed. She turned the key in the lock for the first time since she arrived in Stones End over forty years ago. She stared blankly at the yellowed newspaper article inside.

The headline read: *All Presumed Dead.*

She looked heavenward. *Please, Lord, don't take Arthur from me.*

CHAPTER 25
Pushing Forward

Last night's events played before Constance like a suspenseful film noir. The tartan scarf. The lightheaded sensation. Falling into Arthur's arms. The stares and worried murmurs from her friends.

She lay wondering if Caroline identified the mystery man from yesterday's photographs. Caroline knew she was withholding information, and she feared what Caroline was keeping from her.

The chance of the truth coming out twisted her stomach into a knot. *Would Caroline be discreet? Would Arthur understand?*

The questions pushed her out of bed. She paced. Her anger rose with each step. She glanced at the closet where her wedding packages lay and remembered cutting her beautiful shopping trip short.

With just a few weeks to go, her wedding should be the only thing on her mind. She was tired of thinking about the man lurking over her son's grave—tired of being fearful. Where would this lead? Her anger and frustration spurred on a brave resolve. She passed the mirror and gazed at her reflection. *If my secret comes out, I'll deal with it.*

Arthur stared at her from his photo on the bed table. The thought of their upcoming wedding produced a smile. Another chance for a fresh start. She'd be a member of the Covington family. A warm feeling of love and family filled her heart.

"That's it! The perfect wedding gift." She reached for the phone.

"Good morning, Ari. Did I wake you?"

"It's fine. I had to answer the phone, anyway."

Constance chuckled. "You've been hanging out with Birdie too long. That's a wisecrack she would make."

"What's up?"

"I know what to give Arthur as a wedding present. But I need your help."

"You've got it."

"Call me when Arthur leaves and I'll come by the house."

The newspaper article glared up from the strongbox on her dresser. She slapped the lid shut.

"Go away, ghost! You will not spoil my wedding."

Charlotte straightened the twisted bed covers and strewn pillows. She rubbed her palms against her stinging eyes. The bell on the shop door downstairs jingled. She rushed to the front window of the apartment to see who left.

Martin stood on the pavement, drawing his arms over his head, and swallowing a deep yawn. His mussed hair and shadowy beard reflected a sleepless night.

"Looks like you need a spot of tea," she called down.

He whirled around, searching for the faceless voice.

She giggled. "Up here."

"Good morning, Charley." His arm raised in a wave. "Sounds terrific, but I need to get ready for work. See you at the shop?"

"Yes." Her neck craned out the window, watching Martin lope past the colorful shop awnings and planters filled with mums.

Charlotte twisted around at the sound of her aunt humming.

"Was that Martin I heard?" said Constance.

"Yes. Poor dear. He and Caroline pulled an all-nighter."

"Did he say if they found anything?" Her lighthearted tone surprised Charlotte.

"I didn't ask. Do you want me to run down to the shop? I think Caroline is still there."

"No, dearest. I'm sure Caroline will give…"

Constance reached for the ringing phone. The panel on the answering machine read *Unknown Caller.* She thought it was an obscene hour for telemarketers.

"Hello." She heard erratic breathing on the other end. "Hello. Who is this?" More breathing. "Is anyone there?" A click, then the steady drone of the dial tone.

Constance glared at the cordless phone for a moment before setting it in its cradle.

"Who was that?"

"No idea. They hung up."

Charlotte leaned forward. "You don't suppose it was…"

"Probably a wrong number," said Constance, continuing to stare at the phone.

"A wrong number at six in the morning? We should tell Caroline."

"Let's not fan the fire, dearest. Everyone's nerves are raw. We'll tell Caroline if there are more calls. How's that?"

Charlotte went to persist, but Constance turned and rushed down the hallway.

Something caught Martin's eye before he rounded the corner to his apartment over Rosie's dance studio.

He spun to see Roxy rushing along the side of the church. *Only two reasons to be on that path,* he thought. *Exiting the rear of the church or coming out of the cemetery.* Roxy was no churchgoer. He dialed Caroline.

"I'll be at the cemetery in two minutes."

"Should I meet you there?"

"Negative!"

Martin pulled a fresh shirt from the dresser when he heard a knock at the door. He rushed to hear what Caroline found.

"Good morning, Marty." Roxy stood before him with mussed hair and a misbuttoned coat. Uncharacteristic for a fashion maven. She planted a lingering kiss.

"Are you going to invite me in?"

Martin pulled the door wide. "This is a surprise. What brings you around so early?"

Roxy had never been in his apartment. Martin's old-fashioned morals made him apprehensive about his girlfriend's sensual nature. He didn't trust himself alone with her in an intimate setting.

She glanced around the tidy room with its low-budget furniture and gave a disapproving sniff.

"We need to talk," she said. "Come sit." She patted the couch next to her and flashed a fetching smile. Martin wasn't experienced with women, but he knew *we need to talk* meant trouble.

Fatigue from his sleepless night covered him like a wet wool blanket. Martin lowered himself with a thud. Roxy climbed onto his lap. Martin shifted to put a few inches of space between them.

"I'm crazy in love with you, Marty. And I know you're mad about me. We've been dating for over a month, and I was thinking." Her hand caressed his cheek.

A wary smile crossed Martin's face.

"It's time to take the next step." She brushed the mop of hair out of his eyes. "And get married."

Martin leapt off the couch, throwing Roxy against the cushions. He thought Roxy was leading up to a sexual relationship. Marriage was the last thing he expected to hear.

"Married? Oh, Roxy. I'm not in a position to marry. My career is just starting. I need time to establish myself."

Roxy straightened upright. "That's trash, Marty. We can't put our love on hold. And as far as establishing yourself, it can happen quicker in Manhattan. That's where the money is."

Her proposal alarmed him. Marriage was a monumental step that required time to consider, ponder, and analyze. His tired brain produced a paltry diversion. "And suppose I don't want to leave Stones End?"

Roxy moved within an inch and fixed her best bedroom-eyes on him. She rested her hands on his chest.

"Just think of it, sweetie. You and I in our own place with the city as our playground. We'll save every penny so when it's time to start a family, we can buy a house with a yard for our kids to play."

Martin momentarily warmed to the vision. Roxy saw she hit gold. She pushed in closer and stretched up on her toes. Her open lips moved towards his. He whispered in her ear. "What were you doing at the church this morning?"

She thrust herself from his arms. "Were you spying on me?"

Martin knew her question was a stalling tactic. He'd seen Madge employ the same technique when hiding an extravagant purchase from Oscar.

Roxy's eyes flitted wildly, before composing herself. She pleaded in a demure tone. "It's embarrassing to admit, but I was checking out the church for our wedding. You know, is it proper enough for our big day?"

Martin raised an eyebrow. He never heard of an improper church. "And was it?"

His curt question threw her off balance. "Yes, fine," she stammered.

Martin wasn't as pliable as she thought. Was it possible she was losing him to Charlotte? She saw his eyes following her at the party. She wasn't going down without a fight.

She stamped her foot. "Damn it, Marty. I just proposed marriage. Can you answer me?"

Martin shoved his hands wide. "I have nothing to offer a wife at this stage of my life."

"I don't care about that. I'm in love with you and want to be your bride."

"Well, being established is important to me now."

Roxy had to keep the topic open for further discussion. She rested her head on his shoulder, letting her scent and body heat penetrate his senses. "Will you promise to think about it?"

Martin closed his eyes and inhaled Roxy's essence. Should he consider her proposal? He wondered what kind of life they would have. What kind of mother would she be? He felt the lissome curves of her body pressing into him.

Her dream for their future colored his imagination. He saw a weathered cottage on a hillside. Their children playing in a lush garden. He saw… Martin jumped back. A vision of Charley appeared before him.

"What is it?"

He shook his head, trying to knock the image from his brain. "Nothing." He checked his watch. "I have to get ready for work."

"Without answering my question?"

His mind went blank. Then he saw Charley's face again. He stammered. "What question?"

Roxy spit out through clenched teeth. "Will you think about my proposal?"

Martin needed Roxy to leave. He blurted out, "Yes."

Her eyes brightened. "Do you mean it?"

"Yes. Of course. Now, please, Roxy, I have to wash up and change for work."

He opened the door to find Caroline standing in front of him. She inclined her head toward Roxy.

"I see you're busy."

"Roxy was just leaving."

She gave Martin a lengthy goodbye kiss. Martin pushed from her embrace, a hot, embarrassed mess.

Caroline folded her arms and leaned against the doorjamb, waiting for the soppy scene to end.

"Goodbye, sweetie. I'll bring you lunch," said Roxy.

Martin waited to hear the street-level door slam and invited Caroline in.

Caroline ignored Martin's lipstick smeared mouth and reported her findings.

"No sign of our lurker. The back cemetery gate is still broken. So, he could have slipped through there again. I circled the perimeter. Nothing. No footprints. Checked the church and rectory too. Locked tight."

Martin jerked his head toward Caroline. "Did you say the church was locked?"

"Yes. Why?"

"Roxy said she was in the church just now."

Caroline read the disappointment on his face. She wanted to share what she knew about Roxy. But it wasn't the right time.

Arthur and Ari sat with George watching the soft autumn dawn wake the river, pines and chestnut grove beyond. It was Arthur's favorite part of the day. He and Pop enjoyed many Greek sunrises sitting on a piece of driftwood in their boatyard. The memory spread a sentiment of peace in his soul.

"Have you spoken to Constance this morning?" asked George.

"Constance is not an early riser. I called Caroline. It was a quiet night. No intruder and nothing showed up in the pictures."

"How's the lettering coming for *The Constance*?" asked George.

Arthur slapped his forehead. "In all the craziness, I completely forgot."

"You forgot to take care of your fiancé's wedding gift?" said George.

"I'll get to it today. No, today isn't good either?" said Arthur, rubbing his temple.

"Just let Ari take care of it. He's perfectly capable of painting *The Constance* on the stern of the schooner."

Ari laughed at Arthur's popping eyes. "You're off the hook for one more day. Constance needs my help with your wedding gift."

"My gift?" Arthur suspected it was a secret, so he whispered. "What is it?"

"Don't know, yet. She's coming by this morning to tell me. And don't try wheedling it out of me later."

Arthur laughed. "Ah. It's nice to be talking about the wedding for a change." He spun around, suddenly. "How about this? I give you full permission to design the lettering any way you want, if you tell me what Constance is giving me?"

George howled. "Bargaining won't work. Ari is going with his own design no matter what you say."

Arthur smiled. "I'm going to miss this."

"What?" said Ari.

Arthur stepped toward the front door. "The three of us hanging out." He pulled open the screen door. "And for the record, I trust you with *The Constance*. As long as the background is navy blue, and the lettering is gold." He scooted through the door before Ari could object.

The old man hunched over the kitchen table in the deserted house, eating a cold can of soup. He chanced a single candle. Plenty of time to snuff it out if he heard the nosy deputy pull up.

He jumped at something nuzzling his leg. It was the stray cat that kept coming around. He opened a small cooler and poured milk in a bowl.

"So, what do you think, cat? Leaving the scarf was a stroke of genius, right? I'm counting on it stirring a sentimental memory."

He dipped a crust of bread into the soup and reread his handwritten notes on Constance, Arthur, and the village.

I have all the information I need. He was past his nerves about executing his plan. It was just a matter of when.

CHAPTER 26
Decisions

Wedding plans took off like a race car revving from zero to ninety in three seconds. When Constance saw Arthur bustling to work, she rushed to meet with Ari.

"Can you manage it before the wedding?" She hovered over him, sitting at the kitchen table. "Do you think Arthur will like it?"

Ari studied the sketch Constance brought, then glanced up with misty eyes. "It will thrill Arthur. Emily and Zoe, too. And yes, easily done before the wedding."

"You're a blessing." Constance kissed Ari's cheek and flew out the door to meet Charlotte.

With only 12 days before the wedding, aunt and niece rushed through the week, visiting the seamstress for fittings, with Madge to finalize floral designs, then to Oscar to approve the menu.

Walter and Rosie caught up with them mid-week to review music selections. Mrs. Kruchinski ran out of the bakery to thrust a picture of the wedding cake at Constance before she and Charlotte dashed next door to the hair salon.

"Have you thought about my suggestion for a French twist, Constance? We can also go with a chignon, if you prefer," said Berris, dumping hairstyle magazines into her lap.

"What do you think, Charlotte? My mind is mush," she said.

"Definitely French twist. It's more elegant."

Roxy sashayed out of the back room with a selection of eye shadows that looked like a palette of watercolor paints. "I'm assuming you'll need me to do your makeup, Constance?"

"Oh, yes," said Berris. "Roxy is a professional makeup artist."

Constance winced at Roxy's harshly made-up face. She saw a risk of herself looking like a circus clown walking down the aisle. "Uh... no thank you, Roxy. I wear little makeup."

"I can help with your makeup, Aunt Constance," said Charlotte.

Roxy shoved past Charlotte, holding an eyeshadow palette. "This is your wedding day. Trust me, you'll need a bright look." She glared up and down at Charlotte. "I'm sure I can do something about your looks as well."

Charlotte didn't flinch at the cutting remark and flung one of her own. "Thanks, Roxy, but I'm not partial to looking like a brash neon sign."

Roxy flared her nostrils wide enough to drive a Mack Truck through them. Berris backed away from the rising tension. Constance envisioned breaking up a cat fight. She sprang from the chair. "It's decided then. French twist, no makeup." She grabbed Charlotte's arm. "Shall we go?"

Berris ran after them. "Plan on spraying the French twist pink or maybe purple."

"Don't turn. Just keep walking," said Constance.

Martin muddled through the week in a sleep-deprived stupor. The Roxy proposal plunged his daily routine into an abyss of confusion. He couldn't sleep and barely ate. The only highlight came each evening when he and Charlotte worked on their project to decorate the wedding hall.

Sometimes they went for hours without uttering a word, each working on their own section of the sketch enlargements. Martin stole glances, and his pulse throbbed when he caught Charlotte doing the same.

He loved how she pushed her honey-brown hair behind her ears only to have it fall loose again. She'd do it exactly three times each night before losing patience and gathering it into a ponytail.

By the end of the week, lack of sleep, coupled with long hours, took their toll. Martin's face was pale and his concentration spotty. When he made his third printing mistake of the morning, Arthur tapped his flagging assistant on the shoulder.

"Go home, my boy, you need sleep." Martin resisted but reluctantly shoved his arms through the sleeves of his jacket that Arthur held open. A blast of cold air slapped him in the face when he exited the shop. It didn't revive him.

Teetering across the village square like a drunkard, he heard Horace's good-natured voice. "Martin, my friend, you been hitting the bottle?"

Martin collapsed onto the bench next to him.

"I understand you worked all night earlier in the week?"

Martin nodded. "I fell asleep for a couple of hours in the bookshop. Caroline woke me at dawn. She didn't sleep at all. How does she do it?"

"Personally, I suspect Caroline is a robot who runs on a 30-day battery pack."

Horace's comment drew a weak smile. Sensing his young friend's droopiness was more than a lack of sleep, Horace probed.

"How are matters on the love front? Seems you and Roxy are starting a budding romance."

Martin lifted his bent head. "Don't ask."

Horace winced, recalling the agony of young love. "That bad, huh?"

"Was it ever tricky talking to women for you?"

Horace chuckled. "Like trying to maneuver through a dark room. If you're not careful, you'll bang into a lot of sharp edges you weren't expecting."

"Exactly."

The friends sat in companionable silence, only glancing up when Oscar ran past. Horace waved him over.

"Gotta go back to the diner," cried Oscar. Horace nodded toward Martin and continued to motion to Oscar.

Oscar took one peek at Martin's hang-eyed look and dropped onto the bench across from them.

"What's going on?" he said.

"The perils of romance have dragged our young friend down."

Martin leaned his arms on his lap. "Is it possible to be in love with more than one woman?"

"More than one woman?" said Horace.

"Dangerous territory," added Oscar.

Martin slumped further on the bench. "Forget I asked. There's no chance with one of them."

Walter pulled up and climbed out of his car.

"And where are you coming from, as if I didn't know?" said Horace.

Walter thrust his hands wide. "From the arms of Ana Felicia. And I don't care who knows."

Oscar dropped his head and smiled at Walter's continental, devil-may-care attitude toward romance. Martin blinked and blinked. "Ana Felicia!"

Walter sidled in next to Oscar. "Don't worry, Martin. Constance won't find out until after she and Arthur marry."

Walter looked at the three men gathered. "Did Stones End form a men's club?"

"We're trying to help Martin. He's in love with two women," said Oscar.

Horace added, "At the same time."

Martin leaned toward Walter, who he considered a romantic Italian gentleman. "Are you in love with Ana Felicia?"

"Hopelessly. She's the woman I've been waiting for my whole life."

Martin fixed his eyes on Walter as though his entire world depended on the answer to his question. "What makes you so sure?"

Walter shrugged. "You just know, Martin. The messages of love are written on your heart. And your heart never lies."

Father Gregory loped across the square, stopping when he saw the men. "Is this another secret meeting?" he grinned.

"Trying to solve some age-old questions about love, Father," said Walter.

"Well, that leaves an old bachelor priest like me out." He wedged in between Oscar and Walter.

Walter gave a vague answer that didn't help Martin. He tried again with Oscar.

"Oscar, how did you know Madge was the right woman?"

"I knew the second I met her. It was like reaching home after a hard journey. And the feeling never left. It doesn't seem to matter that our life's interests are completely opposite. She's my home."

Oscar's explanation was closer to how Martin felt about Charley. Still, it didn't shed light on what to do about Roxy's proposal. He tried again.

"And you, Horace? What drew you and Birdie together?"

"Our souls speak the same language. What's important to Birdie are the same things that are important to me, which makes her the only person who truly knows who I am. If anything happens to Birdie, my soul will have no one to talk to."

Martin slumped further into the bench. His fatigue made him cranky. Brain fog set in. It was hard to think. A voice in his head screamed not to let Charley slip away. But what did Charley want?

"Looks like none of this is helping," said Walter.

"I wouldn't say that. You've all given me a lot to consider."

"But?" said Father Gregory.

Martin's hands gripped the sides of his head. "Isn't there a tried-and-true method of knowing if a woman is right for you? Someone's got to have figured this out."

Oscar laughed. "No one told me."

"Martin, are you contemplating marriage?" said Father Gregory.

Martin leaned back slowly, like the effort took everything out of him. "I'm not. But Roxy is. She proposed to me early this morning."

Oscar jerked forward, Walter groaned, and Horace just plain out asked: "What did you say?"

"That I need to be established in my career before I marry."

"Good. Good answer," said Oscar.

"And that I'd think about it," said Martin.

Oscar wanted to say, *Bad answer*, but bit his tongue.

Their silence spoke volumes to Martin. He pushed himself to the edge of the bench. "I know what you think of Roxy, but she has many fine qualities."

"No one thinks badly of Roxy," said Horace. "She's a hard-working, beautiful woman. But know this, women like her satisfy life's needs with material things. It becomes exhausting because material things never satisfy. So, there's always a demand for more."

"If your love for Roxy is worth that kind of exhaustion, and expense, then go for it," said Oscar.

Horace stood and paced between the benches. "Now, if the other woman you're in love with happens to be Charlotte..."

Martin lifted his head. "I guess there's no mystery there, huh?"

Walter chuckled. "There are no secrets in Stones End. You know that."

Horace went on like a lawyer, summing up a case. "Charlotte is a woman whose needs are fulfilled through the heart. And if that's more your style, then there's harmony."

"And you'd save a lot of money with Charlotte," said Oscar.

Father Gregory glared at him.

Oscar shrugged. "Well, he would."

Martin leaned over his knees. "Charlotte wouldn't have me. Look what she's accomplished. We're the same age and she owns her own business already. And where am I? Still struggling with what to do with my life, like a kid."

"There's always hope in love, Martin. Look at me, a barbershop owner in a tiny village about to marry a famous opera singer."

"Marry!" said Father Gregory. He sprang from the bench. "That's fantastic."

Oscar slapped Walter on the back. "Outstanding news. Congratulations!"

"Horace," said Oscar. "Aren't you going to congratulate Walter?"

Horace grinned. "I already knew."

Martin shook hands with Walter. "I'm happy for you, Walter."

Oscar glanced at his watch. "Sorry, gents, but I gotta run. Good luck with your dilemma, Martin. You know we're rooting for you." He strolled a few steps, then swung back. "This was nice. There might be something to this men's club idea."

Father Gregory glanced at his watch as well. "Late again!" He trotted off. "My door's always open, Martin."

Walter yelled to Oscar. "Wait up. I'll walk back with you." He turned toward Martin. "Love knows no limits. You figure out who you love and don't let anything stop you from pursuing her."

Horace slung his mail sack over his shoulder. "My door's always open, too."

Martin watched Horace saunter across the village green. He called after him. "Who would you choose, Horace?"

Horace's eyes twinkled. He gave a mischievous wink. "I won't say. But you might have a trip abroad in your future."

Charlotte halted, seeing Mrs. Kruchinski, Birdie and Rosie sitting at The Café counter. The last thing she needed was to be grilled about Martin. She turned on her heel to escape when she heard, "Charlotte dear, come join us."

Charlotte trudged toward her fate like heading to the dentist chair for a tooth extraction. Birdie took pity and steered the conversation toward the wedding. "How is Constance's wedding ensemble coming?"

Charlotte conveyed a visual thank you. "Wonderful. The only thing we need is something borrowed. I'm sure I have something to lend her."

Mrs. Kruchinski swallowed the last bite of her tuna sandwich and fired off the inevitable question. "And how are you getting along with Martin?"

"The surprise wedding project we're working on is spectacular. I think you'll love it."

Mrs. Kruchinski slapped a napkin on her empty plate. "No use pretending you're not interested in Martin, dear. I saw you two making eyes at each other last week in this very café."

Madge clattered a pile of dirty dishes behind the counter and leaned toward Charlotte. "The two of you are adorable together. And it's obvious you enjoy each other's company."

Birdie wrestled with her *do not interfere* policy. But she had nightmares about Martin ending up with Roxy. He'd be miserable. She ignored her inner voice.

"I've never seen Martin so animated, like when he's around you. Don't end up like Arthur, waiting 40 years to find love. Or like Horace and I, who put obstacles between us for a lifetime."

Charlotte felt emotionally naked. The ladies were shining a floodlight on her feelings for Martin. She felt hopeful and uncomfortable at the same time. The situation overwhelmed her.

Charlotte sighed. "I won't deny an attraction." The ladies moved closer. "But there are some cold, hard facts. Martin is with Roxy, and I'm going home to England at the end of next week. Besides, for me to win Martin, I'd have to steal him from Roxy. Isn't that wrong?"

Birdie slid off the stool and stood before Charlotte. "The only thing wrong is if two people deeply attracted to each other don't pursue their feelings."

Rosie took Birdie's seat next to Charlotte. "This is not all on you. Martin is responsible for pursuing his attraction to you, as well. Sometimes men need a little push. If he doesn't respond, then you'll know. But if you don't take a chance, you face a lifetime of regret."

Birdie raised her finger in the air. "To push or not push. That is the question."

Charlotte eyed Mrs. Kruchinski, who took hold of her hand. "We're not just a bunch of old ladies who like meddling, my dear. This is important. Most of us get only one chance of finding true love. Don't miss yours."

The generous and caring spirit of these women brought tears to Charlotte. And to think, she went out of her way to avoid them. Her head bowed in a sudden twinge of guilt. Mrs. Kruchinski handed her a napkin.

"So, what's it going to be, Charlotte? Are you going to take a chance on love?" said Birdie.

Charlotte raised her head, dabbed at her eyes, and said, "I'm going for it. I don't know how, but I'm going to try."

Rosie slid her arm around Charlotte and patted her shoulder. "Now, that's a department I can help with. You just work your wiles with Martin until the rehearsal dinner next week. And then we go in for the final push."

Charlotte's eyes widened. "And how do we do that?"

"With a complete makeover. Trust me. Martin won't be able to resist your knockout look."

A vision of the leather-clad, big hair, cigarette-smoking Sandy at the end of *Grease* flashed. Charlotte didn't know if the plan thrilled or terrified her.

CHAPTER 27
How Do I Love Thee?

After lunch, Charlotte changed her outfit before going to the printshop. She couldn't decide if the icy-blue vee neck sweater showed too much skin or not enough. After a glimpse in the mirror to apply lip gloss and fluff her hair one last time, she flew out the door, checking and rechecking her reflection in the shop windows as she hurried up Main Street.

When she approached the village green, Roxy strolled out the door of the printshop. Charlotte called out hello. The raven-haired vixen stomped past without so much as a nod. The up-in-her-face reminder that Martin was Roxy's boyfriend stopped Charlotte in her tracks.

Charlotte lowered herself onto a bench across from the shop and wondered how she let a group of delightful ladies talk her into running after Martin. *Work your feminine wiles,* Rosie said. She wouldn't recognize a feminine wile if it introduced itself.

What was she doing? It was just a few days ago she decided pursuing Martin was a fool's dream. And now she sat looking for him with a low-cut sweater on and sticky glossed lips.

The prospect of love intoxicated Charlotte and last year's heartbreak sobered her. Her emotions bounced between the two. She ached to love and to be loved. But she knew love was fickle and carried the risk of heartbreak. Could she handle it? She wasn't sure she was over the last disastrous brush with love.

Her thoughts drifted to how a long-distance relationship might work. It looked impossible. And if the relationship survived, one of them would have to move. For all her frustration with the staid

Cotswolds, she couldn't imagine living anywhere else. She imagined Martin felt the same about Stones End.

Questions without answers sped around in circles like a fever dream. She leaned her head back and breathed deeply. A charming specter of Martin loomed. The base of her spine tingled, remembering the touch of his hand in hers, his breath on her skin, his boyish laugh, how his eyes danced when a brilliant idea struck. Mrs. Kruchinski's opinion echoed: *Most of us get only one chance of finding true love. Don't miss yours.*

She straightened her shoulders and marched toward the printshop.

Arthur sat behind the front desk. Charlotte glanced around the shop. "Where's Martin?"

"He worked too many hours this week. I sent the lad home to rest."

Arthur saw Charlotte's chin drop. She stepped toward the hallway that led to the art room.

"I'll finish the place cards." She turned back. "You haven't peeked, have you?"

"No, my dear. You ordered me not to," he chuckled.

At four o'clock, Arthur brought Charlotte a cup of tea and at six o'clock, he announced it was closing time.

Charlotte stretched her neck from side to side and suppressed a yawn. "Another three hours and I'm done, Uncle Arthur. How do I lock up when I'm finished?"

"I'm not leaving you alone, young lady. Not with a lunatic lurking. And a storm is blowing in fast. Come now, there's always tomorrow."

"Sorry, but I have to complete these cards tonight. When Martin returns, we'll need every minute to finish the wedding project.

I'll be fine. Caroline is parked in the squad car across the street. I'll leave the lights on and lock the front door."

Arthur hated the notion but handed Charlotte a spare key. He'd tell Caroline on his way out to keep an eye peeled. "Just turn the inside latch when you're ready to leave. The key is for the outside lock."

Charlotte was amazed how much she accomplished without the need to sneak peeks at Martin. Three hours of work crammed into two. She touched the Home button on her cell phone. 8:13. Charlotte shut the lights in the art room and strode toward the front door. A loud bang that sounded like cannon fire made her jump. The lights in the front office crackled. Then darkness.

She peered out the front window. The village was inky black.

Sheets of rain drove a moving body of water through the streets. She smirked, an Englishwoman without an umbrella. Unlatching the inside lock, she planned to dash over to Caroline in the patrol car and beg a ride.

She searched in her pocket for the key and turned out a pack of tissues, a tube of lip gloss, and her phone. Remembering the spare was lying on the table in the art room, she dropped the contents from her pocket onto the front counter and went to find the key.

Charlotte felt around in the dark, cursing the power outage. Her hand brushed cold metal. *Got it!* She turned, then froze. Someone was in the shop. She cocked her head. Footsteps by the front door.

My cell phone. I need my phone. A mental picture flashed like an object trapped in the burst of a strobe light. It was on the front counter. Her stomach lurched as though punched. Whirling around, she tried to recall if the room had a phone. The footsteps scratched louder. They moved toward the room.

The sound nailed her feet to the floor. Her heart pounded.

Nausea rose from her stomach to her throat.

The footsteps halted. She cocked an ear. Was he retreating? The electronic plink of a text message sounded. *He has my phone!*

She tiptoed to the right of the door and pushed her back against the wall. Caroline was her only hope. Did she see him through the heavy rain? Charlotte choked on the impulse to scream. Tears trailed down her face. She tasted their salt on her lips. *Why didn't I go with Arthur?*

She willed herself to devise an escape. Her mind refused. Images of being stabbed, choked, or bludgeoned rolled like a film spinning off its reel. How long before they discovered her?

Think, you fool, think, her brain shrieked. *Don't fight him. You won't win. Your only chance is to reach the front door. Wait for him to enter the room, then run for it.* The jagged edge of the key cut into her fist.

The scratchy footsteps stirred. He was so close she heard him breathing. Her heart threatened to explode. Could he hear it pounding? The sudden silence crawled across her skin. Darkness turned to solid black. He stood in the door. Charlotte sucked in a breath and held it.

He inched into the blackness. She waited for him to take a few steps further. He advanced toward the art table. *Now!* hit her brain like a siren. She blasted out the door. His footsteps dogged her. Close. Closer. A strong grip snatched her arm and spun her around. Charlotte screamed and didn't stop.

He yelled something. She heard only her own strangled cries for help. Her fists pummeled his chest. Hands gripped her shoulders and shook her hard.

His voice cried out in the darkness. "Charley, it's Martin. It's Martin, Charley."

She let out a ragged sob and fell against his chest. Martin wrapped her in his arms. "You're safe. I'm here and you're safe."

Charlotte shuddered. Martin held tight. He whispered calming words and stroked her hair. "You're alright. I've got you." She never wanted to leave the safety of his arms.

Wiping her tears, Charlotte raised her head. The sweetness of their mingled breath drew Martin closer. Charlotte closed her eyes. His lips caressed hers, drew back, then caressed them again. This time lingering, passionate. Her body melted to his touch, his scent, his tenderness.

The front door burst open. “Charlotte!” shouted Caroline. Charlotte pushed back from Martin. A beam of light hit her face. She squinted. Caroline lowered her flashlight.

“We’re fine, Caroline,” said Martin.

“The storm blew a transformer. The whole village is out, and the river is breaching. I need to get you home, Charlotte. Your family is frantic. We just lost cell and internet service. They’ve been trying to reach you.”

“You have other people to check on. I’ll take her home,” said Martin.

“Fine but go now. The water is almost ankle deep.”

The umbrella Martin grabbed from the shop proved useless. Gale-force wind blew it inside out before they reached the village green. The water ran fast toward the downhill slope into the two-block business district. Charlotte lost her shoe. It sailed away in the current. Martin chased it, but it was a block away in the blink of an eye.

He slogged back to Charlotte and slid his arm around her waist. “Put your arm around me and hold on.”

Halfway down the first block, Charlotte fell into Martin. “What is it?” he hollered.

“I stepped on something sharp. My foot is cut.” She hopped under the awning of the fruit and vegetable shop and lifted her leg. Blood dripped from a puncture in her heel.

“There’s a shard of glass in it. Look away while I pull it out.”

Martin pinched out the glass and yanked out his handkerchief, which was sopping. He wrapped her foot, then glanced toward the bookshop over a block away.

"I'll have to carry you, Charley."

Charlotte pushed the wet hair from her face. She blanched at the idea. Aside from the embarrassment, it was dangerous in ankle-deep water. She glared at the distance to her aunt's shop. *Not hoppable*, she thought.

Martin stepped close and fixed her arm around his shoulder. "Ready?" A protest rose in her throat, but they were drenched and shivering. She gave a tentative nod.

His knees bent and eyes widened when he lifted Charlotte into his arms. He realized water weighed down her clothes and it didn't help that his clothes hung heavy as well. When they crossed the street, he set her on the sidewalk.

"Need to rest." He stooped over, chest heaving.

The rushing water in the street lapped over the curb at an alarming rate. They needed to reach a safe place, and fast. He lifted Charlotte again and made it to the barbershop before he needed another rest. Walter ran out. "What the heck are you two doing?"

"I lost my shoe and cut my foot," said Charlotte, in a shivery breath.

"Get in here." Walter threw Charlotte's arm around his shoulder. She hopped five feet and plunked into his barber chair. Martin limped in behind them.

Walter unwrapped the handkerchief from Charlotte's foot and winced. "Nasty cut. Not enough for stitches. I'll get the antiseptic."

Charlotte looked down at the widening puddles. "Walter, we're drenching your floor."

Walter stepped from the back room carrying a bottle of peroxide. "It needed a good washing," he smiled.

Charlotte averted her eyes as Walter cleaned and bandaged the wound. She spied a large black umbrella fighting the wind outside the shop window. She pulled herself up in the chair. "Who's that?"

"I can't see," said Walter.

Martin bolted out the door and returned with Arthur, who

rushed toward Charlotte.

"My dear, we were so worried."

"Where were you going in this storm?" asked Charlotte.

"Looking for you. I thought you were trapped in the print-shop." He saw the bandage Walter applied. "You're hurt!"

"It's nothing. I stepped on glass and cut my foot. Martin was carrying me home when Walter saw us."

Arthur turned to Martin. "I'm grateful, my boy. Mighty grateful. You too, Walter. Thank you."

"Well, we've got to get you home and into dry clothes. Your aunts are frantic. You come too, Martin."

"I'm heading home, but thanks," said Martin.

Charlotte sprang from the chair and grabbed the back for balance. "No, Martin. Phone service is out. I won't know if you got home safe."

A softness shone in Martin's eyes. "I'll be fine, Charley. I just live over Rosie's dance studio."

"The dance studio! That's by the village green. Two blocks away."

"Rosie gets nervous in storms. I need to check on her," he said.

"No need. She's next door with Madge and Oscar," said Walter.

"Please Martin, come with us." She reached for his hand. "Please."

"It's settled, then. Walter and I will be Charlotte's crutches. Martin, you'll be the doorman," said Arthur.

Walter pulled on rain gear with reflective strips that made him look like a fisherman from Gloucester. Martin held open the door, then ran past The Café and stood ready at Constance's door.

Constance stood waiting, holding a flashlight in one hand and a candle in the other. "You poor dears, you look like you just climbed out of a swimming pool."

Within minutes, Charlotte and Martin were sitting at the kitchen table in dry clothes, drinking hot, black tea and eating leftover meatloaf. Happy to be warm, Martin didn't even care that the jogging outfit Constance loaned him was bright purple and comically short.

"Charlotte, dearest, you're bunking in with me tonight. Martin can sleep on the couch," she said.

"Where are Emily and Zoe?" said Charlotte.

"In your room. They conked out about an hour ago."

"I'm surprised they can sleep through this storm," said Charlotte, scraping the last morsel of meatloaf and baked potato off the plate.

"We've seen worse back in Greece. Lashing rain and wind tossing ships around like toys and testing the mettle of the saltiest of sailors," said Ari.

Charlotte stiffened as though the storm was more serious than she imagined. Arthur patted her hand. "Don't worry, my dear, the storm is due to blow out at midnight. The village will clean up tomorrow morning. By afternoon, it will be a memory," said Arthur.

"That's good, because Sunday afternoon we're christening *The Constance*," said Ari.

Arthur slapped his hands together. "It's finished? I want to see it," said Arthur.

"Nope. You'll want changes and there's no time. Just put the word out. Day after tomorrow, 1 pm."

"What a week we have ahead of us. Sunday christening *The Constance*, rehearsal dinner Tuesday night," said Constance.

"And Wednesday, we pick up your gown," said Charlotte.

Arthur took Constance into his arms. "And Friday you'll be my bride."

Constance kissed him, then made an eye motion, followed by a slight nod of her head. After forty years of her looks and nods, he knew it was time to leave the young people alone.

Arthur stretched and yawned loudly. Constance stifled a giggle at the exaggerated gesture. Charlotte smiled at her uncles. "Where are you two sleeping?"

"In the fairy tent downstairs," said Ari.

Constance laughed. "It's the storytime area, silly."

"What do you say, Ari?"

"Yep. The fairies call."

An awkwardness settled when everyone left the kitchen. Charlotte sat at one end of the candle-lit table, Martin at the other, and their recent kiss grabbed the seat between them. It felt like those torturous first moments of a blind date.

She grabbed the bed linens Constance left and limped toward the couch. Martin followed her with two candles.

"I can do that, Charley," he said.

She smiled. "A small thank you for getting me home safe."

"Are you tired?" he said.

"Not at all. You?"

He placed a cushion on the coffee table and seated Charlotte on the couch. "Now prop your leg up and I'll find something for us to read."

He took a candle and roamed the bookcases. "Your aunt's collection is impressive."

Charlotte delighted in his look of wonder as he pored over each book. He'd take one out and smile as though seeing a dear friend. She wondered about his heritage. "It just occurred to me I don't know your last name."

"Gallagher." He didn't tear his eyes from the book candy displayed before him.

"Irish?"

"Yes. My grandfather was born in County Kerry."

"Have you ever visited?"

"When I was six. I don't remember much. Hope to make it back there someday." He picked up a book and returned it to the shelf like it was a fine piece of porcelain.

"You in the mood for anything in particular?"

"Nothing heavy. How about poetry?" She pointed across the room. "There's the poetry section. Close your eyes and choose one."

He plucked a book from the shelf and turned it toward the candle. "Ah, Elizabeth Barrett Browning."

Charlotte pulled a blanket over her lap and snuggled into the couch. "Can't go wrong with an English poet."

Martin lowered himself next to her and began to read. He paused at the poem's candlelight reference to glance at Charlotte. The flickering candle on the coffee table bathed her skin in a soft radiance and spun golden color through her hair. He inhaled a sharp breath at the angelic sight next to him. His head bowed toward her lips, and he kissed her with an unleashed passion. Suddenly, he pulled back, then wrapped his arms around her and whispered. "I have to talk to Roxy first. I hope you understand."

"Of course," she whispered.

He rose and extended his hand. "Come, I'll walk you home."

"I can make it down the hall," she giggled, then reached up on her toes and brushed her lips across his cheek.

Charlotte slipped into the bed next to her aunt. Her racing heart hadn't slowed. Martin was a gentleman. He wouldn't officially pursue her until he parted with his girlfriend. She wondered when he'd tell her and how Roxy would react. Time was running out. In eight days, she would be on a plane to Heathrow.

CHAPTER 28
A Spotlight on Roxy

Before the soggy, puddled village opened for business Saturday morning, Karl commandeered his landscaping crew. They hit the streets before dawn, hauling away downed tree branches, mounds of fallen leaves and twigs and shoveling back the muddy earth that washed into Stones End from the sloping hills and overfilled pond.

When the crew pulled out, the shopkeepers bounded outside to put the shine back on the village. They hauled sandbags from doorways, wiped mud-spattered benches and washed windows.

By 10:30, Mrs. Kruchinski realized Berris hadn't stopped in for her daily cappuccino and babka. She dashed next door to check on her. Berris was nowhere to be seen, but she overheard Roxy talking to someone in the back room. She moved closer and saw her at a table with an orange-haired, gum-chewing woman in her early twenties.

"Last night was a drag. I came up from the city to party, not sit in your apartment in the dark."

"Not my fault a storm hit," said Roxy, filing her nails.

"Heard from Marty?" said the friend.

Roxy slapped the nail file on the table. "Yeah, he spent the night with Constance's brood."

The friend snapped a gum bubble. "Does that include you-know-who?"

Roxy squinted her black eyes. "You know it does."

"You better get the situation under control, or you'll lose your main squeeze to that English harpy."

Mrs. Kruchinski saw Roxy strut to the supply cabinet.

"Don't you worry about that. I'm not losing my Marty. I proposed to him the other morning."

The friend's mouth dropped open. "And?"

"He went on about being established in his career before he marries me, but I turned up the sex dial."

"And?"

"And he agreed to think about it. Just a matter of time before he says yes."

"I can't see you with Marty. Don't get me wrong, he's cute, but not your usual muscle-bound hunk."

Mrs. Kruchinski inched closer.

"Tell you the truth, he's not my type, but he's smarter than the jerks we date. He's my ticket out of a life of bratty kids and making ends meet. I'll drag him out of this podunk village and back to Manhattan, where he can make tons of money. I want to live on Easy Street."

"Easy Street might be boring, if you know what I mean."

Roxy's laugh sounded like a witch's cackle. "I'm not worried about that side of things. I can always keep something going on the side."

Mrs. Kruchinski slapped her hand over her mouth. She tiptoed out of the beauty parlor, then sprinted straight to The Café.

"Olga, sit and catch your breath," said Madge, handing her a glass of water.

Mrs. Kruchinski swallowed hard. "Roxy proposed to Martin. But it's just a ruse. She's not in love with him. She says she wants a life on Easy Street. And wait till you hear this. She has no intention of being faithful," she shrieked.

"What!" said Madge.

Birdie and Rosie jumped off their counter stools and huddled around Mrs. Kruchinski.

"How do you know this?" asked Birdie.

"I overheard Roxy just now telling a friend in the shop."

Rosie rubbed her forehead. "This is bad. We have to do something."

Madge noticed Oscar doing that *looking busy thing* he did when keeping something from her. Walter grabbed his newspaper and made a beeline for the door.

"And where do you think you're going, Walter, dear?" said Madge.

She glared at Oscar and then Walter. "What's going on, boys?" Her hands rose to her hips.

Horace and Father Gregory halted at the doorway. Madge's hands on her hips always meant *run for your life*. She motioned a crooked finger for them to come in. The men exchanged a wary glance.

Birdie rounded on Horace. "Did you know Roxy proposed to Martin?"

Horace locked his eyes on Oscar who signaled a *don't say a word* alert with a slight shake of his head.

"I plead the fifth," he said.

Oscar breathed a sigh of relief as Karl strolled in. It felt like the cavalry arrived. "Here's the man of the hour. You and your crew did a helluva cleanup job this morning."

Karl laughed. "Hope you feel the same when the village gets my bill."

Madge spun toward Oscar. "Let's get back to the issue, shall we?"

"I plead the fifth, too," said Oscar.

She stared Walter down. "And you?"

"Ditto." He swiped a napkin across his brow.

The ladies focused on Father Gregory, whose neck was already red from tugging his collar. "Is there such a thing as religious exemption?" he said.

"Yeah, in wartime," said Birdie.

"Feels a bit like war." He choked on a feeble chuckle.

Karl pushed his cap back and scratched his head. "I'm in the dark."

"Roxy proposed to Martin. This is a disaster. We need to do something," said Mrs. Kruchinski.

Oscar whacked the counter. "I vehemently disagree. If Martin wants to marry Roxy, that's his damn business. And by the way, Martin hasn't said yes." He winced, giving up incriminating information.

Horace jumped in to cover Oscar's back. "Bravo, Oscar! I agree. Leave the kid alone." Birdie shot him a scathing look. Horace turned away before he turned to stone. "Yeah, it feels like war," he said.

"Don't get involved. That's my advice," said Father Gregory.

"I agree. It's none of our business," said Walter.

The men looked to Karl, who was their steadfast voice of reason. Surely, he would convince the women to back off.

Karl's corded neck and clenched jaw surprised them. His answer shocked them.

"I agree with the ladies. It's time to get Martin away from Roxy."

CHAPTER 29
What About the Kiss?

Charlotte wondered if Martin broke up with Roxy yet. Time was short. In less than a week, she would return to England. She longed for some unfettered time with him. Time to make plans for when they would see one another again. How would they keep in touch in between visits? Time to have fun and get to know each other better.

She found Martin at the printer running the final sketch enlargement for the wedding hall. She crept up behind him. "Boo!"

He whirled around. "There you are. How's your foot?"

She didn't know what to expect after last night's kiss, but a question about her foot was not in the picture.

"Good," she stammered. "The wound is already closing up. I'm not even limping. See!"

"Excellent." He held up the print. "I colorized the awnings and benches on each one. What do you think?"

Charlotte couldn't think. She wanted to ask about Roxy. Talk about last night. His businesslike manner confused her. What was she expecting—a kiss, an embrace, a peck on the cheek?

"Charley?"

"It's perfect."

"Great, because we're down to the wire. Five days before the wedding and the boat christening will cut that tighter and the rehearsal dinner is Tuesday night."

Charlotte forced herself to focus. "What's left to do?"

"Mounting the enlargements on the standup boards. I suggest we roll a liquid adhesive on each board. It will produce a quality product, but it's a longer process. Or we could take a shortcut and use mounting tape, but there's a risk of them looking uneven."

"Let's go for perfection. We'll start with the liquid adhesive and if we run out of time, we'll switch to tape."

"Agreed."

It was mindless, repetitive work, and Charlotte found her thoughts wandering. There was a different vibe to tonight. She still stole glances at Martin, but he didn't return them like other nights. And he met her small talk with short answers. He worked with a laser focus, like he wished to avoid eye contact or any discussion about last night.

She couldn't read between the lines. Was this how Martin worked under pressure? If it was, she admired his steely concentration. After all, she roped him into helping her with this project, and he certainly was committed.

Still, his lack of intimacy or even camaraderie after last night seemed unnatural. He alluded to breaking up with Roxy before he and she could come together. Did she misread his intention? Maybe he regretted kissing her last night and wanted to be with Roxy after all.

The shop clock chimed ten o'clock. Charlotte put her hands on her aching lower back and stretched. "How about we call it a night?"

"Good idea. Come on, I'll take you home."

Martin talked non-stop about their project on their 10-minute walk to Constance's. His conversation was pleasant and animated, but he kept the topic impersonal. But his chatter ground to a halt when they reached Constance's door. Charlotte fidgeted with her scarf.

"Goodnight, Charley. See you tomorrow." He turned to leave.

"Martin?"

He spun back and gripped her hands. "Forgive me. I'm not myself tonight. It's just that I have a lot on my mind." He stared at her intensely, like he wanted to kiss her. A shiver ran down her spine. Instead, he turned and walked up Main Street without another word and without a kiss.

Charlotte climbed the stairs to her aunt's apartment in a daze. Was she losing her mind? Did she imagine Martin kissed her last night—twice? Doubts about Martin's character crept in. Was he the good man she imagined him to be? Her heart said yes. Her mind refused to answer.

CHAPTER 30
Christening *The Constance*?

With a week crammed to bursting, Arthur and Constance kept the fanfare on the boat christening low-key. Hot chocolate to keep warm on a bitter November day and of course, a bottle of champagne to break across the bow.

Constance did a double take when they pulled into the lot. The 50-foot schooner fashioned of solid teak towered majestically in dry dock at the boatyard. Arthur glanced at the commanding wheelhouse and longed to be at sea with Constance.

"It looks like the whole village is here," she said.

Arthur laughed like an excited child on his first pony ride. "I told everyone."

"Me, too," said Ari.

The crowd applauded as Arthur and Constance strolled to the white-clothed ceremony table that held a single bottle of champagne and a bouquet of red roses. Father Gregory paced off to the side, rehearsing his prayer.

Despite a brisk wind and overcast sky, the boatyard was dressed for a party. Blue and white balloons, representing the colors of the Greek flag, danced, and bounced in the breeze. A purple velvet curtain across the stern waited to reveal *The Constance* in all her glory. A rainbow of streamers hung from the christening platform at the bow.

Constance looked out among the crowd of about 40 people. Mrs. Kruchinski insisted on bringing cookies and pastries and recruited Charlotte to help distribute them. Zoe and Emily worked through the crowd with trays of hot chocolate.

"Birdie, take a cup to keep warm," said Zoe.

Birdie reached inside her coat and wagged a flask. "I got my own warmer-upper."

Zoe glanced over her shoulder, then spun back to Birdie. "Hit me."

Birdie held the thin silver container to Zoe's mouth. She licked her lips and wobbled toward the next guest, wearing a warm smile.

Constance mingled with her friends. She spied Charlotte and Martin huddled close, animated and smiling, and wondered if there was any hope of them getting together. Elaine, the realtor, was busy handing out her card and informing everyone that it was a seller's market.

Arthur ran up behind Constance, rubbing his arms for warmth. "We should start before they turn into human popsicles." Hand-in-hand, they went to find Father Gregory and Ari.

"So, what's the plan?" said Father Gregory.

"Simple as 1-2-3. I'll pull the cord on the drape. Arthur will dedicate the schooner to Constance. Then, you'll say the prayer and Constance christens her with champagne," said Ari.

Arthur, Ari, and Constance stood before the curtain at the stern. Constance waved Emily, Zoe, and Charlotte over.

"No, this is your moment," said Emily.

Constance continued to motion to them. "Please, I insist."

The three women joined Constance and Arthur.

Ari stood gripping the cord. "Ready?"

Arthur nodded and turned to Constance. "Darling, I give you *The Constance* with all my love."

Ari ripped the cord. The crowd whooped in surprise and confusion. Arthur spun around to face the stern. Constance kissed him and whispered, "It's my wedding gift to you."

He bowed his head and wept. "You dear woman. I can't tell you how much this means to me."

Arthur lifted his head, raised his arm, and shouted. "Ladies and gentlemen, I stand corrected. May I present…" he read the lettering on the stern of the schooner. "*The Family Covington.*"

"Group hug," yelled Emily. Zoe laughed and held out her arms. The Covington family, who now included Constance and Charlotte, huddled in an embrace at the sound of roaring applause. No one wanted to let go.

Ari broke away first. "You're up, Father."

Father Gregory waved his arms over his head. "May I have your attention, please?" His call for quiet had no effect.

Ari stepped up. "Allow me." He put his fingers to his mouth and blew a shrill whistle.

All heads snapped around. "Take it away, Father."

"I see a lot of shivering hands hugging their hot chocolate, so I'll keep this brief." He turned to Arthur and his family.

"To *The Family Covington*. May God bless you with warm breezes at your back, calm seas ahead, and peaceful voyages."

Arthur handed Constance the champagne bottle. "You still get to do the honors, my dear."

Constance giggled. "I was hoping you'd say that." She climbed the platform stairs at the bow and with glistening eyes and a beaming smile, she called out, "I christen thee, *The Family Covington*."

The bottle of champagne shattered to thunderous cheers and applause. Constance savored an unhurried gaze of family and friends. *I'll never be happier than this moment*, she thought.

Elaine, waving wildly at someone across the lot, distracted Constance. She turned in that direction. He was over six feet, built like a runner, but in his sixties. A granite jaw and broad forehead grounded his chiseled face. He ran a hand through thick, sandy hair.

Constance buckled at the knees and grabbed the platform rail. Did anyone notice him beyond her and Elaine?

A burst of memories raced. Scotland. Scotland. Cold morning mist. Shadowed glens. Rough-hewn crags. Forest floors of heather. Tawny owls hooting. Fairies, giants, and winter queens.

It can't be, her mind screamed. *He's dead.*

Constance scanned the area. He disappeared. She rubbed her

eyes. Was he a ghost, coming to remind her she was cursed? A curse that brought death to those she loved?

She bounded down the stairs to find Elaine. Arthur met her with two dozen roses. "Thank you, my darling. That was some surprise. And it doesn't matter that she's named *The Family Covington*, she's still yours."

Constance embraced Arthur and whispered close to his ear. "I'll cherish her."

Friends swarmed around the Covingtons.

"This is my first boat christening. I have to say, I'm not disappointed," Horace told Ari.

Walter and Oscar looked up, admiring the schooner. Arthur strolled over. "Not bad for a restored Greek shipwreck."

"She's a beauty, alright," said Oscar.

"Magnificent," added Walter.

Constance pushed up on her toes and stretched her neck. "Elaine!"

Elaine spun around and shoved her card at Constance. "Wonderful event. My, my, a giant boat for a wedding gift. Can't do better than that."

"Yes. Thank you, Elaine. I need to ask: Who were you waving to just now?"

Elaine opened her mouth, then shut it. "I don't know. I waved to a lot of people today."

Constance pointed to where the man stood. "Way over there. A man, tall, sandy hair."

"Oh, he's a client. I'm showing him houses in the area."

"This may sound strange, but did he have a Scottish accent?"

"Now, that's a funny coincidence. No Scottish accent, but his last name is Loch. Not L.O.C.K, but L.O.C.H. That's Scottish for lake." Her chin rose high as though knowing the meaning of loch made her an expert on all things Scottish.

The stranger staring intently at Constance during the ceremony didn't escape Caroline's eagle eyes, nor did the deputy miss Elaine waving to him. She eavesdropped behind the two women, then darted in between them when she heard his last name.

"Do you know his full name?"

Elaine jumped at the deputy's sudden appearance, then laughed. "Of course, I do. I've been showing him houses for almost a month. His name is John W. Loch. A businessman from Chicago who wants to retire in New England."

"Does he have any interest in Stones End?" asked Caroline.

"Indeed, he does. Out of all the townships I've shown him, he asked the most questions about our little village."

Constance leaned closer. "What kind of questions?"

"The usual. What's life like in the village? Do people get along? Are the municipal services adequate? Are taxes reasonable?" Elaine tilted her head back and stroked her neck like she was trying to remember something important. "And he asked one question I don't hear often—never, come to think of it."

Caroline removed her notepad.

"He asked about upcoming village events that he might attend."

"And what did you tell him?" asked Caroline.

"I handed him the *Village Bulletin*."

Constance knew the *Bulletin* listed her upcoming wedding. The deputy scribbled a note, then fired off another question. "And how old would you say he is?"

"I know exactly. He's 58." Elaine stared at Caroline and then Constance. "Why all the questions? Is John someone you know, Constance?"

"I thought he might be, but no. I don't know anyone from Chicago." She felt Caroline's eyes on her.

Constance hugged Elaine. "Thanks so much for coming. It means a great deal to Arthur and me. Now, I must scoot before my family turns into ice sculptures."

When she was some distance away, Constance turned back. The hairs lifted on the back of her neck seeing Caroline walk off with Elaine. *Caroline will not let this go.*

CHAPTER 31
The Investigation Heats Up

Caroline pumped Elaine for information on John W. Loch. Elaine, known for her loose lips, was eager to comply. She gave up his current address, cell phone number, place of business, his widowed marital status, that he planned to buy in cash and that he grew up in New Hampshire and preferred the Northeast over Chicago. The only information the nosy realtor didn't get out of him was his blood type and birthdate.

The background check frustrated Caroline but didn't surprise her. No 58-year-old John W. Loch in Chicago or roots in New Hampshire. The software company he worked at didn't exist, his cell phone number was tied to a throw-away phone and his home address was phony. So, what was the phony John W. Loch's game?

It was obvious he was using Elaine to glean information, but who was his target—Constance, Arthur, Stones End? Was he a con man or was he in cahoots with the stranger in the cemetery—or both?

She called Martin.

"Martin, Caroline here. I need copies of the pictures you took at the boat christening."

"I'll email them right now. What's up?"

"Did you happen to see a stranger in the distance to the right of the schooner?"

"Yes. Tall guy with light brown hair. I noticed him because he kept putting on and taking off his sunglasses. The gesture struck me as odd, but odder was that he had sunglasses at all. The day was overcast."

"Did you get any pictures of him?"

"Maybe. I took shots of the schooner. The camera may have picked him up in the background."

"Let's hope if it did, his sunglasses were off."

"Hold a minute, I'll look right now."

She tapped her pen on the desk. Then drummed her fingers.

"Anything?" No answer. "Martin!"

"Not good. One frontal view with sunglasses on and one of his back. He must have seen me taking pictures and turned away. The guy was out of the focus point, so he's blurry, but I'll email them."

"I'll match it against the photos from the bookshop opening. Maybe we'll get lucky."

Caroline enlarged the photo Martin sent. It was impossibly blurred. The facial recognition software available to her wasn't sophisticated. It kicked out an error message each time she loaded the photograph. She knew Scotland Yard's database was infinitely better.

"Hello, Dad. Need your help identifying a person. All I've got is a blurry photo."

Her father laughed. "Is there any chance of my only child giving me a proper greeting?"

"Sorry. How are you, Dad? How's Mom?"

"Both fine, luv. No need to ask how you are. Your voice is screwed tighter than a drum. What's up?"

"There's a new twist to that stranger we looked into."

"You mean the old man in the cemetery?"

"Yeah. A suspicious character showed up at an event today. He wasn't invited, yet he stood off to the side, staring at Constance. I'm emailing his photo. It's too blurry for my system."

Caroline heard her father's computer ping with an incoming email.

"Got it," he said.

"What do you think? Can you work with it?"

"Don't know. There's something familiar about this face, though. I'll run it through our system. But this photo is a mess. It will take some time. And I can't guarantee results."

Caroline ran a hand over her head. "My gut tells me this guy or our man in the cemetery is going to make a move at the wedding this Friday. Any chance of results before then?"

"Hard to say. We have to sharpen this image, or our program won't accept it. There's no telling how long that will take or if it's possible. My department is working under budget cuts and full plates. So, time and resources are the enemy. But you know I'll try, luv."

"Thanks, Dad."

"Any progress in identifying the old man in the cemetery?" her father asked.

"No. He's held up in an abandoned house the next town over. He hasn't committed a crime, so no chance of getting a search warrant. But I know he's in there."

"Has he been spotted since his cemetery visit?"

"Yes. Staring at Constance's apartment and Arthur's house in the middle of the night. One witness described a tartan scarf he wears. Then the thing shows up in a paper bag in her bookshop."

"Sounds like this guy is checking out his marks. Leaving the scarf is worrisome. It smacks of menacing, maybe sinister. Might mean Constance knows him and the scarf is a message or warning. Is she talking?"

"Negative. She has a history with someone in Scotland, but I've confirmed he's dead. Without identifying the cemetery guy or the boatyard guy, I can't connect either one of them to who Constance knew."

"So, let me get this straight. You have two suspicious characters seemingly stalking Constance and/or her loved ones. If I'm remembering our last call correctly, suspicious character number one is 80ish, lame and wears a tartan scarf. Suspicious character number two is what?"

"58 years old. Posing as an American from Chicago looking to retire in the Northeast."

"I see. Why do you think the old guy left his scarf?" he said.

"No idea. But I agree it's a warning of some kind and now I wonder if the man in the boatyard is an accomplice? Two strangers with a common interest. The old man in the cemetery is lame, but the boatyard guy isn't. He could have slipped in unnoticed and left the scarf in the bookshop."

"Any other data on the boatyard guy?"

"He gave phony information to a realtor he's working with. I ran a background check. John W. Loch doesn't exist."

"Tell me that name again."

"John W. Loch. L.O.C.H. Ring any bells?"

"No. But it might with Interpol. The FBI's facial recognition software is what we need but we don't have enough to get them involved."

"Well, I'll keep pushing from this end," said Caroline. "And, Dad, thanks."

"You can thank me by calling your mother more often."

"Will do."

"And Caroline," her father paused. "Be careful, luv."

Caroline stroked her African parrot's chest. "Hang onto your feathers, Mortimer. Something bad is about to happen in Stones End."

CHAPTER 32
Taking Down Roxy

The final push to finish the wedding project loomed. Martin and Charlotte met at the printshop after the boat christening. Again, he plunged into the project, keenly steering away from intimacy.

"We're in good shape. Last night, I returned and finished adhering the prints to the boards. We just have to attach the stands. Working in the wedding hall will give us more room. But I need to help Caroline with something this afternoon. Would you mind if we tape the stands on Wednesday night?"

"Why wait? It's only Sunday."

He tidied papers on the drafting table. "Tuesday night is the rehearsal dinner and tomorrow night I'm meeting Roxy."

Charlotte had no idea how the meeting would go, and it seemed like he was pushing her away. Swinging emotions sent her frustration level through the ceiling. She admired his decent intentions, but did he have to be so bloody proper?

"Well, I can save time and carry the prints to the hall this afternoon."

"Excellent. I'll help you stack them by the shop door before I leave."

It took three trips each to haul the prints to the front of the shop. Charlotte gathered her hair in a ponytail. "Thanks. You go. I need to get my purse."

She turned toward the corridor when Martin's hand grasped her shoulder. With one twist, she was in his arms. His lips found hers in an urgent, forceful kiss. Before Charlotte knew what hit her, their bodies pressed up against the front window. Charlotte yielded to his hands, drifting up and down her back. She tugged him closer.

Birdie's dog yapped on the other side of the window. Martin and Charlotte leapt apart. Birdie shot an exaggerated thumbs-up at them from the sidewalk. Charlotte giggled and dipped her head into Martin's chest. He whispered, "I haven't forgotten Friday night, Charley." Charlotte opened her mouth to speak, but he was already out the door.

She watched him hurry across the green, shivers still coursing through her body. When he was 50 feet away, she saw him jump as though startled. Roxy running toward Martin caught her eye. Charlotte's eyes widened as Roxy dove into his arms. He tried to escape her clutch, but Roxy kissed him as though she hadn't seen him in a year. He pulled away, said something, then continued across the village square.

Roxy turned a fevered stare toward Charlotte. Her blistering look conveyed a message—she'd seen their kiss inside the shop.

With the prints delivered to the wedding hall, Charlotte turned for home. An edginess pricked at her. Martin's kiss bolstered her confidence, but then seeing Roxy all over him chipped at the fringes. And was it her imagination, or did Martin take a moment too long before backing away from Roxy's embrace?

Charlotte needed to talk with someone, but who? Giving her aunt false hope that she and Martin would get together seemed cruel, especially in the face of her own doubt. The ladies came to mind. Madge's advice smacked of too motherly, Mrs. Kruchinski's leaned toward Great Aunt Prudence's stodgy wisdom and Birdie's advice could go anywhere, including off the rails. A light was on in Rosie's dance studio. Charlotte wandered toward it.

The mirrored walls and polished oak floors of the studio calmed her. Stenciled silhouettes of dancers covered the mirror beneath the ballet barre, and Bach played softly in the background. Rosie, with her hair pulled into a tight bun and the taut muscles of a dancer, stood at the barre in tights bending into a plie. "Charlotte, what a wonderful surprise."

"Have a minute, Rosie? I need to talk to someone before I lose my mind."

Rosie motioned to a table and chairs at the rear of the room. "I'm guessing this is about Martin. Any progress?"

Charlotte grimaced. "Yes. And no. It's like a ping pong tournament and I'm the ball." She updated Rosie on the intimate moments with Martin and how he alluded to breaking up with Roxy, his later aloofness and concluding with their kiss just hours ago.

"Am I wrong to believe he will end his affair with Roxy? He never directly said he would."

"Then, there's no way to tell. Martin is a decent man, but I wouldn't underestimate Roxy. Her kind never surrenders. She'll go down fighting."

"Fight! What will she do?"

"What won't she do? Trust me, women like Roxy live on animal impulses. Anything goes when someone threatens to steal their man."

Hearing this shocked Charlotte. Great Aunt Prudence would grab for her smelling salts if she knew Charlotte considered getting into a catfight over Martin.

"How do you know about such things?"

"I was a flamenco dancer in my former life. I watched women like Roxy claw for men they wanted all the time."

"Doesn't sound like I can win."

"Stop talking crazy. Of course, you can win. But you can't fight a tigress unarmed."

"I'm not sure about this, Rosie. Is a man worth all this scheming?"

"Only if he's your true love, honey. Come early before the rehearsal dinner, and I'll make you look so sexy, it'll hit Martin like a sledgehammer."

A strangled gasp escaped her throat. "I won't look like a mini-version of Roxy, will I?"

Rosie laughed. "No, my dear, whatever gave you that idea? Roxy's brand of sexy is *come and get me.* A demure brand of sexy is so much more alluring. That look will win Martin."

Charlotte bit her lip. "Let's hope you're right." She stood.

"You're in love with him, aren't you, honey?"

Charlotte gave up a lopsided smile. "Well, let's see. I hardly sleep, barely eat, and fantasize about him day and night. What do you think?"

Rosie sprang from the chair and strung her arm around Charlotte. "It's time to take Roxy down. Tuesday. Three o'clock. Be here."

The rehearsal was at five o'clock in the church, followed by dinner downstairs in the community hall. Charlotte escaped her aunt's apartment where Arthur's sisters and Constance were rushing around like someone yelled FIRE!

Only three days away, the wedding that Stones End waited 40 years for took center stage. Shopkeepers made *Closed for the Wedding* signs, Mrs. Kruchinski worked feverishly on the wedding cake, Walter practiced his operatic solo non-stop.

Charlotte sat on the bench outside the bookshop and dragged out her To-Do list. She smiled, seeing only two tasks remaining: pick up Constance's dress tomorrow and decorate the ballroom Thursday night with Martin.

She dashed to the church to take one last glimpse at the community hall for the rehearsal dinner. Paper strings of autumn leaves entwined with gold and green glass beads lined the table. Colorful spider mums in small vases and tea candles set in rust-colored glass holders finished the autumn-themed look.

Leaving the church hall, Charlotte peered at the village clock. 2:45. Fifteen minutes before she and Rosie got to work on her fetching new look. She peeked in the printshop window as she passed. No sign of Martin. She was dying to know how his meeting with Roxy went. Was he finally free to pursue her? Or did Roxy cast one of her spells over him? She whipped out her phone.

"Hello, Charley. What's up?"

She never tired of him calling her Charley or the tingle that ran down her spine hearing it.

"I suppose I can make up a pretense for this call."

Martin blurted out, "Roxy cancelled. I dropped by the beauty parlor twice today but couldn't get in the door. Every woman in town is getting their hair done before the wedding."

"Oh," was all Charlotte could manage.

"I'll try again before the rehearsal. I promise."

"Ok."

Charlotte trudged toward the dance studio. Rosie took one look at her droopy posture and said, "Uh oh."

"Roxy cancelled last night. Martin will try to meet with her this afternoon."

Rosie squinted. "She's up to something."

"Like what?"

"God only knows. All the more reason for you to look drop-dead gorgeous tonight." She led Charlotte by hand. "Come up to my boudoir."

Entering her bedroom was like being dropped into the center of Spain. Bold reds and deep yellows jumped out at her. Paintings of whitewashed Spanish villas atop the Pyrenees, bucolic scenes of shepherds with grazing flocks, and caped bullfighters in prideful stances covered every inch of wall space. Over the queen-sized bed hung a portrait of Rosie in full flamenco pose—chin high, one arm raised and a thrusting leg ready to stomp the floor.

Rosie emerged from her closet holding an exquisite black cashmere dress. The long-sleeved dress, with hemline just above the knee, plunged down half the back. "We can dress it up or down. But let's not go overboard, it's only a rehearsal dinner."

Charlotte slid into the dress. "Perfect!" said Rosie. She attached a delicate gold chain with a long single strand running down the back. Then, wrapped a thick suede belt the color of wet sand around her waist and presented matching suede boots. Charlotte twirled before the full-length mirror.

"Definitely haute couture, honey." Charlotte smoothed her hands over the luxurious fabric. It was the first time she felt the sensual touch of cashmere against her skin.

Rosie pointed to the chair at her dressing table. "Hair and makeup next."

She threw a towel over Charlotte's shoulders and got to work, creating a knotted chignon. She looped a long ivory hair pin through the braid and then buried her in a fog of hair spray. "We can't have stray locks sticking out."

Having someone apply makeup was an unfamiliar experience. Charlotte giggled at the instructions. *Open your eyes, close your eyes, pout your lips, chin up, chin down.* Rosie dropped the last makeup brush onto the dressing table and stepped backward. "What do you think?"

The transformation shocked Charlotte. She squinted toward the mirror. A high-end fashion model stared back at her. Skin of fine porcelain, sculpted eyebrows, outlined sapphire eyes and red lips that whispered the mysteries of starlit nights.

She moved her face forward, then from side to side. "It's remarkable, stunning." She shook her head. "What's the right word? Genius. That's it. Rosie, you're a genius."

"Now, what's the final dazzle a woman puts on?"

Charlotte drew her brows tight. She was not the dazzle type.

Rosie laughed and dangled a long pair of crystal tear-drop earrings. "You always need a dash of sparkle around your face."

She put on the earrings. Rosie appeared next to her in the mirror. "You're a knockout, honey. That painted, flesh-popping vixen doesn't stand a chance."

"Let's go downstairs to the studio. The mirrored walls will give you a panoramic view."

Charlotte rotated in every direction in front of the mirrors, then hugged Rosie. "I don't know how to thank you. I can't wait to see Martin's reaction."

Rosie pointed toward the front window. "Speak of the devil."

Martin ran by the dance studio toward the village square.

"Do you think he's coming from seeing Roxy?" said Charlotte.

"Good chance."

Charlotte scooped up her jacket and purse and ran toward the door. Rosie seized her arm.

"You don't want to appear overanxious. Save the big reveal for tonight."

Charlotte floated from the dance studio with soaring confidence. She couldn't help checking her new image in every shop window. As she passed the beauty parlor, Roxy rushed after her.

"Well, someone's all gussied up. Who are you trying to impress? Hope it's not my Marty because it would all be for nothing." Roxy pushed her face close to Charlotte. "Marty and I are going to be married next month." She shoved her left hand with a sparkling diamond ring in Charlotte's face.

Without another word, Roxy spun and strutted back through

the door of the beauty parlor wearing a smug look. Charlotte stood alone on the sidewalk, dumbstruck. The humiliation of Roxy's words slapped her—*it would all be for nothing*. She looked down at her outfit. A moment ago, it made her feel beautiful and now covered her in foolishness.

Charlotte staggered across the street. She felt Roxy watching her, savoring her mortification. Climbing the stairs to her aunt's apartment, Charlotte sat on the top step. She couldn't bring herself to face her aunts. Laughter drifted from inside. Suddenly, the door flew open.

"I thought I heard… Charlotte, what is it? Are you ill?" said Constance.

Charlotte buried her face in her hands and sobbed. Emily and Zoe ran to the door.

"What happened?" they said in unison.

"We need a moment, dears." Constance pulled the door closed and sat on the step next to Charlotte, waiting for the tears to subside. She dug in Charlotte's purse and handed her a wad of tissues.

Charlotte choked out her words between sobs. "I'm such a fool, Aunt Constance. Look at me," she waved her hand in front of herself. "All dressed up, trying to catch a man who's engaged to another woman."

"Engaged! Who told you that?"

"Roxy just shoved her engagement ring at me."

Constance wrapped her arms around her niece. "Oh, Charlotte. I'm so sorry." Charlotte rested her head on her aunt's shoulders. The tears wouldn't stop.

"I wish I knew how to ease your pain, dearest." She rocked Charlotte in her arms. Salty tears burned her eyes.

Charlotte wiped her face and straightened. "I shouldn't carry on like this. It will ruin your lovely night."

"Don't worry about the rehearsal. I'll make an excuse for you."

"No. I have to be there."

"No, dearest. I don't want you to face Martin tonight or, God forbid, that hussy Roxy," said Constance.

Charlotte jerked her head around. "Is she invited?"

"No telling what that one will do."

Charlotte hunched over her legs. "I can't believe I fell for his line."

Her aunt went rigid. "What line?"

Charlotte gave a sidelong glance. Constance didn't know what transpired between herself and Martin. She didn't want her poor judgment to come between Martin and her aunt, or worse, between Martin and his boss, Arthur.

Constance repeated: "What line, Charlotte? Did Martin make promises to you?"

Charlotte stared straight ahead. "It doesn't matter." She rose and brushed at the tears that wet her jacket. "But you're right. I'm not up to running into Martin or Roxy."

Constance opened the apartment door. "I'll just tell your aunts to give you some space."

Charlotte grabbed her arm. "Please don't tell anyone, Aunt Constance."

"Of course not, dearest."

"Not even Arthur."

Constance paused, then looked at her niece's red-rimmed eyes. "Not even Arthur."

When they heard the bedroom door close, Zoe and Emily rushed at Constance. "What happened?" said Emily.

"I promised Charlotte not to say."

Zoe folded her arms across her chest. "It's Martin, isn't it?"

Emily swatted at her sister. "Don't push." Then she leaned in expectantly.

Constance glanced toward the hall leading to the bedrooms,

then whispered. "Yes, but I can't say more."

Arthur and Ari strolled through the door in high spirits, then pulled up short at the dark mood in the room.

"Is everything alright?" asked Arthur.

Constance grabbed her coat and purse. "Yes, dear. We should go or we'll be late."

Ari threw his hands out and shrugged at his sisters. Emily put a finger to her lips.

Arthur looked down the hall. "Is Charlotte meeting us at the church?"

"Charlotte's not feeling well and won't be joining us." Before Arthur could comment, Constance walked out the door.

They found Father Gregory, Walter, and Martin making small talk and bad jokes when they reached the church. Constance announced Charlotte wouldn't be joining them. She barely looked at Martin. It wasn't clear what he did, but she had a heartbroken niece on her hands. Her fury at the perceived grievance shot from her eyes like a spray of bullets. Martin wanted to ask about Charlotte but thought better of it. He sensed the hostility.

Father Gregory fussed over the rehearsal like it was a fresh experience for everyone. He provided instructions to Ari as the best man, to Walter, who had the honor of walking Constance down the aisle, and Martin acting as usher.

Constance was grateful the rehearsal was quick. She needed a glass of wine and to put distance between herself and Martin.

"Dinner is waiting for us downstairs," announced Father Gregory.

Their friends applauded as Arthur and Constance entered. Arthur kissed Constance's left hand and led her to the table. The women gathered around her.

"We heard what happened. Is Charlotte alright?" said Mrs. Kruchinski.

Constance pulled her head back and stammered, "Who told you?"

"I did," said Berris. "Roxy ran after Charlotte when she passed the shop this afternoon. I stood by the door and listened. It was terrible watching her flaunt her engagement ring in Charlotte's face. Poor Charlotte looked shattered."

"It doesn't make sense. Martin is in love with Charlotte. So how did Roxy convince him to marry her?" said Rosie.

Madge covered her mouth awkwardly. Birdie did a double take then yelled, "Holy crap!" She glanced around quickly to make sure Father Gregory didn't hear her swearing.

Constance looked from Madge to Birdie. "What? What is it?"

Rosie jumped up, eyes blazing. "She's pregnant!"

"Oh my God," shouted Mrs. Kruchinski. "You're right. That's the only way Martin would choose her over Charlotte."

Birdie pulled Rosie back into her seat as Arthur rose and clinked a spoon to his glass.

"My dear friends. I'd like to propose a toast to my future..." He stopped as Roxy sashayed into the hall wearing a red dress that looked as though it was spray-painted on her body.

Martin stood, knocking his chair to the floor. "Roxy! What are you doing here?"

Roxy rushed toward Martin and wrapped her body around his right arm.

"I thought this was the perfect occasion to make our announcement, sweetie." She held up her left hand and wiggled her ring finger. "Marty and I are getting married."

Martin's jaw hit his chest. He yanked his arm away. "We most certainly are not!"

Glances shot around the room like crisscrossing laser beams.

"What are you saying, Marty? I proposed, and you said yes," screamed Roxy.

"I said I'd consider it."

"It's the same thing as far as I'm concerned. And you gave me this ring, so I had every right to think so."

"Are you joking? It's fake. I won it at the carnival last month. And I don't recall giving it to you. My recollection is that you snatched it out of my hand."

Roxy slapped Martin. His right cheek blazed red. "How dare you embarrass me in front of all these people when you have every intention of marrying me?"

Horace burst from his seat, infuriated at Roxy. Birdie tugged on his sleeve. "Let Martin handle it." Father Gregory nearly ripped the collar from his throat.

Martin stepped so close to Roxy he could smell the fear on her breath. "Did you tell Charley we were engaged? Is that why she isn't here?"

"And what if I did?"

Martin spun toward the door. "I've got to find her."

Roxy grabbed his arm so hard threads popped. "I can't believe you'd chase after that British hussy. What kind of slut would try to steal another woman's man?"

Zoe jumped from her chair, ready to punch Roxy's lights out. Arthur and Ari wrestled her back down. Constance burned crimson. Madge leaned over and patted her hand without taking her eyes from the drama.

Roxy thrust her chin at Martin and glared. "You heard me right, she's a slut." For a moment, Martin looked like he would strike her right there in the church room.

Suddenly, a thunderous voice called out. "You have some nerve, missy, calling Charlotte names, when you've been cheating on Martin for the past month," said a man. "That's right. I've seen you two falling out of the storage room half undressed."

It was Karl who spoke.

Roxy staggered backward. Horace let a "Holy shit" escape.

Father Gregory's head snapped around at the expletive. Walter jumped up and yelled, "Go, Martin. Go find Charlotte."

Martin bolted. Roxy was on his heels. The ladies beat her to the door and stood as a wall.

"Get out of my way, you old windbags."

Zoe rushed Roxy and grabbed her right arm. "Emily, I need a hand."

"My pleasure." Emily gripped Roxy's left arm, and the sisters dragged her from the church hall, kicking and howling like an animal trying to escape its captors.

Constance whipped around to Arthur. "Your sisters need help."

Arthur smiled at Ari, who sat with his hands behind his head.

"Trust me. They don't need our help."

Suddenly, Berris sprinted for the door. "Where's she going?" said Mrs. Kruchinski, dashing after her.

"Let's go," yelled Rosie. Constance, Madge, and Birdie chased.

Father Gregory stood before Arthur and Ari. "Your sisters wouldn't hurt Roxy, would they?"

"Oh, crap," said Ari. Arthur was out of his chair and barreling across the room before Father Gregory could pull on his collar again.

Emily and Zoe released Roxy. Zoe wagged her finger. "No more trouble from you. Now go!"

A defeated Roxy stomped down the path in her four-inch heels.

Berris reached the door. Her words had the force of an angry child. "You're fired."

"Way to go," said Birdie, pumping her fist in the air.

Roxy yelled back. "Too late, I quit."

Berris crinkled her forehead. "Can she quit after I fired her?"

Mrs. Kruchinski hugged her. "Don't give it another thought, my brave friend."

Berris beamed as though she was awarded a badge of courage.

Arthur reached the top of the stairs. "Constance!"

Constance swung around. "Everything's fine, sweetheart. We

were just putting out the trash."

Mrs. Kruchinski howled. "Everyone, downstairs. There's still coffee and cake."

The ladies huddled at one end of the table and the men at the other, empty cake plates littered between them.

Birdie leaned across to Rosie. "Sad, isn't it? What made Roxy pull a stunt like that?"

"Desperation," said Rosie. "Charlotte threatened her. She knew she had to act fast. The only problem with her plan was that she misread Martin. Thought he was in love with her, and he would bend to her will."

Constance butted in. "I'm dripping with guilt for being furious with Martin. I should have known better."

"Don't even think about it. Let's put our hope in a double wedding," said Mrs. Kruchinski.

Constance grasped her hands and shook them. "I'd die a happy woman."

Birdie nodded toward the door. "I'd say from the look of them, there's a good chance."

Martin and Charlotte strolled into the room hand-in-hand. Martin marched straight-backed like a soldier on duty and stopped in front of Constance.

"Constance," he turned toward the end of the table, "and, Mr. Covington." He cleared his throat. Charlotte squeezed his hand. "I'd like to request your niece's hand in marriage. I know we've only known each other a short..."

"Yes!" Constance yelled, then burst from her chair and hugged Charlotte. She turned to Martin. "Yes, you dear man, yes!"

Arthur ran to them and extended his hand to Martin. "Well done, Martin. Welcome to the family, my boy." He turned to Charlotte with outstretched arms. "You've made me and your aunt very happy, my dear."

The group drifted from the rehearsal dinner like they stepped out of a fairy tale. Constance kissed Arthur goodnight, and Emily and Zoe told their brothers they were staying with Constance for girl talk. "Tell us everything," said Constance.

Charlotte's eyes glistened, remembering Martin's proposal. "It all happened so quickly. I was drowning my sorrows in a cup of tea when Martin knocked. He called through the door and said that he needed to talk with me. I imagined he came to apologize or explain why he chose Roxy, which was the last thing I wanted to hear. So, I wouldn't answer. Then, his knock turned into pounding."

"Martin pounded?" said Constance.

"It surprised me as well. I stood by the door. That's when he said Roxy lied and that they were not engaged. Before I knew it, I was in his arms."

"Did you kiss?" said Emily dreamily.

Charlotte blushed. "We did. Then, Martin took hold of my hands and said there was something else he needed to say. We sat on the couch. He told me of a conversation he had with Horace and how Horace said if something happened to Birdie, his soul would have no one to talk to."

Constance put her hand over her heart. "That's the most beautiful thing I ever heard." Emily brushed a tear that threatened to spill. "Lucky, Birdie."

"I thought so, too, until Martin said, 'I'll add to what Horace said, Charley. If anything happened to you, my heart would have no one to love.'"

There wasn't a dry eye at the kitchen table. Emily sputtered through joyful tears, "Group hug."

CHAPTER 33
Final Tasks

At the breakfast table the next morning, Constance choked down her disappointment about Charlotte and Martin deciding to be married in The Cotswolds. Arthur, on the other hand, was thrilled.

"I've never been to England. Think of it, darling, we were putting our honeymoon off till sailing season. But now we can plan a European honeymoon. I'd love to see The Cotswolds and we could travel to Brighton, where my father was born."

"You must include Greece. We'll show you our roots," said Zoe.

"I have a shelf of books on Greece in the shop."

Arthur smiled. "She'll have the trip planned before sundown."

Charlotte strolled into the kitchen in a dreamlike fog. "Don't forget, we pick up your dress at ten o'clock, Aunt Constance."

She leapt from her chair and dumped her breakfast dishes in the sink. "I need to see Walter before I pick up my dress."

Charlotte glanced up from spreading jam on her toast. "Did I forget something?"

"No, dearest. Just some last-minute changes."

Charlotte dropped her jam knife. "Anything you care to share with your wedding planner?"

"Nope, it's a secret," laughed Constance, scooting down the hall. "Enjoy your English muffin in our honor!"

Wednesday and Thursday blurred by. Walter wasted no time

rehearsing for the wedding. He serenaded his clients while he cut their hair. Mrs. Kruchinski put the finishing touches on the three-tiered wedding cake and for the first time in decades, The Café wasn't open for Thursday night dinner. Oscar and Madge pulled an all-night cook fest, assisted by Emily and Zoe.

Ari was horrified to discover that Arthur intended to wear a business suit to his own wedding and dragged him shopping for a tuxedo.

"Constance said I could wear a suit," said Arthur. Ari held the door to Arthur's 1969 antique Renault. "Stop being a knucklehead and get in the car."

Charlotte insisted Martin keep his eyes closed for the big reveal of the ballroom at the conservatory. Martin's head jerked when he walked in. "What the...?"

"Surprise," Charlotte yelled.

"It's spectacular. How did you do this?"

"I didn't. Karl suggested the scaffold, so I handed him yards and yards of sky-blue silk fabric, a thousand feet of white twinkle lights and he did the rest."

The ballroom resembled a charming replica of Stones End, complete with a silken blue sky and real-life touches of potted ficus trees, colorful mums and strings of red, yellow, and orange leaves strung over the shop posters.

Martin pulled Charlotte into his arms. "I'm going to love being married to you." Charlotte giggled. "I was just thinking the same about you."

A full harvest moon closed on the frantic day before the wedding.

Tired bodies and minds met their pillows with dreams of happily-ever-after for Constance, Arthur, and their newly bonded families. They all forgot the lurking stranger. All but Caroline.

"Hello, Dad. How goes Scotland Yard? Anything to report?"

"Nothing, luv. We've been sharpening the photo of the guy from the boatyard, but our facial recognition system hasn't found a match yet. We'll keep trying. Has he shown his face since the boatyard?"

"No."

"How about the other guy? Still holed up in the abandoned house?"

"Yes."

"You're giving me one-word answers, luv. Talk to me."

"My gut tells me no, but am I imagining a threat that isn't there?"

"No. The suspicious behavior from the cemetery guy says he's planning something. Standing over Constance's son's grave, in front of her shop, in front of Arthur's house. He's casing these places. And planting that tartan scarf in the bookshop was designed to send a message. The situation appears sinister to me."

"I agree, but Constance's connection to Scotland is with some dead guy. Leading me to dead ends. And this new lurker in the boatyard has me stumped. Something tells me I'm not dealing with two suspects. I think the guy in the boatyard is the same guy from the cemetery."

"That's a new twist."

"We must ID him, and fast."

"Gotcha. If he has a rap sheet, it might map what he's about to pull in Stones End."

"I understand what you're dealing with, Dad, but we're out of time. Tomorrow's the wedding."

"And you think that's when he'll make his move?"

"Yes."

"I'll stay on it...double time!"

CHAPTER 34
The Wedding

The radiant bride emerged from the limousine wearing a three-quarter length cream satin dress, matching shoes and a silver and gold beaded jacket. And Charlotte's crystal earrings for *something borrowed*. Charlotte handed Constance her bouquet of white rosebuds with a small spray of blue forget-me-nots for *something blue*.

"You look positively stunning, Aunt Constance."

Constance fidgeted. "I should have gone with a veil, don't you think?"

"Don't worry about a veil. I'm just glad your French twist isn't pink."

Walter extended his arms to Constance and Charlotte and escorted them up the path to the old stone church with its pointed arches and sloping slate roof. Martin greeted them at the entrance, as did the rich scent of incense and the spicy fragrance of the fall mums decorating the narthex.

When they entered, Charlotte spied Martin poking his head out the door and jabbing a thumbs-down to Caroline sitting in the squad car across from the church.

Caroline checked her phone, praying her father texted or emailed information from London on the suspect in the boatyard. Nothing. She exited the car and hurried to the church.

"Ready when you are, Constance," said Martin.

Charlotte took her position ahead of the bride. Constance wrapped a shaky hand around Walter's right arm.

"Everyone's cell phone off?" said Walter. Constance dug hers out of an inside jacket pocket. Charlotte's eyes widened. Constance laughed. "Crazy, isn't it? I can be without a purse, but not my cell phone."

Martin opened the door and nodded at the organist. The soft, rolling chords of *Ave Maria* played.

A familiar voice soared to the rafters of the candlelit church. Arthur turned toward the altar as Ana Felicia stepped from the sacristy. His eyes brightened, seeing his childhood love and his heart swelled hearing the famous opera singer's angelic voice. Then he whirled around to check Constance's reaction. She flashed a dazzling smile and a wink.

Walter whispered, "Thank you. Ana Felicia and I are very grateful that you included her."

"I understand you're next," said Constance, acknowledging the well-guarded secret. He smiled and squeezed her arm.

The attendees nestled shoulder-to-shoulder in the oak pews. The jasmine-like scent of the hydrangeas spread around the altar, scented the entire church. Arthur and Constance held hands, waiting for Ana Felicia's last note. Mrs. Kruchinski and Madge held their handkerchiefs at the ready. Horace wrapped his arm around Birdie and Ari couldn't wipe the smile off his face if he tried.

Father Gregory cleared his throat. "Dearly beloved…" He stopped at the steady clunk of a pole against the marble floor. The sound reverberated off the walls of the cavernous church. Panicked eyes darted around the room.

Madge pointed at the corridor to the right of the altar and screamed. "It's him!" Oscar, Horace, and Karl burst from the pews. Martin and Walter rushed to the altar.

The old man banged his walking stick with surprising force, then bellowed in a voice stronger than his frail, hunched appearance suggested. "The wedding must stop!"

Father Gregory spun toward the intrusion. "What's the meaning of this? Who are you?"

The color drained from Constance's face. Arthur grabbed hold of her right arm. The old man shuffled closer, then stopped at the right side of the altar, ten feet from the wedding party.

"Do you not remember me, Connie? Do you not remember your husband?"

The rear door of the church burst open. Martin ran to Caroline. "The guy from the cemetery is Constance's first husband."

"No, he isn't," she said, sprinting toward the altar.

Constance took a few shaky steps forward. "Colum?"

Caroline blocked Constance from advancing further. "You recognize this man?"

A weak "yes" escaped before Constance fainted headfirst into Caroline's arms.

An explosion of speculation pelted the air like a paint gun shot. The church erupted in hand-covered whispers and loud talk. "Birdie, you're closest to Constance. Did you know about a first husband?" said Mrs. Kruchinski.

"No. She must have been very young because she married William in her early twenties."

"Clearly, the first marriage was annulled, or she couldn't have married William," said Rosie.

"What could have happened?" said Birdie.

Mrs. Kruchinski noticed Ana Felicia lurking and listening. She grabbed hold of her arm. "You're in this now, whether or not we like it. What do you think?"

Ana Felicia's eyes brightened at being included by her top critic. She gave her fellow Greek compatriots a smile. Emily and Zoe introduced themselves to the famous daughter of their home village. Ana Felicia leaned into the group. "I'm more concerned with why Constance's first husband is here now. Aren't you?"

Emily choked on a sharp breath. "You don't think he wants to take Constance from our brother, do you?"

The women turned and looked at the old man leaning against the far-right wall off the altar. He suddenly looked like a villain planning to swoop in and steal the bride from her beloved.

"I can't bear our baby brother coming this close to marriage and losing," said Zoe.

"We're forgetting that Constance would have to agree to go with this guy, and I can't see her leaving Arthur. We don't know what kind of relationship she had with her first husband, but it obviously didn't end well," said Madge.

"True," said Rosie. "Constance has been with Arthur for decades. Her first marriage was over 40 years ago. She doesn't even know this guy anymore."

"Constance will choose Arthur. You'll see. At this point in her life, only happily ever after will do," said Birdie.

They took another look at this man who claimed to be the first husband. Despite Birdie's positive opinion, it was anyone's guess if there'd be a wedding.

Constance was woozy. Her thoughts spun like a mirrored ball ricocheting a dizzying light. *It's not possible. He's been dead for over forty years.*

Opening her eyes, she found herself on the couch in Father Gregory's office. The room smelled of beeswax, lemon oil and worn missals. Sunlight hitting the stained-glass border around the windows threw splotches of color across the threadbare carpet.

Caroline stood by the door. Arthur's family, Charlotte and Father Gregory huddled by the window and Arthur sat in a chair holding her hand. Constance wondered where Colum was and couldn't imagine what was going through their friends' minds.

Charlotte brought a glass of water. "Take a sip, Aunt Constance." She pulled herself up on her elbows. "Please, may I have a moment alone with Arthur?"

The small group departed amid murmurs and whispers, looking like they stepped on a live wire. All except Caroline, who marched out with a tightly drawn unibrow and a determined set to her jaw.

Constance buried her face in her hands. "I can't look at you."

Arthur leaned his head on hers and uttered softly. "You can tell me anything."

She wept. "I'm so terribly sorry. I never wanted my secret to cause you pain."

Arthur offered his handkerchief. "We all have past secrets. You dealt with mine, now I'll deal with yours." His voice sank to a somber tone. "Now, tell me, sweetheart. Is it true? Is this man your husband?"

She wiped her eyes and stared at the makeup smudges on his handkerchief.

"His death certificate dissolved our marriage. But, yes, he was my first husband. We met in Scotland where my family spent summers. It was the last vacation before I started university. We fell in love, and he asked my parents for permission to marry me. They immediately said no."

"What was their objection?"

"My age, for one. I was only 18. Colum was 21. But they considered our love as a youthful fancy that would fade."

Arthur stared into Constance's teary eyes. "And was it?"

"It didn't seem so at the time. In retrospect, I must have been out of my mind."

"How did you end up married? Did your parents give in?"

"We eloped. Colum signed on as a crew member with his uncle's expedition to Antarctica. He was leaving the week before my family returned to England. We faced a six-month separation. He was worried I wouldn't wait."

"Your parents must have thrown a fit."

Constance lowered her head. "They never found out. We hoped when my parents saw all his letters, they would realize how earnest he was and accept our marriage."

"And did they?"

"He never returned. I saw Colum off in Scotland. Saying goodbye was painful. We stood between wedded bliss and immediate separation. He tore himself from my arms and handed me his itinerary so I could track his journey. They flew from Heathrow to Buenos Aires. Then trekked to the southern tip of South America to board a ship in the town of Ushuaia."

"What happened?"

"A violent storm overtook the ship. There was an explosion. It disappeared off the coast of South Shetland Islands. In 1973, I found out from a BBC broadcast. Certainly no internet back then. It was the day we were returning home. I didn't know if he was dead or alive."

Arthur drew a hand over his face. "I recall this story. You must have been out of your mind with worry."

"The search crews gave up after a week. One morning, my mother shuffled into the kitchen and spread the newspaper across the breakfast table. That awful headline blared up at me: *All Presumed Dead*. My parents knew Colum was on the ship and there they were chatting about the tragedy like they would about a tree landing on someone's car. The casualness of their conversation enraged me. I wanted to scream: *You're talking about my husband.*"

"But you didn't?"

"No. I snatched the paper and stormed out."

Constance sat up. Arthur moved next to her on the couch.

"I have to ask?"

"Why I never told you?" Constance twisted the handkerchief into a knot. Her eyes stared past Arthur. "Simple. I'm cursed and didn't want you to find out."

"Cursed!"

"I know it sounds crazy. But don't you see? You witnessed the deaths of William and Willie. If you learned my first husband was killed, you'd come to the same conclusion and want nothing to do with me."

"Sweetheart, you are not cursed."

"Somewhere in my mind, I know that. It seemed too real to ignore when Willie drowned, though. One by one, the men in my life died. So, I suppressed my feelings for you all those years, thinking if the gods didn't know I loved you, they wouldn't take you from me. But when you proposed, something told me to give up my foolishness."

Arthur put his arm around Constance and pulled her close. "I can't explain the bad things that happened in your life, but you are not cursed. And nothing will happen to me or us."

He couldn't imagine how this development affected their future. It terrified him to ask. He stood and peered out to the church cemetery where her son and husband were buried. "What you must have gone through—no hope of saying goodbye, no closure. Did anyone ever contact you with the details of what happened?"

"No. Just what I read in the newspaper, that reported an explosion. The two-day storm trapped their ship in the Drake Passage. It's a dangerous region where the Atlantic, Pacific and Southern seas collide."

"I read about the vicious currents in the passage."

"By the time a search team reached the ship's last known location, there was nothing."

Constance rested her head on the back of the couch. "You're the first person I told this story to."

Arthur turned from the window. "You didn't tell William?"

"No. I saw no point. My marriage to Colum was never consummated. Everything was so rushed that last week. There was barely time to squeeze in a civil ceremony. We stepped from the judge's chambers into a tearful goodbye. He was dead in less than a week."

"Did Colum's family learn about the marriage?"

"I don't know. He had no family other than his uncle and his cousin, Ian. I assumed his cousin was on the ship as well."

"At first, I half-heartedly convinced myself that it never happened. A summer fling, a rushed wedding, a hasty goodbye. No one knew. So, it was easy not to speak of it. I was responding like a small child who believes they're invisible when they cover their eyes. The shock of it twisted my thoughts. Keeping it hidden made perfect sense."

"How did you cope with such a tragedy? You were only a teenager."

"Going off to university saved me. I grew up in those years and saw my youthful insanity for what it was—selfish and irresponsible."

Arthur rubbed the rising hairs on the back of his neck. None of it made sense. A first husband, presumed dead, stood on the other side of the door. How would this end? "You must speak with him." Constance squeezed her eyes shut.

Suddenly, Arthur went down to his knees, his eyes brimming. "My love, am I going to lose you?"

Someone knocked. Before they could answer, Caroline marched in and halted the tender scene.

"I'm sorry. I must speak with you." She dragged over a chair.

"I need for you to hear this, Constance. The real Colum MacGregor died on that ship. There's no disputing it. So, explain why you believe this man is him?"

Constance leaned forward. "There's no mistaking his face or those eyes. They're the blue that only shines when the sun hits an iceberg. I've been on this Earth 62 years and have never seen eyes that color on anyone else. It's him."

Caroline shook her head. "It's not him, Constance. It's not."

"Why are you so sure? Do you have proof?" asked Arthur. He prayed she did.

"No one could have survived that explosion."

Arthur turned to Constance. "Caroline's instincts are never wrong. And as a sailor myself, I must agree with her."

"This is confusing. Do I trust my eyes? Or Caroline's instincts?" She pushed herself from the couch and smoothed the wrinkles in her dress. With that one motion, she appeared as the strong, confident woman Arthur loved. "There's only one way to find out. I must speak with him."

Caroline jumped up. "Arthur and I should be present."

"Please, Caroline, no. I need an unguarded conversation to tell if it's really Colum."

Arthur's eyes locked on Caroline. The steely look in her eyes gave him a shiver. She was scared. The acid in his stomach rose and burned his throat. In that moment, he imagined losing Constance. He just didn't know if she would be a victim at the hands of a madman or would she willingly leave with her first love.

Caroline shook her head at the red flag waving before her. This plan broke police procedure. Never leave a suspect alone with an involved party. The perp could be armed. He could attack her.

"I don't like it," she said.

"Sorry, Caroline. It can't be helped," said Constance.

The two friends glared at each other.

Caroline broke the standoff. "If you must, then keep your guard up. Ask him what happened on the trip, but don't talk about your shared past. Let him bring up the memories. Listen carefully if he does. Don't fall for generalities. You want to hear details. Keep your distance."

Caroline's instructions stoked more stress on an already tense bonfire. Constance's hands trembled. She nodded agreement.

Constance stood at the window overlooking the cemetery. Caroline's words of caution unnerved her. Why was the deputy so sure he wasn't her first husband? She had no proof. It was just a theory that no one could have survived the shipwreck. But Arthur agreeing rattled her further. Why would he be here if he wasn't Colum? She stopped herself from speculating. The question frightened her.

Colum scraped into the room. The door closed. "I've caused a right mess for you, Connie." Her heart pounded out of her chest. She swallowed hard, turned, and faced his piercing blue eyes.

"What happened to you, Colum?"

"Do you mind if we sit?"

Constance motioned toward the round table in front of the window. Colum held a chair for her, then dragged himself to the opposite side with his back against the window. He winced as he lowered his crooked body into a chair and kept his left leg extended like it no longer bent.

Colum reached across the four-foot table. "Will you hold my hand?" Constance pulled her hands to her lap. The distance between them felt as far as the ocean that separated them all these years. He dragged his arm back. The flinching pain in his eyes stirred her compassion, but not enough to drop her guard.

He raised his shoulders sheepishly. The gesture struck her as familiar. "I can't blame you, lass. Me showing up after all these years. And on your wedding day, no less."

"Please, Colum. I need to hear what happened."

He folded his arms across his chest. It did not appear as a defensive gesture, yet her nerves tingled. She might have recognized Colum's face, but the man who sat across from her was a stranger. They sat in silence for a few moments. Colum looked off into the distance when he spoke.

"I'm sure you read about the storm that trapped us in the passage. It blew in fast. I was on the deck near the bow, trying to make my way below, when the explosion hit. It was like the devil himself threw me into the icy water. I woke draped across a piece of wreckage. Within seconds, everything went black. When I opened my eyes again, I was aboard a ship."

"How badly were you hurt?"

"I don't remember much, lass. My head felt like someone split it with a hatchet and my leg was mangled. Consciousness came and went for some time. Then one day I woke up in a hospital in Buenos Aires. The staff said two men dropped me and left. I couldn't tell the hospital personnel my name or what happened."

"You don't know who rescued you? Who brought you to a hospital?"

"I suspected they were smugglers. Must have been a few seamen aboard. Smugglers wouldn't care what happened to me, but fellow sailors would."

"You couldn't remember your name. Amnesia?"

"For a while. Partial memory came back eventually." He leaned across the table again. Constance twisted her hands in her lap tight enough to draw blood. Colum curled his arm back once again. The corner of his eyes softened. "You were the first person I remembered, Connie."

Constance shifted in her chair at his intimate tone. She wasn't ready to walk down memory lane or hear why he came. She blurted out, "How long before your memory returned?"

"About a year. I spent that time in the hospital. My leg was all shagged up. They operated a bunch of times and then they tried to get me to walk again." He slapped his bad leg. "This was the best they could do."

Suddenly, the story seemed fantastic to Constance as well. How could anyone survive an explosion that blew a hundred-foot vessel clear out of the water? And what are the chances of being spotted in icy seas and rescued in a violent storm—zero? He left too many gaps. Gaps a convenient case of amnesia couldn't fill. Yet here he was staring with those icy-blue eyes.

"I can see you dunna believe me."

"I want to, but I have so many questions. How is it that the hospital staff didn't link your Scottish accent to someone from the expedition?"

"They never heard my accent. It was Buenos Aires, so I spoke Spanish."

She recalled Colum was a student of languages. He proudly announced that he was fluent in five and how it would come in handy when they explored the world.

Colum gripped his walking stick, pulled himself from the squeaky chair and faced the window. Pity pricked her heart as he struggled to hold himself to his over six-foot height. She saw a proud man trying to hide his deformity.

His voice dropped low and thick. "The thought of you kept me going. I pushed beyond human endurance, wanting to return to you a whole man. The hardest blow came when the doctors said I'd never walk straight again."

Colum stared out at the cemetery. Birdie's ghost story came to her mind.

"Why did you stand over my son's grave?"

His weight shifted, tilting his body toward his stick. "I canna say for sure. Paying my respect to your son is something I had to do. It might have been our son under different circumstances."

His tender explanation jolted Constance into the past. She and Colum were back in Scotland in front of a campfire, sharing dreams about starting a family. She imagined their first child as a boy who would grow up like his dad and hunger to travel the world.

Colum shifted again as though standing was painful. "What kept you from contacting me?"

He turned from the window. "My injuries and the fact that my memory didn't fully return. Oh, I remembered my name eventually, and that I was Scottish born but there were many missing pieces." His eyes fixed in a tender gaze. "But I never forget our afternoon in that shady glen. We ate bread and cheese and feasted on the wild berries strewn across the forest floor."

Constance's mouth was as dry as a dustbin. No one knew about that day. The church room was suddenly stifling. He moved closer. The scent of salty air and pine filled the space between them.

"Ah, Connie, have you forgotten all of it? We got into a fit of laughter because the berries turned our tongues blue. Remember?"

Constance felt dizzy. She held her head as he pounded out memories only Colum would know.

"We laid on my jacket under the tall pines. Your chestnut hair flowing free like the mane on a wild filly. Our first kiss was under those pines. I can still hear your sweet voice. I thought my heart would burst hearing you whisper, *I love you*."

The color crept up her neck under Colum's stare. It wasn't possible to think past the impossible. A blinding scream echoed in her head: "It's him!"

Constance staggered from her chair, needing to put space between her and the ghosts from her past. A war between *possible* and *impossible* raged in her head. She fought to summon Caroline's advice. "What did you do after the hospital released you?"

"I flew back to Scotland. It's a sad day when a man canna see his future. With a bum leg and a scrambled mind, how would I support my bride?"

Constance couldn't bear any more. The account of his suffering rose a self-loathing bile in her throat. *I shoved the news of his death in a box and hid it away. Like our marriage never happened.*

Colum continued his relentless story. "By the time I plucked up enough courage to find you, you already re-married. I don't blame you, lass. It was good that you made a life for yourself without me."

Constance was reeling. Her worries were always hiding her teenage marriage. Not coming face-to-face with her first husband. She held Arthur's handkerchief tightly. It smelled fresh like a summer morning. The scent grounded her thoughts and lifted her courage. It was time to ask the question she dreaded. "Why now, Colum? After all these years?"

He clumsily maneuvered his round-backed body and stiff leg into the oak chair. Constance wondered if he was stalling, but then he gazed upward as though pleading for God's help.

"I wanted to talk with you one last time. Explain what happened and tell you how sorry I am for not coming to you after William's death."

"How did you know about William dying?"

"My father had two brothers. His younger brother was the explorer who died. And his older brother lived in Kent, Connecticut. His wife, Kathleen, knew of you through your articles in the village newspaper. She kept me informed about your life all these years."

"That's how you knew about Willie?" Constance rubbed her temples. "Forgive me, but I don't understand why you didn't come to me after William's death."

Colum's voice rose. "Can you not see I would have been a burden to you?" He pushed back in his chair and inhaled deeply. His words softened.

"It took all my courage to make this trip, then I lost my nerve when I got here. Convinced myself just seeing you from afar would be enough. But I stood outside your bookshop one night and glimpsed you passing the window upstairs. That one look awakened sleeping memories and my love burned as if we were still lying under the tall pines."

His breathing was raspy, the same breathing she heard on the phone that morning. Her thoughts skid out of control, like a car sliding on ice. "Please, Colum, tell me what you want?"

A single tear wet his cheek. He rubbed his eyelid like a sad child.

"A cruel twist of fate stole our happiness, lass. And took with it my home, my fortune and even my pride, but I wouldn't let it have my love for you. So, I'm asking—does your heart hold another chance for us?"

Constance froze in the impossible moment. Colum's life of tragedy, lost love and lost hope, crushed her. She owed this sad, broken man before her. But what? Arthur's handkerchief, wrapped like a bandage around her hand, reminded her she owed Arthur as well. But which man needed her love more?

She shambled across the room and sat at the table. Colum tugged his cap toward his face as though hiding from the shame that was about to fall. Constance sat, twisting the handkerchief. Colum drew in a long breath and held it.

She spoke without lifting her eyes. "Did you say you lost your home?"

The question provoked a sad chuckle. "A minor point…and a classic diversion." His grip tightened on his walking stick. "But it gives me my answer." He hauled himself from the chair and placed his hand on Constance's cheek. "Goodbye, my bonnie lass."

He limped past her toward the door.

"Wait."

Arthur paced the length of the corridor outside Father Gregory's office. "What's going on? It's taking too long."

"It's going to be fine, Arthur. They have a lot to catch up on," said Father Gregory.

Ari put his arm around his brother and shook him. "Why are you so worried?"

Arthur glared wildly. "This man is a stranger. I know nothing about what he and Constance had together. Or what he's asking of her now. But I know this, the woman I love has an ironclad sense of obligation. And if this man convinces her she owes him loyalty, then Constance may choose him."

Martin and Charlotte strolled up the corridor.

"What's going on with the guests?" asked Arthur.

"Patiently waiting," said Charlotte.

"And?" said Ari.

"Speculating like crazy," said Martin.

Caroline looked at the door to the office. "That's enough!" She turned the knob, the door creaked open. Arthur pushed past her. "Constance!"

She shoved her cell phone into the pocket of her beaded jacket. "Everything's fine, darling. Colum is just leaving."

Colum tipped his cap and quickened his limp, exiting the office.

"What happened?" asked Arthur.

"I'll tell you later." She smiled and bolted from the chair. "Right now, we have a wedding to attend."

Caroline blocked her. "Constance, this man is under investigation. You need to update me with what transpired."

Zoe and Emily, who were listening at the door, barged into the room. "Please, Constance, tell her," said Emily.

Constance faced the deputy. "I have a great deal of respect for you, but I can identify my first husband. And I'm telling you, it's him."

Caroline blew a long, frustrated sigh. "What did he want?"

"He told me his story. It was one of tragedy and hardship. He also spoke of things only my first husband would know. Then he asked for a second chance." She turned to Arthur. "I said no. But his life of infirmity has left him penniless, sweetheart. I'll explain later, but I felt obligated to help him. He wouldn't hear of it. We argued, but in the end, I convinced him to accept my gift. Now, he'll be able to return to Scotland and live comfortably."

"Comfortably! How much money did you give him?" asked Caroline.

Constance pulled her head back. "I'm sorry, but that's between Arthur and me."

Zoe rubbed her eyes. Emily covered her gaping mouth and Ari mopped his brow. Arthur spun around to Constance. "Tell me now."

Constance hesitated at their reaction but knew helping Colum was the right thing. She looked Arthur in the eyes. "Half my life savings. I wire transferred the money to his RBS account just now."

Caroline slapped a hand to her forehead. “I wish you hadn’t done that.”

“He’s my first husband, who’s suffered unspeakable tragedy and pain. I’m happy to help him. Now, it’s done, and that’s the end of it.”

“I’ll say this one last time. That man is not Colum MacGregor, and I will prove it,” said Caroline.

Constance bristled, then straightened her dress. “In the meantime, we have a wedding to attend.”

They entered the corridor. Father Gregory was talking with Colum. Constance rushed ahead. “Are you staying for the wedding?”

“No, I’ve caused enough trouble. I’ll be on my way.”

Colum limped past Martin as he stepped into the church. Martin blinked at something that glinted in the light as he edged by.

The wedding guests took their seats as Colum struggled down the center aisle toward the exit. Caroline dogged him. If information came through from her father at Scotland Yard, she was ready to pounce. And if information didn’t come, in a few quick minutes, Colum would disappear with Constance’s money. She whipped out her phone, praying for something, anything. She jammed the phone back in her uniform pocket.

Madge leaned forward to the pew in front of her. “Caroline’s sweating.”

Mrs. Kruchinski fanned herself with her handkerchief. “It is warm in here.”

“No,” said Madge. “Caroline never sweats!”

Mrs. Kruchinski and Karl twisted backward in their seats.

Rosie leaned over Oscar toward Madge. “And why isn’t Martin sitting?”

They glanced toward the side wall. Martin stood with unblinking eyes trained on Colum.

"Something's up," said Birdie from the third row.

Horace stood, then Walter, followed by Karl and Oscar. They didn't know why they were standing, but something told them to be at the ready.

Charlotte, Arthur, and Ari stiffly moved into their positions at the altar. Father Gregory opened and closed the prayer book in his hands several times as they waited for Constance.

Caroline hit Refresh on her phone. She and Martin suspected the guy in the cemetery wasn't lame. It explained how he was getting away so quickly. She bet that the guy from the boatyard was the same guy in the cemetery. But who the hell was he? And why the elaborate ruse?

Her father was six hours away in London, operating some of the world's best crime-fighting technology. Would he and his colleagues find a photo match with the facial recognition database before this suspect escaped? Colum was 15 yards away and five rows of pews from the door. She hit Refresh again.

Martin inched down the side wall not taking his eyes off Colum. What was the tiny flash of light he saw?

Arthur turned for a last look at the man who was escaping with half of Constance's retirement savings. Ari leaned in and whispered. "Caroline told me his story. What are the chances he survived that explosion?"

Arthur stared at his brother. "A million to one."

"Are you thinking what I'm thinking?" said Ari.

"We need to have a little talk with Colum before he leaves."

"Cover for us, Father," said Ari. The priest threw his arms up in the air.

"Where are you two going? The bride will be here any moment."

Constance appeared from the corridor to the right of the altar. The brothers glared at Colum's back and then at one another. "Caroline will have to nail him," whispered Ari.

The bride slid next to the groom.

Father Gregory attempted a humorous opening. "Let's try this again, shall we? Dearly beloved, we are gathered…" He stretched his neck, seeing Martin tear down the side aisle. "Oh, what is it now!"

Arthur and Ari spun around when Martin hollered, "Caroline! Stop him!"

Caroline hesitated as she twisted toward Martin.

"Contact lenses. He's wearing blue contact lenses."

Colum spun and threw his walking stick at Caroline like a warrior throwing a spear. Constance gasped. The frail man she thought was her husband rushed, sure-footed, for the double doors.

Father Gregory yelled, "Get down." The wooden stick cut through the air.

The guests ducked at the same moment Caroline body-slammed Colum to the floor. She cuffed the writhing suspect, then whipped out her ringing phone and hit Speaker.

Her father's voice screamed. "Caroline, you're dealing with a dangerous man. Whatever you do, proceed with caution." Caroline tried to interrupt, but her father talked over her. "His name is Ian MacGregor, and he's wanted here in the UK and throughout Europe for conning people out of enormous sums of money. He's violent when cornered. And get this, he's the cousin of the dead Colum MacGregor, the explorer who died on the ship that exploded."

"Dad," Caroline yelled. "Our suspect is already in custody."

"Where?"

"Cuffed to a pew. Here in Stones End."

There was a pause, then her father's laugh rang through. "Well done, luv."

The church echoed in applause.

Caroline grabbed the suspect's arms and pulled him to his feet. Horace, Walter, and Oscar formed a human jail cell around him in case Caroline needed help. Martin cut through the pews to the middle aisle. Charlotte ran to his side.

"Meet Ian MacGregor," said Caroline. "A dangerous con artist wanted throughout Europe. And I suspect, if Martin's correct, is wearing ice-blue contact lenses. And I bet he's not as old as he's made up to be." She tugged at his hair. A white-haired wig slid off, revealing sandy hair.

Constance burst forward to MacGregor. "Why?" she demanded.

He shrugged nonchalantly. "Nothing personal, lass. Europe is crawling with cops hunting me. I escaped, but my money didn't. Colum and I were like brothers in our youth. It helped that we looked like twins. Except for the eyes. He told me every detail about you and him. It made you an easy mark."

She lifted a clenched fist. Father Gregory yelled, "Constance!" She lowered her arm just in time. Arthur's punch landed squarely on MacGregor's jaw. He staggered back and lost balance. A second round of applause erupted, mingled with a few whistles and shouts of *Bravo!*

"That's all, folks." Caroline pulled the suspect toward the door.

"Wait," he said. His eyes found Martin. "My bloody cap shadowed my eyes. How the hell did you figure out I wore blue lenses?"

"I startled you when you entered the church from the corridor. When you lifted your head, the candlelight from the altar caught the edge of your lens. It was just a matter of figuring out what caused that tiny glint of blue light."

Charlotte hugged Martin. "You're positively brilliant!"

The wedding party resumed their places. Father Gregory cleared his throat again. "Dearly beloved…"

"Wait," yelled Arthur.

Father Gregory slapped the prayer book shut and glared. "What in the name of the good Lord is it now?"

"Constance needs to cancel that money transfer."

"Oh, my gosh." Her fingers blurred as she tapped away. She tucked her cellphone into her pocket and kissed his cheek. "Done!"

Ari pointed to Father Gregory. “Hit it, Father.”

“Dearly beloved, we are gathered here...”

George called to the gentle breeze blowing across Arthur’s front porch. “Congratulations, son. Welcome to our family, Constance. May you live happily ever after!”

Book Club Discussion

My Stones End Series is popular with book clubs. Here are some discussion topics you may enjoy. Your comments and suggestions are always welcome. — Ceil Warren

Email: contact@ceilwarren.com
Website: www.ceilwarren.com

1. Constance never told a soul about her marriage to Colum. Was she right to keep it a secret from her second husband, William, and her soon-to-be husband, Arthur?

2. With so much doubt and suspicion about Colum, why did Constance fall for his story and give him half her life's savings?

3. Martin told Roxy he needed to establish his career before he married. Why, then, was it alright for him to propose to Charley?

4. For all his talk about living in England, Martin loves Stones End. When he marries Charley, what would it take for him to leave his beloved home and move to The Cotswolds? Or what would it take for Charley to permanently move to Stones End?

5. The next wedding in Stones End will be between Walter and Ana Felicia. What would keep him from retiring and moving to Ana Felicia's homeland in Greece?

6. If Ana Felicia moves to Stones End after the wedding, how would she get along with Arthur, Constance and all the folks she hurt?
7. How will the village react to the possibility of Martin and Walter moving from Stones End?
8. If you see a book 4 in the Stones End series, I would love to hear your ideas.

About the Author – Ceil Warren

Native New Yorker Ceil Warren builds on a long family line of storytellers and characters faced with life's impossible challenges. Born into a close-knit family of eight children, she grew up with amazing tales and people from Newfoundland to Belarus. Stories of survival: from Manhattan tenements in the 1920s to an exploding ship in World War II.

Living 17 miles north of Manhattan in Westchester County, Ceil takes full advantage of Broadway theater, museums, ballet and opera. All nourish her creative passion for storytelling, characters and drama.

Ceil shattered the glass ceiling for business women and corporate leaders in the 1970s, when women were just beginning to advance into higher-level management and corporate positions. She self-taught her way to a successful career in finance, becoming CFO of a sales operation for a Fortune 500 company at the age of 34.

In her second career in writing, Ceil gladly trades building business plans, telling company stories and crunching numbers for weaving remarkable tales about people against all odds and places you want to visit or even make your home.

The reader continues the journey in this exciting third book of The Stones End Series. If you enjoy Arthur's adventure, please consider leaving a review or rating on my Amazon and Goodreads homepage.

www.ingramcontent.com/pod-product-compliance
Lightning Source LLC
LaVergne TN
LVHW091129080826
845145LV00008B/2091